Chicks with Sticks
(Knitwise)

Chicks with Sticks
(KnitWise)

ELIZABETH LENHARD

DUTTON BOOKS

DUTTON CHILDREN'S BOOKS
A division of Penguin Young Readers Group

Published by the Penguin Group
Penguin Group (USA) Inc., 375 Hudson Street, New York, New York 10014, U.S.A. · Penguin Group
(Canada), 90 Eglinton Avenue East, Suite 700, Toronto, Ontario, Canada M4P 2Y3 (a division of
Pearson Penguin Canada Inc.) · Penguin Books Ltd, 80 Strand, London WC2R 0RL, England ·
Penguin Ireland, 25 St Stephen's Green, Dublin 2, Ireland (a division of Penguin Books Ltd) ·
Penguin Group (Australia), 250 Camberwell Road, Camberwell, Victoria 3124, Australia (a division
of Pearson Australia Group Pty Ltd) · Penguin Books India Pvt Ltd, 11 Community Centre,
Panchsheel Park, New Delhi–110 017, India · Penguin Group (NZ), 67 Apollo Drive, Rosedale, North
Shore 0745, Auckland, New Zealand (a division of Pearson New Zealand Ltd) · Penguin Books
(South Africa) (Pty) Ltd, 24 Sturdee Avenue, Rosebank, Johannesburg 2196, South Africa ·
Penguin Books Ltd, Registered Offices: 80 Strand, London WC2R 0RL, England

This book is a work of fiction. Names, characters, places, and incidents are either
the product of the author's imagination or are used fictitiously, and any resemblance to actual
persons, living or dead, business establishments, events, or locales
is entirely coincidental.

The publisher does not have any control over and does not assume any responsibility for author or
third-party websites or their content.

CIP Data is available.

Published in the United States by Dutton Books,
a member of Penguin Group (USA) Inc.
345 Hudson Street, New York, New York 10014
www.penguin.com/youngreaders

Designed by Irene Vandervoort

Printed in USA   First Edition
ISBN 978-0-525-47838-6
1 3 5 7 9 10 8 6 4 2

For Mira

Acknowledgments

This book was written during the first months of my daughter's life, and for that reason, I owe my mother tremendous gratitude. While I wrote, she gave us hours and hours of childcare, as well as love, support, and household S.O.S. I could *not* have done it without her. (And PS, my father cheerfully *did* do without her while she spent all that time at my house.) My sister-in-law, Wendy, was also an adoring nanny when needed.

Equally valuable support came from my wonderful agent, Jodi Reamer, and my peerless editor, Julie Strauss-Gabel, who completely gets the writer thing *and* the mom thing, and whose affection and compassion for these characters has inspired me through three years of Chicks.

Huge thanks to Sarah Shumway for all her help, not to mention her lovely knitting projects. Sarah Pope Greene's knitting patterns are also beautiful.

As always, I was lucky to have many friends and family members cheering for me and the Chicks. In particular, I relied on my cousin and partner-in-pregnancy, Ellyn Davidson, for always being there to pump up my confidence, and Laurel Snyder, who, among other things, helped me whip my scattered thoughts into formation one fateful afternoon.

Most of all, I'm grateful for my husband, Paul, who completely *respects* the writer thing and the mom thing, who took amazingly sweet care of me whenever the going got tough, who delights me every day. Quite simply, he—along with Mira—is the point of it all.

Chicks with Sticks
(KnitWise)

1 ✦ (Work over a multiple of 4 stitches)

If there was such a thing as pre-nostalgia, Scottie Shearer was aching with it.

And her friends had no sympathy whatsoever.

"Scottie, senior year hasn't even started yet," Amanda said, shading her eyes. They were sitting on a picnic blanket in a cozy park flanked by rows of Chicago apartment buildings. In a few hours, the place would be overrun with people settling in for one of the city's greatest summer rituals—an outdoor flick called Movies in the Park. But for now, Scottie and her three best friends were the only ones there, knitting, picnicking, and absorbing the afternoon's last bit of sunshine. "Please don't get all squashy about the year *ending*."

"I'm not!" Scottie protested. She tossed the square of seed stitch she was knitting onto the blanket and looked at Bella and Tay. "You guys, am I squashy?"

All of them, of course, knew exactly what this meant. "Squashy" was the not-particularly-attractive thing that happened to Scottie's face when she got weepy over a sappy chick flick. Or a cute text from her boyfriend. Or, apparently, the thought of high school ending in nine fleeting months.

"You're definitely pre-squashy," Tay said bluntly.

Huffing in frustration, Scottie swiped a compact of sparkly face powder out of her backpack, popped it open, and examined her face. Her fair skin was smattered with summer freckles, her lips were gloss-free, and there was a definite sheen on her nose. She'd looked better, but she honestly saw no signs of squashiness: the downturned mouth, the crinkly eyes, the expression that flickered between pathetic and tragic. . . .

"What makes you think so?" Scottie demanded of Tay.

"Because Trader Joe's finest treats lie before you, and you—snacka-holic—haven't touched them," Tay said coolly. She paused her clicking, clacking circular needles to point at the vast spread of junk food on the picnic blanket. "Because you're knitting a *memory* quilt, which, I'm sorry, is just maudlin. *And* because Bella just got chocolate on one of your quilt squares and you didn't even notice."

"What?!" Scottie and Bella cried together.

Scottie's gaze swung from Tay—all spiky hair, midnight-colored bicep tattoo, and eyebrow ring—to barefooted Bella, who was wearing her hair in beaded braids these days. If Scottie hadn't been completely accustomed to the vast difference between her two friends, she might have gone into instant culture shock. Instead, she only gaped at Bella's long, thin fingers, which were holding a knitted lace square of silver silk.

Chocolate-smeared silver silk.

"Bel-la!" Scottie complained.

Bella dropped the square and stared in horror at the finger-shaped brown smudges already melting into the yarn.

"Oh *nooooo*," she wailed, slapping a sticky palm to her forehead. "What did I *dooooo*?"

"You totally wrecked Scottie's square, that's what," Tay said. "You see, B? That's what you get for straying from the path of the righteous, the true, the vegan."

"Tay!" Amanda said. "How do you know that wasn't some sort of organic, single-origin chocolate? Or even carob? And besides, doesn't Bella feel awful enough?"

"No, Tay's right," Bella cried dramatically. She grabbed a napkin and attempted to wipe the chocolate off the silver yarn, which only made it smearier. "This was a peanut butter cup with no social value whatsoever. No wonder I messed up Scottie's square! It's karma! It would have been fine if it had been *my* knitting."

She held up the webby, olive-colored shawl she was working on a floppy circular needle. "But it was yours, Scottie! I just wanted to take a closer look. Your lace is so pretty. Or it was until I *ruined* it."

Scottie gazed at the square, crumpled up on the picnic blanket. She hadn't blocked it yet, but she'd been so excited about the circle-within-a-square pattern she'd invented that she'd brought it to the park to show her friends.

"Tell you what," Scottie said, delicately picking up her besmirched lace. "This square *was* going to commemorate the night that Amanda dragged us to that karaoke club with all the disco balls. But now, I think it'll be about this—our annual Chicks with Sticks back-to-school picnic at Movies in the Park. The chocolate smell will only enhance the memory, right?"

"Back-to-school picnic?!?" Tay yelled as she reached across the blanket and dug into a bag of chili-laced tortilla chips. "Could you make us sound any more dorky? This isn't an annual anything. This is just us doing what we do. Y'know, knitting, gorging . . ."

"Ex-cuse me?" Amanda said, one bite into a chocolate truffle. "*I* don't gorge."

"Uh-huh." Tay stared at Amanda for a long, deadpan moment—prompting a fit of giggles from Scottie and Bella—before continuing her kvetch.

"I think we need to stop naming things," Tay declared. She popped a chip into her mouth and crunched it noisily. "I mean, it's cool, I *guess*, to call ourselves the Chicks with Sticks. But then you went and named our slumber parties Sacred Sleepovers, which was definitely pushing the boundaries of dweebiness. Now we're having a Back-to-School Picnic? What's next? The Chicks with Sticks Bi-monthly Ice Cream Social? The Chicks with Sticks Second Wednesday in November Diet Coke Run?"

"Dude," Scottie said, adopting Tay's boyish drawl for a moment, "hyperbolize much?"

"Ooh, you *are* a senior, aren't you?" Tay said. "Check out the vocabulary."

Tay was a year younger than Scottie, Amanda, and Bella, not that you'd know it if you lined the four of them up for a compare-and-contrast. Tay—a survivor of her parents' nasty divorce—slouched through life with a sneer. It didn't matter that she never wore makeup and had an all-cargo-pants-and-T-shirt wardrobe. Her world weariness made her seem way older than sixteen.

Amanda could easily pass for twenty-one. She had perfect curves, perfectly arched eyebrows, and a devastating wardrobe stocked with Imitation of Christ, Tuleh, and old Chanel suits of her mother's that she'd ripped and reknitted into cut-up couture.

Bella—with cut cheekbones and a gangly/gorgeous bod—would have looked older than her years, too, if not for the extreme earnestness she broadcast to everyone.

I guess I'm the only one who looks completely and hopelessly my age, Scottie thought, glancing down at her not-terribly-tight jeans, her goofy knitted wristbands, and her *Sticks Happen* baby tee.

A beat later, Scottie realized with surprise that she was pretty okay with looking like a perfectly average seventeen-year-old.

Maybe that was because—despite her straight, pale brown hair, her unbreakable addiction to Gap-wear, and the fact that she couldn't wear a B-cup without the help of several wads of tissues—Scottie knew she didn't melt anonymously into the background. Not anymore. The Chicks with Sticks didn't exactly blend.

Take their picnic. The girls could have chosen a quiet sliver of grass on the lakefront for their junk-food fest, but instead, they'd plunked themselves into the absolute center of Movies in the Park.

And in honor of tonight's flick, *Willy Wonka and the Chocolate Factory*, they were camping it up. Bella had planted chocolate-scented candles at each corner of the blanket and worn a cinnamon-colored knitted tank and shimmery green skirt. Amanda had gone to Teuscher Chocolates and Trader Joe's to stock up on a ridiculous bounty of cocoa-packed snacks. Then she'd dabbed her neck with Demeter's Brownie and donned a rakish top hat she'd found in a thrift store. It was the image of Willy Wonka's hat. Of course, on Amanda, it looked completely cool.

Tay had contributed by setting up lounge chairs around the blanket and Scottie had made each of the girls cardboard fans with pictures of Augustus Gloop, Veruca Salt, and the rest of the chocolate factory baddies glued to them.

Tossed into the mix was the knitting: Scottie's scattered memory quilt squares; the sensible striped hat Tay was knitting herself in prep for fall; Bella's shimmery shawl; and the sleeveless sweater Amanda was freeforming out of fat wool tendrils and shredded grocery bags.

Suffice to say, the Chicks were a total spectacle.

And Scottie was feeling anything but shy about it.

Yup, she thought incredulously. *I'm knitting in public and worshipping at the altar of Gene Wilder and somehow I don't care who knows it.*

Scottie grabbed one of Bella's peanut butter cups and popped it into her mouth. *And I know Tay feels the same way, no matter how much she complains. She can't deny that if we're dorky, we're dorky and proud.*

Scottie grinned as she scanned the growing crowd of moviegoers around her and indeed caught quite a few people shooting bemused glances in her direction. Then her gaze fell on the family settling in right next to the Chicks' blanket.

While the parents busied themselves unpacking a grocery bag full of sandwiches, chips, and cookies, their two kids eyeballed the Chicks. The older one, a twelvish-looking girl jangling with bangle bracelets and big hoop earrings, cast sidelong glances with a curled lip. The younger one, a curly-headed boy hopping around the grass in his bare feet, gaped.

"Wow!" he said. "Lookit all that candy!"

"Mind your own biz, Zeke," his sister hissed at him, before shooting another furtive look at the Chicks.

"Hey, what are they doing with all that string?" Zeke pressed on.

"Duh," the sister huffed. "They're knitting. Now would you stop being so hyper? You're *completely* mortifying."

"You're just mad cuz *you* don't know how to knit," Zeke said. He glanced again at the Chicks' picnic and bounced on the balls of his feet as if he were absorbing caffeine from the *smell* of their chocolate.

"I can too knit," Big Sister retorted, lowering her voice to a guttural whisper. "Mom taught me years ago. I just don't *want* to knit. It's lame."

Scottie almost laughed out loud. She could remember when she'd felt exactly the same way. In fact, she'd been horrified when her great aunt Lucille had roped her into executing her first stitches. She hadn't fallen in love with knitting until weeks later, and even then, she'd picked up the sticks begrudgingly. She'd knitted, not because she'd wanted to, but because she'd *had* to. The blue yarn Aunt Lucille had foisted upon her had wormed its way into her brain and taken hold of her. Permanently, as it turned out.

"If knitting's so lame, why are *they* doing it?" Zeke said, pointing at the Chicks and not even trying to whisper.

Amanda and Scottie exchanged a smirk. Just like Scottie, Amanda had been an accidental yarn girl. In fact, all of the Chicks had strung their first knits and purls with major skepticism.

Well, Scottie corrected herself with a glance at Bella, *maybe not all of us. Bella was into it from the start. Knitting fit into her whole crunchy yogini thing perfectly.*

But there was no good explanation for Scottie, Amanda, and Tay's

•• Chicks with Sticks

yarn addiction. Amanda was about as non-homespun as they came. Nobody in her family even cooked, much less did cozy stuff like sewing or knitting. And why should they, when they had a full-time maid/nanny to do that kind of thing for them?

Scottie had a filmmaker older sister, a mom who was a big-time painter, and a dad who made his living selling her mom's "works" at his art gallery. For most of Scottie's life, there'd been so many creative juices pumping away in her family's loft that they'd threatened to wash her away, so she'd long ago decided to steer clear of anything remotely artsy.

And Tay should have rejected knitting as way too femme and fusty for her skateboarding, baseball-watching self.

But somehow—Bella insisted it was fate—all four of the Chicks had found themselves in the same knitting shop on the same night a couple of years earlier. They'd left the store with the first bits of what would become massive yarn stashes, mongo needle collections, and an itch to knit that would send them stitching and bitching all over town, even in the cafeteria of their hipper-than-thou school, Olivia Stark.

And that's why Scottie just *had* to say something now.

"Y'know," she called across the blankets to the sullen girl, "knitting doesn't *have* to be lame. Check out Amanda's top. She *made* that."

Scottie pointed at the halter Amanda was wearing. She'd knitted up dozens of skinny strips of fabric, felted them until they were raggedy, then woven them together in an elaborate geometric pattern.

"Scottie," Amanda said through gritted teeth. "Puh-leeze."

Zeke's sister was looking at Scottie like she'd just offered her one of those Scientology personality tests. But when her oh-so-skeptical gaze fell on Amanda, Scottie thought she detected some admiration in her eyes. So she kept on talking.

"And look at what Amanda's knitting," she declared. "Those are shredded grocery bags!"

"Uh, cool," the girl said, though it was clear she was underwhelmed.

Only cuz she has no idea how hard it is to knit up grocery bags, Scottie told herself before pressing on.

"We could help you get back into knitting if you want," she offered. "We have a stitch 'n bitch every Tuesday at Joe, you know across from the Olivia Stark School? Totally fun. It's called Never Mind the Frogs."

"Because apparently it's a law among knitters that *everything* has to have a cute name," Tay said with faux chirpiness.

"Tay," Scottie whispered with an irritated squint. "Thanks for the undercut."

"Frogs?" The girl squirmed, sighed, and fiddled with a few of her bangle bracelets. "Um, well that sounds *neat* but . . . I think I'm busy Tuesday."

"Oh, that's okay," Bella chimed in sweetly. "We meet every Tuesday, so you can come to another one."

"I'm kinda busy every Tuesday," the girl said before she pulled a cell phone out of her purse and began texting intensely. She might as well have slammed a door in the Chicks' faces.

Scottie felt her cheeks flush.

Okay, maybe I kinda overdid it with the dorky-and-proud bit.

"Um, Scottie?" Amanda said carefully, "remember when you used to be so shy that you were embarrassed to knit in public, much less knit-evangelize to complete strangers?"

"Shut up," Scottie wailed. She snatched up a chocolate Twizzler and began twirling it between her fingers. "I'm completely embarrassed."

"Why embarrassed?" Bella said, looking up from her WIP and blinking in surprise. "You only wanted to share your knitty joy with that girl. You were being nice."

"Sweetie," Scottie said to Bella, "you wouldn't understand."

It was true. Bella was one of those rare birds who did *not* embarrass. Not only would she go to the movies with her parents on a Saturday night, she'd tell everybody about it on Monday morning. She didn't just knit in public, she did *yoga* in public. And her hair—her voluminous tendrils of honey-colored hair, tied atop her head so they undulated like a graceful anemone—meant you could spot her from blocks away. Her oddness was adorable, precisely because she had no idea she was odd.

Scottie turned to Amanda and Tay for support.

"Way to alienate the local youth, spaz," Tay said, shaking her head.

"Yeah, freak," Amanda said, grinning at Scottie.

"Traitors!" Scottie shrieked. "Whatever happened to our whole 'knitting is cool' thing? Stark is awash in yarn and Frogs is so crowded that it's spawned an outpost at Intelligentsia Coffee. So why was that girl so snubby?"

"Because you were so desperate," Tay said. "Dude, nobody likes a telethon. The way to draw folks in is to be aloof."

"Well, you would know," Scottie teased.

"Why do you want to draw people in anyway?" Amanda said. "Nobody likes a trend, either."

"I know," Scottie said with a frown. If anything, she'd always been annoyed by all the knit-poseurs out there—those girls who couldn't do anything but garter-stitch scarves out of novelty yarn; who knitted just to have an excuse to hang at stitch 'n bitches, then yammer about it on their MySpace profiles. "I guess I just wanted that girl to know what she was missing. She looked so alone."

Nobody had a retort for that one, because there was no denying that all of them were a lot less lonely since their knitting had strung them together.

For now, Scottie thought, tossing her Twizzler onto the picnic blanket. *But next fall, Amanda, Bella, and I go to college and Tay stays here. What happens then?*

Scottie picked up her silver square and lifted it to her face, breathing in the scent of chocolate. Her pre-nostalgia kicked in again.

Y'know, she thought, propping her chin on her fist and shooting Bella an affectionate glance, *I think this square is perfect, just like it is. I want to remember this whole day, chocolate overdose and all—*

"Oh no, she's getting beyond pre-squashy now," Tay announced.

Scottie looked up, startled. Tay was shaking her head at her, a rueful smile on her face. Between crunches on another handful of chips, she said, "Scottie, if you're going to turn everything we do into the *last time* we ever do this, or the *last time* we ever do that, it's gonna be a very long year."

"How do you *do* that?" Scottie complained. "How do you know exactly what I'm thinking, especially if what I'm thinking is completely humiliating?"

"What are friends for," Tay said with a grin, "if not to humiliate you?"

"And remind you that we're not going anywhere," Bella said, throwing her arms around Scottie's shoulders and giving her a squeeze. "Not for a long time, anyway."

"Yeah, so get a grip," Tay said. She pointed at the deep indigo sky. "The movie's about to start."

"And the day after tomorrow," Amanda said, slumping onto her back on the blanket and stashing her knitting in her bag with a sigh, "school starts. Ugh. If I wasn't gonna be a senior, I'd be so depressed right now. Only knowing that this year is gonna be about nothing but senior skip days and senior pranks and all those pull-you-out-of-class senior assemblies I've heard about, keeps me from hurling myself off my bedroom balcony."

Great, Scottie thought as she flopped down next to Amanda, tucking her yarn bag beneath her head to use as a pillow. She'd just retired her cavernous Suki bag for an even more enormous canvas backpack covered with psychedelic flowers and lined with enough pockets to hold every conceivable knitting tool. *Now* I'm *depressed.*

She was grateful for the dark, which hid her definitely-squashy-now face from her friends. She scooped up a handful of M & M's as Tay and Bella arranged themselves on the chaise lounges. And when the projector began to flicker an old-timey cartoon onto the movie screen, Scottie clinked bottles of mocha Frappuccino with Amanda and tried to seem jovial.

But in the back of her mind, she was trying not to worry that all these beginnings were really the beginning of the end—the end of her life in Chicago and, even worse, the end of the Chicks.

2 * (Knit through back loop)

"Now, seniors, before you begin your search for the perfect senior service project, I'd like you to take a moment to close your eyes. That's right. Now take a deep, cleansing breath. Heck, take three of 'em!"

Scottie and Amanda, sitting with Bella in one of the back rows of the Olivia Stark School assembly hall, gave each other a weary look. Up on the stage, their principal, Dr. Heath, was taking off her bedazzled reading glasses and smiling benevolently at the seniors squirming before her.

Clearly she had no idea that they were *all* shooting each other weary looks.

All except Bella, of course. When Scottie glanced over at her, Bella's eyes were obediently closed. Perhaps unconsciously, she'd pulled her legs up onto her chair, folded them into a lotus, and rested her upturned palms on each knee. Her cleansing breaths *whooshed* out of her loudly.

"Check out Bella's exemplary pranayama," Scottie whispered to Amanda of Bella's yoga-ready breaths. "She's totally gonna make valedictorian."

"If this new principal has anything to do with it," Amanda sighed, giving the woman an irritated glare. Dr. Heath's very large bosom was heaving and ho-ing through her own cleansing breaths.

"So this is how it's gonna be this year?" Amanda went on. "Not only do the seniors have to do these major community service projects, we also have to get all spiritual about it?! I can't believe the Stark parents approved of this Heath person. Could she be any more corny?"

"Are you kidding?" Scottie said. "Dr. Heath is my parents' McDreamy! For one, she's a semifamous author."

"I guess," Amanda said. "Not that I'd ever heard of her before she came to Stark." Next to her, Bella did a few neck rolls and another moany cleansing breath.

"What was her book called?" Amanda whispered. *"When You Wish Upon a Child?* Dor-ky!"

"Tscha," Scottie said with an eye roll. "My parents had never heard of her, either, but believe me, when they found out she'd been hired, they ran right out and bought her book. That way they could brag to any buyer who came over to look at my mom's art: 'Look! Our daughter's school principal is a semifamous author!'"

"Just like your mom's a semifamous painter?" Amanda said with a wink.

"Exactly," Scottie said. "Semifamous is very big in my parents' circle. When you're semifamous, you're impressive and alluring, but not so much that you make other people feel like losers."

"The way a *truly* famous person would, right?"

"Uh-huh," Scottie said. She nodded at Dr. Heath, who was now instructing the kids to "visualize the universe guiding you down a path" or something like that.

"So McCrunchy is perfect for Stark parents," she said. "She's super-progressive and new agey. And with the whole semifamous thing, the parents can rest assured that their kids are in super-accomplished hands, but deep down, they can *also* believe that *they're* just as smart as Dr. Heath is."

"Wow, what happened to our starry-eyed Scottie?" Amanda said with an incredulous laugh. "You sound just like Tay."

So, maybe some of Tay's bite has *rubbed off on me,* Scottie thought with a grim smile. *So much the better. I'm gonna need some more edge now that I'm a senior.*

She sighed. *A senior. I still can't believe it.*

She glanced over at Bella, wondering if she was feeling as freaked.

Apparently not. Bella had opened her eyes and was gazing placidly at Dr. Heath, her wide mouth settled into a relaxed smile.

Amanda, too, seemed unperturbed now. She'd tuned out Dr. Heath and delved into her Prada tote for some covert action with her crochet hook and a puff of wine-colored cashmere.

Scottie sighed and turned back to the stage.

"It's appropriate, as seniors, that you give back to the village that brought you up," Dr. Heath said. She clasped her chubby hands—clacking with turquoise rings—before her. "This is your last chance, after all. For next year, you will swim upstream to new waters. To college. To new cities. To life in a world that is bigger than the microcosm of the Olivia Stark School."

Okay. We get it already. We're SENIORS. Life as we know it is about to CHANGE DRASTICALLY. We're GROWING UP.

Scottie rooted around in her own backpack, seized up some comfort knitting—a loopy scarf that she was working in super-soft, whiskery acrylic—and began purling furiously.

Now can we just stop talking about it so much?

After the assembly, Dr. Heath led the seniors into the gym. The basketball court was filled with volunteer-manned folding tables, each bedecked with posters, placards, and leaflets advertising their various causes. Every save-the-world organization seemed to be there, from Planned Parenthood to Illinois PIRG. Since dozens of non-profits had set up shop for the community service fair, Stark had bussed in kids from several other private schools on the North side. Hundreds of people were already perusing the options when Scottie, Bella, and Amanda began to make their rounds.

•• *Chicks with Sticks*

Bella gasped in excitement as they approached the first row of tables.

"Ooh, wouldn't it be interesting to be a guide for a visually impaired person?" she said, pointing at a table near the door. "Or I could work with senior citizens. And, hel-lo! Check out all the environmental causes, you guys! Oh, how am I gonna decide which thing to do?"

"Yeah, how *are* we?" Scottie complained. "We're going to spend two hundred hours on these service projects, yet we have to pick a passion in the next forty-five minutes? No pressure or anything."

Since she knew Bella would just encourage her to prana her way through her panic, Scottie looked to Amanda for commiseration.

But Amanda only shrugged.

"I already have to do two hundred hours of service this year so I can deb," she admitted with a wince. "So my mom called the school and asked them if that could count for my senior service project, too."

"Oh, I almost forgot," Scottie said with a grimace of her own. "It's your debutante year."

"Scot-tie," Amanda hissed, glancing around to make sure nobody had heard. "Not so loud."

"Whoops." Scottie cringed apologetically. The kids at Olivia Stark were not your average prep school richies. Sure, plenty of the students had money, but flaunting it in the usual way—with Mercedes and Manolos—was verboten. It was way more acceptable to use your bucks to go to a writers' colony and pen morose poetry or fund an underground film festival—something Scottie's trendy-beyond-words older sister had done back when she was a Stark senior.

Also, most of the kids here had money because their parents had made it big making a difference in the world. They were activist lawyers or research doctors or semifamous artists like Scottie's mom. Amanda's version of money—inherited from a bloodline that went back to the Mayflower—was more rare at Stark.

And it definitely wasn't cool.

But Bella, who didn't know from cool, said loudly, "Oh, Amanda, don't be embarrassed! I mean, sure it's gonna be *painful* going to all those cotillions in a white gown and gloves. And the whole being-paraded-around-by-your-dad thing is sorta like being a cow at auction, isn't it? You could say that it's about as anti-feminist as you can get!"

"Not to mention being anti-vegetarian." Scottie elbowed Bella and grinned. "You know what happens to those cows."

"Make me feel worse, why don't you?" Amanda wailed.

"Wait!" Bella cried. "I was trying to make you feel better."

"Um, okay. *How?*" Amanda sneered.

"By reminding you how much this means to your family," Bella said. "Didn't you tell me that if you didn't make your debut, it would be the equivalent of your mom showing up at a society tea in a micro-mini and an 'I Voted for Kerry' button?"

"Basically," Amanda agreed with a laugh. "We're talking complete ostracization."

"So you're doing it for your mom," Bella announced.

"Yeah, I *know* Bella," Amanda whined. "What I don't know is how this can be a good thing."

"Okay," Bella said as the three girls strolled through the service fair, "think of all the deb stuff you have to do this year—"

"The brunches and lunches and teas?" Amanda listed. "The cotillions and balls and parties? The etiquette lessons and deb class meetings, all masquerading as community service? Uh, thanks, but I'd rather not."

"Lemme finish," Bella chided as she swiped a Greenpeace flyer off a table covered with plush Orca whales and baby seals. "Think of all this deb stuff and then think of my yoga practice."

Scottie screeched to a halt and started laughing.

"I'm pic-picturing," she gasped, "Amanda doing downward dog in her white deb gown. With the bustle poking up in the air!"

Bella started tittering with her and even Amanda had to join in with some very un-debutante-like snorty giggles.

• • Chicks with Sticks

"Okay, I'm game," Amanda said. "Tell me, Bellissima, *how* is debbing like yoga?"

Bella fluttered her arms into a graceful knot and said, "Well, you know I've always had a love-hate thing going with my practice. I mean, I can live with my vinyasa, but my poses? My balance is forever out of whack. Still, I've been doing yoga every morning with my parents since I could walk. I haven't always loved it, but in the end, I think it's done me a lot of good. Plus it's totally helped me and my parents bond."

"You're definitely good at that cleansing breath thing," Scottie said. While the girls strolled and chatted, she'd been scanning all the tables for her perfect service project. So far, though, none of the various feed-the-hungry and help-the-homeless organizations had spoken to her and *she* was starting to feel a bit hyperventilatish.

"Bella, you and your parents are closer than anyone I know," Amanda said seriously. "It's *not* because of yoga. It's because your parents respect you and let you be who you are. Your 'rents are totally into your knitting, for instance."

Amanda huffed with disgust. "Not only does my mom not get my knitting," she went on, "she doesn't get my knitty friends. She just wants me to be BFFs with all the other Mayflower kids. But I can't *stand* the girls in my deb class. They're all so . . . so blond! And the guys who are lined up to be our escorts? They're *bland*. Which is even worse."

"Aren't you stereotyping just a little?" Scottie said. "I mean you seem like a total WASP too, even if you're not blond. And *you're* different."

"Well, these folks aren't," Amanda said. "Trust me. I had hopes, but when Curtsy Class started this summer—"

"Curtsy Class?!" Scottie screeched before doubling over with laughter once again. "Tell me they don't really call it that."

"No, they don't call it that," Amanda said sourly. "They call it Etiquette Instruction, but it seems like we spend all our time perfecting our deep curtseys, so that's what *I* call it. Anyway, I started going and I was all ready to bond with the other girls about the lameness of our debbing burden. But it turns out? They're completely into it. They think it *matters*. They're Stepford Muffies."

The three of them had reached the end of the long rows of tables. Bella had swiped up two fistfuls of pamphlets, most of which were the telltale forest-green and earthy brown of environmental groups. But Scottie? She was flyer-free.

She looked at her watch.

"Oh my God," she said. "We've only got ten minutes left. I'm gonna be stuck wearing an orange vest and picking up trash on the freeway!"

"Um, I think that's a different kind of community service," Amanda giggled. "You know, the kind that comes with a permanent record?"

"Still, I've gotta decide on something!" Scottie glanced at her watch again. "And now I've only got *nine and a half* minutes left."

Scottie wrung her hands and gazed desperately around the gym. All the brightly colored posters, canvas awnings, and flyers were making her eyes cross! And the bright-eyed volunteers sitting behind the tables were starting to look more intimidating than inviting.

Especially to someone like Scottie, who was completely decision-challenged.

I mean, I can spend forty-five minutes agonizing over a yarn *purchase,* Scottie thought. *I can't pick a year-long service project in the next nine minutes, fifteen seconds. I just CAN'T.*

"Uh-oh," Bella stage-whispered to Amanda. "She's panicking."

"Completely," Amanda said back.

"Is it that obvious?" Scottie said—okay, shrieked. Loudly.

Amanda answered by wincing, wiggling a finger in her ear, and saying to Bella, "Oh yeah, she's *completely* panicking."

Then she turned to Scottie and said, "I'm off the hook here, so . . ."

"So?" Scottie asked.

"So let's get going!" Amanda announced. "I'm helping you find a service project."

"Really?" Scottie cried. Immediately, the nervous chatter in her head subsided.

"No prob," Amanda assured her. "Eight minutes, forty-five seconds is *plenty* of time."

Scottie followed Amanda gratefully as Bella went to perch on the bleachers and peruse her flyers.

Now that she had an ally at her side, Scottie felt her vision clear a bit. She spotted the familiar Rush Hospital logo at one table and stopped.

"Okay, what about this one?" she proposed. "Am I a candy striper kind of girl?"

"The girl who gags if I *talk* about throwing up?" Amanda said. "I think not. What about an organization that helps homeless people?"

Scottie perused the sign-up clipboards at a couple more tables and shook her head.

"Looks like everything's filling up," she said.

"Hey," Amanda said, "how about the Humane Society?"

She pointed at a sign a few rows over featuring a heart-tugging picture of a fluffy kitten and puppy, nestled together in a cage.

"No way. My parents are already anti-CC, ever since she clawed up their Eames chair," Scottie said. "They've made a 'no more pets' rule."

"So?" Amanda said.

"So, *you* try working with a bunch of doomed doggies," Scottie shrilled. "Within a month, I'll be keeping a small zoo in my bedroom."

"Okay, okay," Amanda laughed. She craned her neck to check out the posters at the end of their aisle. "Don't lose it. There's got to be something here."

Scottie's eyes wandered to the table right next door. Its poster was almost identical to the Humane Society's. But in place of fuzzy animals, it had a picture of sort-of-scruffy, round-cheeked children.

BIG SIBS/LITTLE SIBS, it said. BE THERE FOR A CHILD . . . TODAY.

"Look at that," Scottie complained to Amanda. "Isn't it annoying how people seem to get animals and little kids mixed up? It's like they think buying a kid a squeaky toy and a Frosty Paw is going to make everything better."

"Yes!" Amanda cried.

Scottie jumped and turned to Amanda. "Um, I didn't know you felt so strongly about the plight of the children!"

"Me?" Amanda said breathlessly. "I'm talking about *you*. Scottie, you should be a big sib."

"What?" Scottie squeaked. "Have you forgotten about the one and only time I tried to babysit?"

"Okay, that kid?" Amanda said. "He was two. And it would have been just fine if not for the projectile vomit."

"Ack," Scottie gagged. "Don't say that word."

"Anyway, I think your little sib would be older," Amanda said, already leading Scottie toward the Big Sibs table. "Maybe twelve or thirteen. Which is just your size."

"Why do you say that?" Scottie said, trailing behind her reluctantly.

"Hello?" Amanda said. "Did you or did you not practically arm-wrestle that tweeny girl at Movies in the Park into coming to Frogs?"

"Okay, did I or did I not completely bomb with that girl?" Scottie protested. "She thought I was a complete geek."

"So . . . you'll request a snark-free little sib," Amanda declared, pushing Scottie toward the table.

"I don't think you can be that specific," Scottie hissed.

"Hello!"

Scottie jumped as a bright-eyed young woman sitting behind the table beamed up at her.

"Would you like some information about Big Sibs/Little Sibs?" the woman asked.

Scottie groaned inwardly. *Okay, escape at this point would be extremely awkward.*

She gave the woman a sheepish smile and a little wave.

And then, because she basically had no other choice, Scottie actually followed Dr. Heath's advice. She closed her eyes for a moment and searched her soul, picturing herself with one of the apple-cheeked kids in the poster. She imagined taking the little boy to a Cubs game, and sipping pink lemonade with the girl at American Girl Place.

Huh! Scottie was surprised to realize that the image actually sent a thrum of warm static through her. *As long as she doesn't ever throw up, maybe a little sib would be kind of cool. I could introduce her to the best chocolate in the city. I could teach her how to knit. . . .*

Scottie was still pondering when Dr. Heath's voice burbled out of the gym's announcement system.

"Time's up!" she said. "I hope you've discovered a service project that's in harmony with your goals."

Scottie's mouth dropped open. *What do I do?*

"C'mon, Scottie," Amanda said, swiping a pen off the table and thrusting it at her. "It's this or dozens of doomed puppies. And besides, you know you want to."

Only two hours into her senior year, Scottie felt like she didn't know which end was up, much less that she *wanted* to risk vomit and yarn-scorn for her senior service project. Then again, she had little choice. So she grabbed Amanda's pen, and signed away her school year.

3 *(Divide at the center)

At exactly 3:18 that afternoon, Scottie plunged through Stark's front doors, ducked between a couple of huffing yellow buses, jaywalked across the street, and burst into Joe. She heaved her book-weighty backpack onto the counter and perched on a tall stool while her eyes adjusted to the gloom.

Joe had been turned from an Irish pub into a coffeehouse when Scottie was in elementary school, but the joint still had a barry feel to it. From the yeasty darkness and shiny wooden bar to the notoriously crabby baristas and craggy wood-plank floor to the always-roaring fireplace in the loungey back room, it was the perfect place to hunker down with a sludgy dose of caffeine for some serious chit-chat.

When Tay loped into Joe a few minutes after Scottie, she looked like she needed both. Her shoulders were hunched and she was scowling more than usual. But before she had a chance to tell Scottie what was up, the barista ambled over.

"An extra-tall mocha, full-fat, with two shots of chocolate and one of almond," Scottie blurted at him.

"I'll have the same," Tay growled.

"No, that's for you," Scottie said with a smile. "That's what you always order when you're feeling put-upon."

"Do you ever get the feeling that we're in a rut?" Tay asked, shaking her head.

"Whatever," Scottie laughed. "I bet you don't know what I'm gonna order."

"Uh, yeah I do," Tay said. She turned to the barista, who looked like he couldn't have been more bored by their girlie exchange. "She'll have a vanilla frap with whipped cream and then she's gonna douse it with cocoa."

"What," the guy asked, his surfer-dude voice dripping with sarcasm, "no pink sprinkles with that?"

"What," Tay retorted, pointing at the barista's shaggy locks, "no shampoo with *that?*"

While Scottie tried to stifle a snort of laughter, the guy shrugged with grudging respect and wandered over to the espresso machine to get started on Tay's mocha.

"Maybe you shouldn't have ordered an extra-tall," Tay grumbled. "I've gotta bolt this down and get home."

"What?" Scottie gasped. "Why? We're supposed to be here all after-noon, comparing notes on the first day."

"Speaking of notes," Tay said, slumping backward against the bar, "didn't you take nineteenth-century lit last year? I could really use your notes from *that*. That class is gonna be bo-ring."

"Yeah, I wasn't talking about *those* kind of notes," Scottie said. "We need to talk about how it feels to be back. And about the fact that Tom Castellucci got shipped off to military school and Annie Milstein shaved her head. And hello? What was up with Dr. Heath doing that haiku slam in the courtyard at lunch? *Those* kind of notes. You know. . . ."

"Yes, yes I do," Tay said. "Because that is exactly what we did on the first day of school *last* year."

Tay pulled a crumpled wad of coffee cash out of her jeans pocket and gave Scottie a suspicious look. "Scottie, if you've given this little pow-wow a name, I swear I'm gonna have him put my mocha in a to-go cup."

Scottie's mouth fell open. As usual, Tay was *so* onto her.

"Um, okay, maybe we are in a rut," Scottie admitted with a guilty smile. "But is that so wrong? I *like* our ruts. They're like home, y'know?"

Tay shrugged and looked around for a subject change. Conveniently enough, she found a stack of 'em next to the cash register.

"Hey," she blurted. "Did you change the Frogs flyer?"

She pointed at some hot pink flyers. Scottie spotted a familiar, loopy font and a cartoon of a frog. It was almost exactly like the Chicks' "Never Mind the Frogs" notices—except Scottie always stacked those on the torn-up coffee table near the fireplace. And *her* flyers were purple.

"What the. . . ." Scottie snatched up one of the pink flyers.

NEVER MIND "NEVER MIND THE FROGS." KNITTING IS *SO* LAST YEAR. FOR THE NEW, THE NOW, THE COOL, CHECK OUT BABES WITH BATTING.

ON OUR LAPS NOW: A CRAZY QUILT LIKE YOU'VE NEVER SEEN. BRING YOUR OWN NEEDLE AND THREAD, WE'LL SUPPLY THE TREATS. MEET BY THE FIREPLACE AT JOE, EVERY WEDNESDAY AFTERNOON.

"OhmiGod," Scottie exclaimed, waving the slip of paper in Tay's face. "This is a declaration of war!"

"No way," Tay scoffed after she'd had a chance to read the flyer herself. "They're just riffing on us is all. It's nothing."

The barista slammed their drinks down at the end of the bar and barked, "That's $7.25."

He pointed at a big coffee can parked near the quilting flyers and added, "Note the tip jar."

Scottie grabbed her frap, took a desperate gulp, and gaped at the flyer some more.

"'Knitting is so last year?'" she screeched at Tay. "Quilting is 'the now, the cool?!' How is that not a direct hit against us?"

Before Tay could find some other way to shrug off Scottie's outrage, Bella bounced through the door.

"Hi Chick-a-dees!" she called out, grinning her super-wide grin. Then she called to the barista, "Reuben? Can I have one of your awesome honey milks? In a to-go cup?"

"Sure thing, B," the barista said. The gruffness in his voice melted away and he even shot Bella some semblance of a smile as he grabbed a gallon of two-percent out of the fridge.

"Oh. My. God," Scottie said again, but this time she was gaping at Bella. "The grouchiest barista in the history of Joe has a name and you know it? Okay, who *can't* you charm?"

"Apparently," Tay said, handing Bella a hot pink sheet, "the Babes with Batting."

Bella skimmed through the flyer. "Hee! They made their flyer just like ours!"

"Hee?!" Scottie said. "Am I the only one who's freaked by this?"

"Ooh, she's right," Tay said to Bella. "I mean, it always starts with an innocent flyer. But before you know it, they'll have a website. Then a club at school. Eventually, of course, they'll challenge us to a rumble at the playground. Between all the knitting needles and quilting needles, somebody'll definitely put an eye out."

Bella giggled.

"I'm sure they don't want to be mean," Bella said, as Reuben gently placed her honey milk before her. "They're just trying to get people excited about quilting. You know, like Scottie tried to get that girl at Movies in the Park excited about knitting?"

"I'm never going to live that down, am I?" Scottie groaned.

"You should be glad," Bella said, wiping off her milk mustache with the back of her hand. "It helped you find your destiny!"

"What, knitty nerd?" Scottie said. She motioned at the memory squares poking out of the top of her backpack. "I think that's been pretty well established for a while."

"No," Bella said. "I heard you're gonna be a Big Sib! Amanda told me in Euro history."

"Oh, that," Scottie said. "I'd say that was more default than destiny. But you never know. There might be a little fate going on there, too. Maybe as a big sib, I can right all the wrongs done to me by *my* big sister."

"What's Jordan's latest?" Tay said.

"Oh, nothing terrible," Scottie said sarcastically. "She's only making a movie about her *childhood*. In which *I* am prominently featured."

"Ooh!" Bella squealed. "You're gonna be a movie star."

"Okay, a twenty-seven-minute movie by an NYU film student?" Scottie corrected her. "That's not exactly movie star material, thank Gawd. But it is enough to *mortify* me. I'm sure she's gonna make me out to be completely evil, with buck teeth and smelly feet and a toenail-biting habit."

"But none of that stuff is you," Bella protested. "Anybody who knows you can see that."

"Actually . . ."

At the sound of Amanda's voice, Scottie glanced over her shoulder. Amanda had just stumbled into Joe, bowed under the weight of a big, lumpy garment bag.

"Don't even, Amanda," Scottie warned her.

Completely ignoring her, Amanda grinned at Tay and Bella and announced, "It is a little known fact that Scottie Shearer *did* bite her toenails once upon a time."

"Even though you had smelly feet?" Tay said to Scottie with a curled lip. "Scottie, I hang out with skaters who do farmer's blows in the middle of their airs and even *I* think that's disgusting."

"One time!" Scottie protested. "One time I had reeking feet, and only cuz my parents went to Spain and brought me back these ridiculous sandals with soles made of old rubber tires. But Jordan will never let me live it down."

"And now," Tay grinned, "neither will we—Bucky."

"Okay, so I also had buck teeth!" Scottie bellowed. "But hello . . ."

Scottie bared her perfectly normal teeth to her friends.

". . . I wore a retainer for three years. I'm completely cured."

"Okay, okay, I guess you're not a freak," Tay allowed.

"Anymore," Amanda added.

"Thanks a lot," Scottie said dryly. "Just promise me you'll remember that when you see Jordan's movie and she totally *Welcome to the Dollhouses* me."

Amanda giggled as she heaved her garment bag onto a stool and waved at Reuben. He ignored her, of course.

"Speaking of freaks, Amanda," Scottie quipped, "is there a reason you're toting half your closet around town with you?"

"Ugh," Amanda sighed, still trying fruitlessly to get Reuben's attention. "I've got deb duty in forty-five minutes, but I couldn't remember this morning if it was a tea, penmanship critique, or Curtsy Class. So, I just brought outfits for all of 'em."

Bella lifted one slender finger in Reuben's direction. "Can you bring Amanda a cappuccino with a double shot?" she asked. "She's got a long afternoon ahead of her."

She turned casually back to Amanda.

"Not that I approve of all that caffeine," she scolded. "It's totally unnatural. Then again, so is being a debutante, right?"

Amanda gaped at Bella as Reuben began foaming up milk for her cappuccino. "How did you—" she stuttered. "But that guy never looks twice at me—"

"It's Bella-magic," Scottie said with a grin. "Don't question it, for ye shall never understand it."

"Reuben's very nice underneath all his bristles," Bella insisted. "I don't know why I'm the only who sees that. Anyway," she continued, looking Amanda up and down, "why can't you wear *this* outfit to your deb thing? You look so pretty."

Amanda really did. She was wearing a pencil skirt that she'd hemmed with a little flounce of orange, hand-knitted lace. Her sheer T-shirt was also DIYed. She'd cut it down the front, then cinched it in with a bit of webby knitting. On anybody else, the get-up might have looked raggedy and threadbare, but Amanda wore it with such confidence that it looked like couture. Her makeup—all smoked-up eyes and matte-beige lips—made her look even more hip.

"This," she said, glancing down at her carefully constructed outfit with regret, "would totally get me tried for WASP treason. Or at the very least, it'd get me noticed. And I want to get through this whole deb year as inconspicuously as possible. I'm just gonna knit my way through all these classes, play wallflower at the cotillions, be home from all the balls by pumpkin hour, and hope nobody *ever* hears about my dirty-deb past when I'm designing clothes at Parsons next year."

Scottie flinched. Amanda couldn't wait to ditch Chicago and head to the Parsons School of Design. At the end of their junior year, one of Stark's guidance counselors had told Amanda that she was a shoo-in. She'd been more giddy after that meeting than Scottie had ever seen her.

"I mean, I've been worrying about college *forever*," she'd confided to Scottie. "It's just been *expected* that I go Ivy. My parents met at Columbia. My uncles went to Cornell and Yale. And my brother's practically being recruited for Harvard out of the fifth grade."

But the only part of Amanda that was Ivy League material was her DNA. Even though she'd made major strides in dealing with her learning disability the past couple years, she wasn't exactly giving the kids in the honors classes a run for their money.

Now that she knew she could get her degree by sketching, sewing, and knitting, she was saved. She was already working on her Parsons early-admission application.

And that's great, Scottie thought, taking a slurp of her frap, *except for the fact that Amanda and I have been going to the same school since we were seven, and I don't know* what *I'm gonna do without her, not to mention Bella and Tay.*

Not that Scottie wanted to think about that *now*. She quickly came up with a new topic.

"Wait a minute," she said, taking an indignant gulp of coffee. "Amanda, you have to be at deb duty in forty-five minutes. Bella's drinking from a to-go cup. And Tay, you're leaving, too?! Whatever happened to our traditional post-first-day-of-school dish?"

"See, I knew it!" Tay exclaimed. "You're probably all ready to knit up a quilt square memorializing this precious moment."

"Well, maybe I would if you guys weren't all bailing," Scottie retorted. "Explanations, please?"

"I've got to start my senior service project," Bella said apologetically. "I'm collecting signatures to protest Alaskan oil drilling."

"*That's* what you picked for your service project?" Scottie said. "Wow, I never knew you were so into the Alaskan wilderness."

"It's a respect-the-earth-in-general thing," Bella shrugged. "My parents used to take me to no-nukes rallies when I was a little kid. This just made sense."

"Sort of like Amanda curtsying to the landed gentry," Tay joked.

"Shut up!" Amanda said. "And besides, you're not one to talk. You're leaving, too. What's up with you?"

"What's up is the lease on my dad's apartment," Tay said. Her glower, which had begun to melt away under the influence of Chick-time and chocolate-laced coffee, returned. "I've gotta start packing."

"No way." Scottie laughed. "Your dad's leaving his ultimate bachelor pad? I thought he'd finally gotten the place perfect. A flat-screen TV in every room. A second medicine chest to house all his date-night cologne. And hasn't he finally managed to upholster every bit of furniture in leather?"

"Why should I care," Tay snapped, "when it's all being shipped out anyway?"

Scottie's grin faded. "Shipped out?" she said. "Don't you mean 'shipped to a new apartment?'"

"Yeah, I do," Tay said, slamming back the last of her mocha. "A new apartment in Milwaukee."

Instantly, a hot lump formed in Scottie's stomach. "Wait . . . what?" She gasped. "You are *not* moving to Milwaukee. You *can't*. You're, like, more Chicago than the Sears Tower—"

"Scottie," Tay cut in. "Of course *I'm* not moving to Milwaukee. My dad is. He got a job transfer there. He told me over breakfast this morning . . . way to make my first day of school even worse."

Scottie blinked as major tragedy quickly morphed into a mere blip. Relieved, she took a swig of frap, then went in for details.

"Okay, so your dad's moving," she said. "Are you moving in with your your mom full time?"

"Yesssss," Tay groaned sullenly.

"Wait a minute," Amanda said. "Isn't that good news? I mean, you're always complaining about your parents' joint custody thing. You hate having to drag yourself back and forth between their apartments every other day. And your mom definitely annoys you less than your dad. Girlfriend! You've got a reprieve!"

"That's what I thought at first, too," Tay said. She swiped a cardboard cup insulator off the counter and began popping it open and closed. "I started plotting out what I'd do with no commute between my two bedrooms. I'd have more knitting time. More hang time. More John time."

Scottie raised her eyebrows. Tay hardly ever talked about John. She didn't have to. When he wasn't at basketball practice, he was pretty much always around, stealing potato chips off Scottie's lunch tray, trading knitting quagmires with Amanda, and most of all gazing at Tay with his moony blue eyes. In her own mega-reserved way, Tay loved John's omnipresence, Scottie knew. Tay loved John, period. But she never talked about it.

So this tiny revelation was noteworthy.

But if Scottie called her on it, Tay would probably never let such a slip happen again. So Scottie stuck to the topic at hand.

"So what's the problem with the Milwaukee thing?" she asked.

"How much do you think I see my dad these days?" Tay asked her friends.

"Well, you're at his place at least three nights a week, right?" Bella said.

"Yeah, but unlike you and your folks, B," Tay said, "we don't sit down together for a nice, sprouty, vegan meal, followed by a kabbalah reading or drum circle or something."

"Stereotype me, why don't you!" Bella protested. "There's no drumming in our house. That's *so* men's movement."

"Well, then it *is* a surprise my dad hasn't glommed onto it," Tay said, her face going dark. "Anyway, if I see my dad for dinner at all—you know, if he doesn't have a dinner with a client or a *date*—it's him and me scarfing takeout in front of the TV."

"Oh, Tay," Bella said, clutching her to-go cup with both hands. "That's so sad."

"No, what's sad is *now* I'm going to have spend entire weekends with him," Tay exclaimed. "Since I'll be spending the week days with my mom, I have to go to Milwaukee two weekends a month and spend forty-eight hours with the guy. *Weekend* hours, with no school for me or job for him. We'll have no buffers at all! It's going to be completely boring and awkward and *annoying*. And spending every weeknight with my mom? With her touchy-feely, 'You know, Tay, we should really *talk* more?' That's gonna be almost as bad."

"But—" Scottie began.

"What about—" Amanda offered at the same time.

Tay held up her hand.

"You guys," she said. "Please don't try to be all silver lining-y. This sucks, plain and simple. And unlike you, I have two whole years of suckage to get through before I can escape. Now, I gotta go."

"So do I," Bella said, cringing.

"And I better change into something dowdy," Amanda sighed, heaving her garment bag off the coffee counter and peering toward the bathroom to see if it was occupied.

"O-*kay* then," Scottie announced, sliding off of her stool and heaving her bag back onto her shoulders. "Maybe I'll see if *Reuben* wants to dish about the first day of school. Something tells me, though, that I'm gonna get a big, fat no."

"Scottie . . . let's try again tomorrow," Amanda said. "I don't think I have any more deb dreck to deal with until Thursday."

"All right," Scottie sighed. She tucked her quilt squares more firmly into her backpack as she got ready to leave. "But y'know, tomorrow won't be the first day of our last year of school. It won't be the same."

"And maybe that's a good thing," Tay declared. "Cuz I gotta say, if we put major expectations on our *every* interface this year, just because it's the last one? I think life is gonna start to be a real drag."

Scottie was about to retort when Tay cut her off.

"And by 'we', I mean *you*, Scottie Nostalgia-is-my-middle-name Shearer. Now—see ya on the second day of school!"

4 *(Join main color and contrasting color)

As Scottie tromped to the L, she flipped open her cell and speed-dialed. Beck answered on the first ring.

"Tell me again, why am I taking philosophy *and* physics in the same semester?" he said. "I mean, how many ways can they think up to be existential? My head is so full of the big picture I feel like a gnat."

Scottie smiled gratefully. Celling with her boyfriend—just starting his second week at Northwestern University—wasn't the same as coffee-clatching with the Chicks, but it *did* give her crushy shivers that no amount of vanilla frappé could create. And not just because she adored Beck, but because this boyfriend-girlfriend thing they were doing? It was totally working—at least this time around.

The previous fall, when Beck had moved into the old bread factory where Scottie lived, the two of them had instantly fallen in like.

And that was the beginning of all our troubles, Scottie thought with a wry smile. *Basically, Beck understood that he liked me enough to take me out on a couple of dates. And I understood that we were complete soul mates, to be joined at the hip from that day forward.*

Needless to say, the couplehood Scottie concocted hadn't gone over so well with Beck. Adjusting to his new city and school was hard enough without navigating a new, suddenly-serious relationship, as well. Before

Scottie had even had a chance to recover from their first kiss, Beck had broken up with her.

Sort of.

Somehow, instead of going their separate ways, they'd started hanging out even more than they had before.

Turns out, Scottie remembered, *accidental dating is a lot more fun than "official" dating. The whole don't-call-him-he'll-call-you, schedule-Saturday-night-dinner-and-a-movie-on-Wednesday thing was* such *a drag. But once we broke up? I could wander down the hall to Beck's loft on a random Tuesday night because the Sci-Fi channel was having a* Firefly *marathon and I knew there was microwave kettle corn in his pantry. Or he could show up at my place on a Sunday morning with Apple Jacks and the funnies and I wouldn't even care if I'd just rolled out of bed and still had morning breath.*

Before Scottie and Beck knew it, they were coupled off again. Not that either of them realized it at first. It was Tay who'd pointed it out to Scottie one wintry evening. They'd just left Never Mind the Frogs and were heading to their favorite falafel joint for dinner. Scottie was keeping herself busy until nine because her parents were having an opening at their loft/gallery. There was nothing that made Scottie squirm more than being waylaid by some middle-aged, desperate-to-be-hip art aficionado who would try to bond with her over their mutual love of the Decemberists.

The girls had tromped up the slushy stairs of the L stop, then huddled under the heat lamps as they waited for the train. While she waited, Scottie bounced on the balls of her feet, scrunched her mittened hands around in her pockets, and squirmed her face deeper into the orange-and-gold scarf that she'd looped around and around her neck.

"Okay, either you have to pee *really* bad," Tay said, jokily edging away from Scottie, "or you're desperately waiting for a call from your boyfriend."

"I'm desperately waiting for the train," Scottie protested. "This is how I keep warm. I've refined my L dance over many years and it works perfectly *while* being perfectly unobtrusive."

"Then why did I *just* notice that you had to pee really bad or you were desperately waiting for a call from your boyfriend?" Tay teased.

"Oh, just because I'm not cool to the point of frozen, like you. . . ." Scottie teased back. "And meanwhile, let's rewind for a sec. 'Desperately waiting for a call from my boyfriend' would mean that I *have* a boyfriend. And I don't. We can't all have an eternal love like you do with John."

"Gross," Tay complained. "John is not my 'eternal love.'"

"Um, dating the same guy for two years?" Scottie quipped before burrowing her chin more deeply into her scarf. "When you're in high school, that's eternal love."

"Then what do you call snogging Beck exclusively for six months?" Tay said. "Cuz that's what you've been doing, Scottie."

Scottie stopped bouncing, squirming, and burrowing. Immediately, a chill began to creep through her outerwear, but she barely felt it.

"Has it been six months?" She gasped.

"It's February," Tay pointed out, her words gusting visibly in the 25-degree air. "And you got together in September, right?"

"Yeah, but we're not *together* together," Scottie protested. "Remember? Because I got incredibly spazzy about the whole boyfriend-girlfriend thing?"

"Yeah, well seems to me that you've been doing the boyfriend-girlfriend thing anyway. Sans spaz," Tay said, with a hint of pride in her voice.

"Huh," Scottie said. She was so stunned, she forgot to return to her L dance. She was frozen by the time the train arrived, but she didn't even care.

The previous year, when Scottie had decided that she and Beck were a couple, she'd never bothered to inform Beck of that fact. This time, she went straight to the source.

(Knitwise)

"Okay, don't freak out, but Tay seems to think that we're an official item," she said to Beck that night while they were doing their homework at Mandrake's, their favorite coffeehouse. "Which is stupid, right? Because we're not doing that forced boyfriend-girlfriend thing? Right?"

The moment the words left her lips, Scottie broke out in a sweat. Because suddenly, she realized that she *did* want to be Beck's girlfriend.

In fact, I don't think I ever stopped *wanting to be his girlfriend.*

And now that she'd been reminded of that annoying fact, it'd be really hard to go on being his *non*-girlfriend if he didn't feel the same way.

Beck looked at Scottie seriously. "Well, are you dating anybody else?"

"No!" Scottie had squawked. "As if I have the time. I'm always hanging with you or the Chicks."

Plus, no other boys are half as cute as you are. In fact, since I met you, I've sort of stopped noticing that other boys exist.

Scottie's breaths got even shorter.

"Wait a minute," she said. "Are *you* dating anyone else?"

"No," Beck said immediately.

Scottie and Beck gazed at each other across the table. It was their regular table—tucked into a corner far away from the busy counter and so time-worn it looked like it had been dipped in tea, which was precisely why they both loved it.

Then Beck leaned over and kissed Scottie. When he pulled away, he was smiling.

"Hello, girlfriend," he said.

"Wait—are you sure that's what you want?" Scottie stammered, trying to ignore the zingy feelings shooting through her. "I mean, when I called you my boyfriend in the fall, you freaked."

"Well, now it feels right," Beck said. "It's been six months, you know."

"You've been counting," Scottie said, feeling her face go pink.

"What, and you haven't?" Beck said. "Scottie, I know you. . . ."

"Seriously!" Scottie protested, her eyes going wide. "I totally lost track."

"See?" Beck said. "That's the very definition of feeling right."

"But you don't think it's going to feel weird?" Scottie pressed on. "Having, y'know, *declared* something? That's what happened before, remember?"

"Like I keep saying," Beck said, still all crinkly-eyed and smiley, "this isn't before. This is now. And the only thing that would be weird is if I didn't kiss you again right now."

What could Scottie do but succumb to the PDA?

And after that, surprisingly, it *hadn't* gotten weird. In fact, things had stayed pretty much the same. They'd still IM'd each other their most random thoughts in the middle of the night and staged spontaneous dates whenever the mood struck. Beck had still spent plenty of time with his friends from their school's underground 'zine, *Starkers,* and the Chicks had remained at the top of Scottie's speed-dial list.

Somehow Scottie—queen of the spazzes—had scored both a boyfriend *and* some balance.

And that was why her current cell chat with Beck was so effortlessly breezy.

"Philosophy and physics were part of your master plan, remember?" Scottie said. She paused to let a nanny pushing a stroller full of triplets edge past her on the sidewalk. "What was it you said? 'The only way I'm going to be a truly great film critic is by studying the scope of humanity?' It was something like that, right?"

"Oh my God, was I really that pretentious?" Beck said. "Well, I've changed my mind. The way to become a great film critic is to forget about books and just go to the movies. At least twice a day. I wonder who would give me a degree to do that. Maybe Brown?"

"Who knows," Scottie mused. Now she paused in front of Mortally

Wounded, one of her favorite boutiques, and spotted a wild knitted hat—a bright orange newsboy number with a crown so bunched and bumpy it resembled cauliflower. As she often did when she spotted new knitty wonders, she found herself trying to imagine the pattern behind the hat. She was quickly stumped.

If only Amanda were here instead of at her dumb deb thing, she sighed to herself. *Not only could she figure out the how behind that hat, she'd be able to do it one better.*

Scottie knew that one day she'd be seeing Amanda's designs in shop windows. She was as certain of that as she was that Beck was destined to be the next Ebert (but a young, hot version of Ebert with shaggy dark hair, hazel eyes, and very kissable lips).

"You know," Scottie said suddenly to Beck, "you don't know how lucky you are."

"That I have so much philosophy reading to do that my brain might turn to grey goo by morning?"

"That you know exactly what you want to do with your life," Scottie said. "That there's a *point* to liquefying your brain in philosophy class. Meanwhile, I'm floating around with no point except the ones on my knitting needles."

"Scottie, you're in high school," Beck said. "The whole point of high school is to get through it so you can leave and go to college."

Oh, really, Scottie thought dryly.

In the past week, Beck had described every corner of college life to her. He was living in a cell of a dorm room with a roommate named Jurgen who gnawed on cold sausages when he came home from parties at 2 A.M. He was loving his three cafeteria meals a day. Most fabulous of all, he was living parent-free for the first time in his life, which meant staying out as late as he cared to, eating burgers for breakfast and cereal for dinner if he wanted, and worrying about no one but himself.

It sounded like heaven, yet college still felt like a black hole in Scottie's future. She never dreamed about the cool stuff she might

·· *Chicks with Sticks*

learn, the friends she might make, the non-Chicago town she might live in. All she could picture was the life she'd have to give up to get there; the life that she'd finally, somehow, gotten *right*.

How is it possible, Scottie thought, staring glassy-eyed at the cauliflower hat, *that I suddenly have three best friends, a completely cute boyfriend, semipopular status at school, and even parents that I can stand? Finally, everything's fallen into place—just in time for me to kiss it all good-bye.*

She sighed heavily.

"What's wrong?" Beck said. "Hey, did the first day of school suck? I totally forgot to ask you."

Scottie peeled herself away from the window and resumed her walk to the train. She knew if she wanted to dish about her first day with Beck, she could. He'd laugh about the redesigned cafeteria that had all the cliques jockeying for turf; about her English teacher, Mr. Brody, coming to class with a woolly beard and lecturing about his summer hike up the Appalachian Trail; about the fact that Charlie Whitfield and Zoe Cochran had *finally* broken up, much to the relief of all the Starkers who'd witnessed their operatic fights over the years . . .

But she figured Beck would only listen to her little high school stories to be nice.

Oh great, Scottie thought with another sigh. *Squashy alert.*

She quickly searched her mind for a subject change and found one.

"So guess what's new in Chickland?" she began.

She spent the rest of her commute home telling Beck all about Tay's clueless dad, her needy mom, and her new hands-on living arrangements. By the time Scottie arrived at the artfully rusted door of the Bread Factory, she was no longer feeling pangs of self-pity. She was just feeling terrible for Tay.

"See," Beck pointed out to her. "Even if you don't have a 'point' yet, at least you have tolerable parents. Which is more than Tay can say. Or me, for that matter."

Scottie gulped. She actually adored Beck's mom, a fashion designer who bustled around her loft in patchwork skirts, fingerless gloves, or striped stockings—whatever handmade eccentrica had struck her fancy that day. But Hannah didn't just *dress* on impulse. She ran her life that way, and it had always been hard on Beck. It was one of her never-look-back epiphanies that had inspired her to leave Beck's dad last year and drag Beck from New York to Chicago to start a new life. It had taken Beck months to adjust to it all, and even longer to forgive his mom for the nonchalant way she'd turned their entire family upside-down.

"You're right," Scottie shrugged as she hauled open the heavy door and fished her mailbox key out of her backpack. "Yes, my parents are dorks in funky glasses, and my mom is pretty loopy when she's in her painting zone, but lately they're pretty tolerable. I mean once my mom stopped trying to groom me into being some 'fiber artist' on the fast track to the Whitney Biennial, I guess my parents have some-how struck a balance between ignoring me and being all up in my Kool-Aid."

"All up in your *what?*"

"You know," Scottie said. "'Why're you all up in my Kool-Aid when you don't even know the flava?' You've heard that one."

"Uh, *no*," Beck guffawed. "Must be a high school thing."

"Oh piss off," Scottie said affectionately. She opened her family's mailbox and pulled out the usual stack of bills, flashy invites to art openings, and catalogs.

"Hey," she said, making her voice go low and flirty. "I'm standing in the place where we first met."

"Oh really," Beck said, flirting right back. "Anything good in the junk mail trough for me?"

Scottie sifted through the bin where people tossed their supermarket circulars, takeout menus, and ads for everything from psychics to pizza.

"Hmm," Scottie said, fishing out a crude flyer. "There's a dermatologist in Rogers Park who'll give you package deal on Lasik surgery and hair implants. Looks like you can even get them simultaneously."

"What, you don't think bald and bespectacled is a good look for me?" Beck cried. "Scottie, I'm hurt."

"Hey, I'm just trying to help," Scottie giggled.

"Then read a hundred pages of Immanuel Kant and call me with a report in the morning," Beck proposed.

"Never heard of him," Scottie retorted. "Must be a college thing."

"Well, how would you know?" Beck shot back. "You haven't even been up to visit me yet."

Scottie bit her lip. Beck was right. Even though his campus was just a twenty-minute L ride away, Scottie hadn't gone to see his new digs yet. The fact was, she'd much rather hang with him in his mom's chaotic loft, sifting through the takeout containers in the fridge while his vast CD collection played in the background. Their last date before Beck had left for college the previous weekend, they'd spent hours at Mandrake's. Beck had read through his orientation packet while Scottie knitted up a wide, get-your-hair-off-your-neck headband to get her through the swelter of Chicago's Indian summer. It had been so cozy, so familiar, and frankly, much more appealing than the cinder-block digs Beck kept telling her about.

"Oh, come on," Scottie said. "Chicago has Mandrake's, the Music Box, and Hot Doug's hot dogs. Chicago's where it's at."

She paused.

"Okay, that sounded like a bad commercial for tourists," she said. "But you know what I mean."

"The thing is, Scottie," Beck said, "Evanston is where *I'm* at." Some of the breeze had gone out of his voice.

"You're right, you're right," Scottie said vaguely. She pushed through another rusty door and headed down the long hall to the elevator. "Listen, I better go. I'm about to go into no-cell-ville."

"The elevator?" Beck said. "*Our* elevator?" The flirty lilt came back and Scottie's cheeks went pink. The clunky freight elevator was super-slow and thus, usually empty. In other words, it was an excellent place to make out.

"See," she said to Beck, "you *do* miss it here. We don't have our own private elevator in your dorm."

"Hmm, you're right," Beck said. In the background, Scottie heard a thud and a clatter.

"What are you doing?" she said.

"What do you think?" Beck said. "I'm pulling out my laundry basket. And it looks dangerously full."

"Whoops, better come home," Scottie said. "If that basket's too heavy for the stairs, the elevator's here for you."

"I'll count on it," Beck said.

Scottie laughed as she clicked her phone shut. She was still giggling when she got off the elevator and reached her loft door.

Both of her work-at-home parents were likely to be home. *I guess I could tell* them *about Mr. Brody's new Grizzly Adams thing,* she thought with a shrug. *They're probably dying to hear about my first day anyway, so might as well throw them a bone.*

With that, she unlocked the loft's massive, rusty door and pushed her way inside.

5 *(Work in ribbing)

Scottie's parents were indeed right there when she came in. Of course, they were so busy talking to her *sister* that they didn't even notice that Scottie had arrived.

Okay, maybe that bone-throwing won't be necessary, Scottie thought with an eye-roll.

She stepped into the kitchen, where her parents were sitting shoulder-to-shoulder in front of the family iMac. The computer's webcam was aimed at their faces and on the screen, Jordan was peering into *her* webcam in New York. Their mom was covering her thin mouth with her hand as she chortled, and their dad was gesturing wildly as he told a story.

A story Scottie recognized in about half a second.

"You see, back in the day," her dad was saying, "your mother was very anti-baby talk. None of this 'wee wee' or 'poo poo' for her. She taught you girls how to talk like little grown-ups."

On the computer screen, Scottie saw the fuzzy image of her sister, nodding and giggling. Her nose ring glinted in the light of her computer monitor, and behind her two of the willowy girls who shared her NYU dorm suite were doing Pilates.

"Um," Scottie began, "what's going on he—"

"And your mom *hated* the third person thing," her dad went on. "You know, when women would say to their kids, 'Mommy has to go to the store now.' She would always say 'I' and 'you.'"

"Jordan?" Scottie called over her parents' shoulders. "You're not taping this, are you?"

"Shhh, honey," Scottie's mom whispered, peeking back at her. "This is for your sister's movie."

"No," Scottie breathed, dumping her stuff on the kitchen island. "You guys can *not* be telling this story on film."

"So one night, we're at a patron's party," her dad said, ignoring Scottie. "You know that kind of scene—a bunch of artists trying to act respectable for a bunch of socialites. There were ice sculptures and stuffed mushroom caps and no music at all. I mean, you could hear a pin drop in there. And three-year-old Scottie toddles up to your mother. . . ."

"Dad!" Scottie whisper-shrieked.

Her dad glanced over his shoulder, winked at Scottie, and turned back to the webcam to press on.

"And she tugs on Carrie's dress," he said, "and then she announces, very loudly, 'Mommy! I have to myinate!'"

"You know," Scottie's mom explained, as if Jordan hadn't heard this story a dozen times already, "instead of 'urinate?' *Yourinate.* Isn't that cute?"

"Adorable," Jordan said, flatly as she scribbled some notes on a clipboard. "Wasn't this during that period when Scottie was really, really fat? Do we have any home movies from that time?"

"Oh my God," Scottie broke in. "That was baby fat. I was *three!*"

"And *so* cute," her mom chimed in. "Remember what I used to call her, Ted?"

"Our little Jabba," her dad crooned, giving Scottie a playful chuck under the chin.

"Okay, guess what?" Scottie protested, knocking her dad's hand away. "I'm no longer three years old. So . . . Jabba? What was that?"

This was a babyhood story she actually hadn't heard.

"You know, from that *Star Wars* movie," her mom said absently. She peered at her reflection in the computer monitor and pulled at her short red hair to make it go spikier. "It was just a little joke."

"Wait a minute. Jabba?!" Scottie exclaimed. "As in Jabba *the Hut?!* Mom! I wasn't *that* huge! It was just *baby fat!*"

"Of course, we knew that, sweetie," her mom said. "Which was why we could joke about it. I mean, you went through this period where you just . . . *sat* there while Jordan ran circles around you."

Okay, next time I start to think of myself as even remotely cool? Scottie told herself. *All I have to do is do a little check-in with the fam. Jeez!*

"I can't believe you called your own daughter Jabba!" Scottie squeaked. "That's, like, cruel and unusual!"

"Oh, Scottie," her mom said, waving her off. "I meant it with affection."

"I ran circles around her?" Jordan said from the computer screen. She made more notes. "Interesting choice of words. Very interesting."

"Jordan," Scottie shrieked. She shoved between her parents and thrust her face up to the webcam. "I forbid you to use this stuff in your stupid movie. You're violating my privacy. You're violating my *civil rights!*"

"Well, if you think it's just a stupid movie," Jordan sniffed, "then it doesn't really matter, does it? Besides, this story isn't just about you. It's about our *family.* Which includes me. So your stories are my stories, when you think about it. And my stories are material for my *art.* So . . . sorry. There's nothing I can do about it."

Scottie blinked for a moment, trying to make sense of what Jordan had just said. When she couldn't, she turned to her parents. "Mom!"

"Well, Scottie," her mom said with a guilty shrug, "she does have a point. I mean, you've never complained when I've put you in my paintings."

"Yeah, because most of your paintings are *abstracts!*" Scottie fumed. "You painted me as a wavery angel splashed with coffee or as a big, blue dot. The only one who knew those pictures were me was *you.*"

"I really don't see a difference," Jordan piped up from the computer screen, "between you painting Scottie as a big round object and me using video from the Jabba years. Do you, Mom?"

While her dad propped his chin on his fist and tried to hide his extreme amusement, Scottie's mom looked from Jordan to Scottie.

"Well," her mom squeaked into the webcam, "now Jordan, Scottie has a point, too."

"Yeah," Jordan sniped. "And it's *just* the kind of point I'd expect a non-artist to make. She doesn't understand."

"Oh, whatever," Scottie sputtered. She stomped over to the kitchen island and began sifting angrily through the pile of mail she'd tossed there. "I don't know why I even bother protesting. We all know Jordan's just gonna do what she wants to do."

Scottie was fuming so hard, she barely even glanced at the letters and catalogs as she flipped through them—until she spotted a familiar pink pamphlet. It was the monthly newsletter from Stockinette, a ridiculously hip yarn shop in super-trendy Bucktown. KnitWit, where Scottie's yarn addiction had first taken hold, would always be her first local-yarn-shop love, but as LYS's went, Stockinette ran a close second. It had white leather couches for stitching and bitching, galvanized tin buckets brimming with fuzzy goodness, and a ton of cool classes, readings, and other events on its calendar.

Just the thought of catching some fiber therapy at Stockinette calmed her down a bit. She decided to pointedly ignore her sister while she flipped through the knitty news.

Of course, Jordan was never one to be ignored.

"Hey, where did Scottie go?" she said, squinting at her computer screen to try to get a glimpse. "Is she still there?"

"*Yes*, I'm here," Scottie growled, repositioning herself between her parents in front of the webcam. "I'm just looking at a newsletter from Stockinette."

"Oh, that yarn place?" Jordan yawned. "So you're still knitting?"

Scottie stopped reading and turned to glare at her sister's image on the iMac. The previous year, when knitting was at its trendiest, Jordan had scooped up some sticks. She'd founded a Stitch 'n Bitch at some fabulous New York coffeehouse and started dropping Stollerisms into all her conversations. She'd even made a knit-flick for one of her film classes.

"Of course, I'm still knitting," Scottie snapped. "Aren't you?!"

"Oh, not anymore," Jordan said dismissively. "I'm kind of over that scene. I mean, yeah, knitting *was* the new yoga, but now yoga is the new Pilates."

"O-kay," Scottie said slowly. "So what's the new knitting then?"

"Quilting, of course," Jordan blurted.

"No. Way," Scottie breathed. She could literally feel her nostrils flaring, she was so mad.

But the last thing she needed was for her nostril-flaring to be caught on the webcam, so she rolled her newsletter into her fist, grabbed her backpack off the island, and headed for the kitchen doorway.

"Quilting, huh?" she said, just before she left the room. "That sounds just about right for you, Jordan."

"Thanks!" Jordan said brightly. Of course, she had no idea that Scottie was lumping her with the venomous Babes with Batting; the insult didn't even nick her.

So what else is new? Scottie sighed. *I guess nothing can hit her if she's running circles around me.*

Scottie waved at her parents, who were turning back to the iMac.

"So, Mom," Jordan said, "remember those kind of cheesy portraits you did of Scottie when she was little? Can you dig those out of storage for me?"

"During my Cassatt period?" Mom protested. "Oh, sweetie, are you sure you want something so staid?"

"Oh yeah," Jordan said. "Staid would be perfect."

Scottie let out a long-suffering sigh and began to trudge to her bedroom.

Eow, eow, eow!

Scottie's cat suddenly tottered into her path, yawning and stretching after what had clearly been a long nap.

"Hi, CC," Scottie murmured, scooping up her runty blue-gray cat and kissing the top of her head. "Looks like your day's been *much* more relaxing than mine."

"No doubt! It was your first day of school."

Scottie glanced over her shoulder. Her dad had snuck up behind her while, back in the kitchen, her mom continued to plot Scottie's humiliation with Jordan.

"Yup," Scottie said with a shrug. "First day of school. It always seems like this big event, until you actually get to it. Then it's kind of like any other day."

"Maybe it is this year," her dad said, with a gleam in his eye. That's when Scottie noticed that he was hiding one hand behind his back. "But not *next* year! That's gonna be a doozy!"

Suddenly, he whipped his hand out. He was clutching a sizeable stack of big, glossy folders and pamphlets. The top folder read, WILLIAMS COLLEGE: ARE WE IN YOUR FUTURE?

"Dad," Scottie squawked, "I haven't even memorized my class schedule yet and we're already on to next year?"

"Well, honey, with college applications due in January," her dad countered, "you really need to narrow down some favorites soon, don't you think?"

Scottie shrugged and glanced downward. CC was curled up beneath one arm. With her other hand, she clutched her backpack and Stockinette newsletter.

"I'm kind of loaded down," she said with a crooked smile. "Can I grab those pamphlets later?"

"How about I leave them on your desk," her dad said, walking into Scottie's room ahead of her and plunking the stack next to her computer.

"Thanks, Dad," Scottie said. She plopped onto her bed and unzipped her backpack. Letting CC scramble to the foot of the bed, she began unloading the detritus of the school day, from crumpled service fair flyers to an errant lip gloss to a quilt-square-in-progress. Only when she began to pull some actual books out of her pack did Scottie notice that her dad was still there, standing awkwardly in the middle of her white shag rug.

"Listen, are you mad about the Jordan thing?" Scottie asked, kicking off her shoes and crossing her legs beneath her. "Sorry if I was harsh, but I think I have a right to be a *little* peeved. I mean, is she including *her* baby pictures? The ones that show she was basically bald until she was two?"

"Oh that," Dad said. "Listen, honey, don't worry about Jordan's movie. Even if she does use some stuff from your childhood, it's possible nobody will even see it."

Scottie gave her dad a sly grin. It was a well-known fact in their family that Scottie and her Dad were multiplex fans and neither of them ever really got Jordan's films.

"Right," Scottie agreed. "There's no way this film'll get further than some NYU screening room filled with black beret types."

She laughed and flipped open the little notebook where she'd jotted all her homework assignments. *You'd think the teachers might want to ease us in, but no! I've got thirty pages of reading for history alone. And let's see, just a journal entry for English. That's not too har—*

Suddenly, Scottie glanced up. He was still there!

"Um, Dad?" she said. "Is there something else?"

"Oh, well," her dad said, pulling at the neck of his mock turtleneck, "I just want to let you know that if you want to talk about any of these schools, I'd be happy to discuss them with you. More than happy!"

He gave the stack of catalogs a tap.

"And these are just the ones that *I* came up with," he said. "The ones I thought might appeal to you. But there are so many more options, Scottie. Maybe you'd like to make an appointment with your guidance counselor to talk about those."

Oh, that *sounds fun.* But with another glance at her dad's big, excited grin, Scottie realized that that was exactly what he thought.

So she relented.

"That's a good idea," she said with a thoughtful nod. "I should do that. You know, just to get started."

"Right," her dad said, clapping his hands and rubbing them together. "Because there is a *lot* to do, honey. I know at this moment, senior year probably seems endless, but believe me, it'll fly right by before you know it."

He said it as if that was a *good* thing.

Scottie nodded vaguely and grabbed the closest book she could find. She opened it purposefully, and buried her head in its pages.

"Thanks," she said. "But, Dad? I've sort of got a ton of homework to do."

"Oh, sure honey," her dad said, finally turning toward the door. "Just know that I'm here if you have any college questions. Any at all."

"*O-ka-ay,*" Scottie sing-songed.

As soon as the door shut behind her dad, she tossed her book aside, flopped back onto her pillow, and stared at the rough, metal rafters of the loft's faraway ceiling. Then her gaze wandered to her bedroom walls—drywall partitions that stopped a good six feet shy of the looming ceiling.

Here's a college question, she mused. *Do you have less privacy living in a dorm room with a roommate? Or having an open cake-box for a bedroom, just across a loft from your parents?*

She shook her head, looked back at her messy school stuff, and plucked out the most interesting item in the pile—the Stockinette news-letter. As usual, the shop had breathless yarn news: a new shipment of elusive Risdie yarn and a sale on some end-of-season cotton.

On the events calendar was a spinning workshop that intrigued Scottie, especially since it took place in a shop in Evanston.

Hmm, she noted. *Noon to three. Perfect opportunity for a knitogether with the Chicks* and *a visit with Beck.*

Further down the calendar, Scottie spotted a name that she recognized!

ALICE BIERMAN WILL READ FROM AND SIGN COPIES OF HER MEMOIR/PATTERN BOOK *PURLICUE* IN OUR LOUNGE, SATURDAY, DECEMBER 8TH AT 2 P.M.

Scottie felt a thrum of pride in her chest. Of course, she knew all about *Purlicue,* and Alice's book signing.

But why go to a for-the-masses reading, she thought with a grin, *when earlier that week, you're invited to the book's private launch party at the author's house?!*

If there could possibly be a fifth Chick, she would be Alice. The dearly departed KnitWit had been her shop, her baby. She'd transformed a shabby old flat on an Andersonville side street into a magical den of the knit, stocked with mismatched vintage furniture, a different paint color for every room, and knitting needles everywhere. Alice's yarn stash was as gorgeous as it was obscure. Even now, she wouldn't reveal some of her fiber sources, though KnitWit had been shuttered for more than a year.

Alice had other mysterious talents as well. The moment she laid eyes on someone, she could match that person with the perfect yarn. She'd done it for Scottie the day they'd met. Later that day, she'd done it for Amanda, Tay, and Bella as well. For a while after that, she'd been the fulcrum around which the Chicks revolved.

Now that Alice had moved on, Scottie still felt occasional twinges of yearning for those KnitWit days.

Maybe that's why I've been making these quilt squares, she mused. She dropped the Stockinette newsletter, reached down to a basket next to her bed, and pulled out a fuzzy, half-finished square.

If I don't knit up all my Chicky memories, she thought, looping the yarn around her finger so she could finish knitting the square, *I might wonder if this amazing time in my life had ever really happened.*

6 ✳ (Remove marker)

"Y'know, it took me six and a half weeks to knit my last sweater," Tay said as she and Scottie walked down Central Street in Evanston. Tay shoved her hands into her jacket pockets and shivered a bit. Three weeks had gone by since school had started and all evidence of summer had disappeared.

"That's not too bad. Especially since you had some major cabling going on in that sweater," Scottie said. Unlike Tay, she wasn't shivering. That was because, at the first hint of autumn cold, she'd happily pulled an arsenal of hand-knitted outerwear from the depths of her closet. She was decked out in a long, skinny scarf fringed with fuzzy tendrils, a knitted headband, and some hand warmers edged with tiny feathers.

"Still, six and a half weeks is pretty long time," Tay said. "Which makes me wonder . . ."

Scottie shot Tay a sidelong look. She sensed some serious snark coming on.

". . . why on earth would I want to add, oh, six months to the process by *spinning* my own yarn?!"

"I knew it!" Scottie said, glaring at Tay through a grin. "I knew you'd be all neg about this spinning workshop."

"Well, it seems a little *much*, doesn't it?" Tay said, gazing at the slate-gray sky as they walked. "I mean, it's bad enough that I feel compelled to knit at all, when I could just *buy* my sweaters at Old Navy for far less money and *way* less time. But add spinning to the mix and I might veer out of control. Do you think they have a twelve-step program for yarn addiction?"

"Yeah, it's next door to the glass-half-empty hotline center," Scottie said. "You should give 'em a ring some time."

"Or maybe I should just confiscate your Stockinette newsletter," Tay countered. "I swear, Scottie, every time you get that thing, you end up dragging us to yet another weird knitting event. Remember the 'Knitting in Motion' workshop?"

Scottie giggled. "You *know* I thought we were just gonna learn how to knit möbius scarves," she defended herself. "I had no idea they'd make us do that interpretive dance, flinging all that yarn around. And why should you complain about it, anyway? You just sat there and laughed while the rest of us made asses of ourselves."

"If only I'd had a video camera," Tay sighed. "I could have blackmailed *all* of you."

"Not Bella," Scottie retorted. "She was *all* about the interpretive dance."

There was a moment of silence as Scottie and Tay recalled Bella, with long bundles of yarn clutched in each fist, twirling giddily around the gymnasium where the Knitting in Motion workshop had been held. She'd leaped and spun and whirled all over the place, her long, skinny legs kicking out in every direction and her arms fluttering over her head. She'd looked completely ridiculous and stunningly beautiful all at once.

"Anyway," Scottie went on, "if you're *that* anti these little workshops, you didn't have to come today. We could have just met up for a stitch 'n bitch after."

"Yeah, well, the 'all-day' aspect of this little outing had its appeal," Tay admitted. "My mom's been angling for a little 'us' time."

"Is she freaked that you're heading off to Milwaukee next weekend?" Scottie asked with a sympathetic wince.

"*Tscha,*" Tay said. "Now that I'm in Andersonville full-time, the woman is pure Cling Wrap. I *had* to get out. And since John's got an away game today . . ."

". . . you had no choice but to hang with us," Scottie said. "Tay, I'm touched by your devotion."

"Shut up," Tay said. "I'm all about hanging with *you* guys. It's the Charlottes that I'm worried about."

"Charlottes?"

"You know," Tay said impatiently, "The spinners. They're all gonna be wearing high-collared shirts and their lips are gonna be thin and pinchy and their names'll be Olive and Shirley and Charlotte and they'll be about a hundred years old. Either that, or they'll be a bunch of organic farming types named Adelaide and Junebug. You know, with two long, gray braids and Birkenstock clogs and lots of beaded jewelry."

"Wow," Scottie poked at Tay, "when you stereotype, you really stereotype!"

"Hey, guys!"

Scottie looked across the street. The sound of Bella's squeaky voice—and her halo of wild braids—was unmistakable. She'd been doing community service hours in another northern suburb that morning and had taken a bus to meet the Chicks. Now she was heading toward them from the bus stop, waving wildly.

"How was the PIRGing?" Scottie asked Bella as they resumed their walk toward the workshop. "I bet all those folks in Winnetka were *way* into your save-the-world pitch."

Tay snorted. Winnetka was a famous bastion of super-rich folks who lived in gated estates.

"Oh, I'm not doing PIRG anymore, didn't I tell you?" Bella said. "Those people were so . . . angry. So today I went door-to-door for the

Save the Prairie Society. Do you *know* how important grasslands are to the Illinois ecosystem? If so much real estate development keeps happening, the prairie's gonna be, like, gone!"

"I did *not* know that," Tay said with a half-smile. "I'm sure the Winnetkans are *really* concerned about the prairie."

"Well," Bella shrugged, "I didn't get any donations, actually. But people were *really* nice. Two different ladies invited me in for tea!"

"Sounds like a couple of Charlottes," Scottie said, elbowing Tay in the ribs.

"Huh?" Bella asked. But before Scottie could explain, Bella snapped her fingers. "Oh, I almost forgot. Amanda celled me. She said she's just finishing up her deb luncheon and she's driving up in her mom's car. She'll be here in fifteen minutes."

"And here *we* are now," Scottie said coming to a halt. "Ten-thirty-two Central."

She pointed at the address on a woodsy shingle hanging above the storefront's door. Below the number was the shop's name: We R the World.

Tay sighed and squinted at Scottie.

"Adelaide and Junebug it is."

Actually, the instructor's name was Carmody.

But other than that, Tay's prediction was dead on. Carmody had the frazzly, gray pigtails, the clogs (though hers were Crocs instead of 'Stocks), and ropes of beads around her neck. Several of the students in the class looked like her crunchy clones.

But there were also a fair amount of Charlottes, and a handful of young Stockinette types who could easily have been the Chicks' classmates at Stark.

"See?" Scottie whispered to Tay as they settled themselves at a long table stocked with tufts of soft, gray roving and some drop spindles. "I told you this class would be cool."

"I reserve judgment until Carmody starts talking," Tay hissed back.

"Hello!" Carmody announced at that moment. "Welcome. I'm so happy to be here. I've come here from my farm in Wisconsin, where not only do I spin my own yarn, but I also shear my own wool from a barnyard full of goats, llamas, and sheep. There's something quite profound, I must say, about nurturing every aspect of a garment—raising the animals who give us the wool, washing and preparing the fiber, spinning it into yarn that's as unique as a snowflake, and finally, knitting something beautiful from that yarn."

"Oh, wow!" Bella squeaked.

"Oy vey," Tay groaned.

Just at that moment, Amanda slipped into the seat her friends had saved for her, smoothed down her deb-ready Chanel suit, and whispered, "CoCo? We're not in deb-land anymore."

Over the next three hours, the Chicks learned everything from how to card wool to how to identify the lazy kate on a spinning wheel.

Around the two-hour mark, Scottie and Amanda began dissolving into giggles as they imagined setting Carmody up on a date with Dr. Heath.

By two and a half hours, Bella had a small pile of broken yarnlets at her elbow and an expression that was anything but zen.

"And I thought yoga was tough," she whispered to her buds as yet another attempt spun wildly off her spindle. "Spinning's even harder. I should have known. I mean, have you seen *Gandhi?*"

After three hours, the class ended and Amanda, Bella, and Scottie gratefully began to pack up their supplies. It was only then that they realized what was going on with Tay.

She was still working her spindle. Her fingers were drafting her roving with a steady, easy rhythm and the yarn that was emerging looked *fabulous*. It was evenly spun and it wound around the spindle's shaft in a soft, graceful coil.

"Oh my God, Tay!" Amanda exclaimed. "You're a natural."

"Look at her face," Bella added, pointing at Tay's smooth, serene fore-head. "Where's the scowl?"

Only then did Tay's eyes unglaze and her fingers slow. As she emerged from her spinning haze, the small, contented smile that had been on her face for who-knew-how-long gently melted away. Then she blinked at her beautiful yarn, at her stunned friends, and at her swiftly develop-ing spinner's callous.

"You're totally addicted!" Scottie crowed, marveling at Tay's fresh yarn.

"You're right," Tay realized. Then she shot Scottie a glare and said, "Shearer, I'm gonna kill you."

Scottie laughed and shook her head.

"I'll do a Google on that twelve-step program for yarnheads," she breezed. "Now, come on. Beck's waiting for us."

As Amanda drove them all to the Northwestern campus, Scottie sank into the car seat with a happy sigh. This was the first long, lazy Satur-day the Chicks had had together since their chocolate fest at Movies in the Park. And when they pulled up in front of Beck's dorm and Scottie spotted him sitting on the front steps—looking all cute with a book propped up on his skinny legs—she sighed in double-time.

If I squint hard enough, she thought to herself, only half-joking, *I can pretend we're all in Chicago. Then this would* officially *be a perfect day.*

As it was, she felt so giddy that she skipped up to Beck and planted a sloppy kiss on his mouth.

"Hey!" Beck said, grinning as he emerged from his studying. "You're finally here!"

"Oh, are we late?" Scottie said, checking the time on her cell phone. "I thought I said 3:30."

"I mean, you finally made it to Evanston," Beck said, reaching over and tucking Scottie's hair behind her ear. "I've been holding my laundry hostage until you decided to come."

"So you're saying that this shirt is totally dirty?" Scottie said, gingerly touching the collar of his long-sleeved tee.

"Oh yeah, filthy," Beck grinned. "I'd keep my distance if I were you."

"That's okay, *we've* got that covered," Amanda said, breaking into their flirt-fest. "Man, you guys. Talk about PDA."

Scottie was about to tease Amanda about *her* checkered PDA past, but stopped herself just in time. Ever since Amanda had broken up with her boyfriend, Toby, the previous year, she'd been doggedly single. Sure, she'd consented to the occasional date, usually with boys who had the same pale intensity and dark-haired, rocker/geek vibe as Toby. But those guys rarely lasted more than a few weeks.

Amanda wouldn't have ever admitted it, but Scottie was sure she put every one of her suitors through a point-by-point comparison with Toby. And when they, inevitably, didn't measure up, she made a clean exit.

Now she had another excuse to blow off the boys—just about every free moment she had seemed to be eaten up with deb life.

And of course, Scottie knew, *there's no way she'll* ever *find a Toby-clone at some country club cotillion.*

So that was that, it seemed. For Amanda, romance would be deferred until further notice. She didn't seem to mind, really. She rarely talked about it and didn't seem at all sad when Scottie got all Beck-mushy or John hung around the Chicks' lunch table shooting Tay swoony glances.

Still, Scottie didn't want to rub Amanda's aloneness in her face. So she stuffed her hands into her pockets as she told Beck, "We've been spinning wool for the past three hours."

"I assume," Beck replied, "that means you're desperate for some coffee?"

Scottie and Amanda nodded vigorously and even Bella murmured, "A little chai *would* be nice."

Tay on the other hand, looked bright-eyed and happy.

"Wow," she said, placidly rubbing her new spinning callous with her finger. "I feel so mellow. This is *weird.*"

She pointed at Scottie. "If I start growing my hair out, wearing Birkenstocks, and singing folk songs," she threatened, "you are in major trouble."

"Or you can just accept your fate," Bella teased Tay, "and move into my house. I'm *sure* my parents would be happy to give you some yoga instruction. Maybe my mom would throw in a little acupuncture."

"Argh!" Tay cried.

"Let's head to the Unicorn Cafe," Beck said, motioning to the Chicks to follow him. "Not only do they have excellent coffee, but you can watch N.U.'s most obnoxious brainiacs go at it there. Someone is always playing a showy game of chess and there are usually a couple grad students having a loud argument about semiotic theory or something."

"Okay, I don't even know what semiotic theory is," Amanda said with a flinch.

"Neither do I," Beck said with a shrug and one of his cute, lopsided smiles. "That's the entertainment factor."

Scottie subtly slipped her hand into Beck's as they walked into a quad behind his dorm. Even though the weather was starting to chill, the lawn was dotted with students leaning against trees, flopped on benches, or lying on the grass with their heads on their backpacks, all studying.

"These are mostly dorms," Beck said, pointing at the pretty red brick buildings that bordered the courtyard. "I heard that right before finals, everybody leans out their windows at the same time and lets out a primal scream."

"That sounds a little terrifying," Bella said, turning to look at all the windows facing the quad.

"A lot less terrifying than finals," Beck said. "It's a blowing-off-steam thing, I guess."

"I think it's cool!" Tay said with a fierce look.

"Desperately trying to get your edge back after the whole spinning episode, are we?" Scottie giggled.

"Is it that obvious?" Tay asked with a grimace. Then she spotted something at the far end of the quad. "Hey, what's that?"

Scottie followed her gaze to a huge, craggy rock painted bright red. It was nested in a little plot of gravel and set off from the rest of the action with a low wall.

"Oh, that's the Rock!" Beck said proudly.

"Uh, we can sort of see that it's a rock," Tay said.

"No, it's *the* Rock," Beck said. As they got closer to it, Scottie saw some Greek letters spray-painted messily into the red, followed by STASH BASH! 11 P.M.

"So that's an ad for some frat party?" Scottie said. "Wouldn't a flyer have been a little easier?"

"Yeah, and when was the party?" Amanda wondered. "That could have been painted years ago."

"More like a few hours," Beck said. "People repaint the Rock every night."

"No way," Scottie breathed, though when she squinted at the rock, its jags and crags did have the gummy texture that came from layers upon layers of paint.

"Way," Beck said with a grin. "People do everything via the Rock here—protest wars, propose marriage, shout out to the astronomy club, whatever. It's totally okay by the school, but you still *have* to do the painting in the dead of night."

Scottie laughed as she pictured the Chicks in black clothes and knit caps, skulking across the quad to paint *C w/ S* all over the rock.

Then Scottie cocked her head, and conjured another image: the four of them lounging around a dorm suite littered with knitting needles, books, laptops, and snacks. She imagined them primal screaming out their dorm windows together, drilling each other for finals, trooping to the cafeteria in a congenial clump . . .

Wait a minute, she realized. *Why did I always assume that the Chicks could never end up at the same school? I mean, yeah, to outsiders, it would look totally Dawson's Creek-dorky if we all went to Northwestern. But who cares? At least we'd be together.*

Scottie looked around the quad. The scene was straight out of Lincoln Park in Chicago, except everyone was just around her age and had the cool, lopey presence of the curfew-less.

For the first time ever, it all looked kind of . . . appealing.

Especially if we could go, say, here, Scottie thought. *Going to Northwestern would be kind of like staying in Chicago, but not. Kind of like still being in high school together, but not. It would be perfect!*

In the back of her head, a voice that sounded suspiciously like Amanda's whispered, *But not.* Scottie pushed it away.

Then she turned to Beck. "Didn't you tell me they have an amazing art school here?" she said brightly. "What about fashion design? How's the fashion design department?"

"Um, I don't know, actually," Beck said, looking at her quizzically.

"I doubt it," Amanda said absentmindedly. "I mean, if you want to go into fashion, you go to New York. Everybody knows that."

"Maybe," Scottie said. Beck had just led them out of the quad and now they were walking down another picturesque avenue. In front of one severe-looking building, Scottie spotted a sign.

"Hey look," she said to Tay. "The Hogan Biological Sciences Building. I bet all the pre-med people just *live* there. Looks pretty nice, doesn't it?"

"It looks like a prison!" Tay said. She gaped at the building with a curled lip. Scottie took a second look with her. The building was a sheer face of gray rock, folded up like an accordion and dotted with a few skinny, vertical windows.

"I guess that makes sense," Tay added. "From what I hear, being pre-med is pretty much all toil and agony. That's the only reason I'm glad it's two years away."

"Yeah," Scottie said with a nervous giggle. "Lucky you."

Their group tromped along in silence for a few minutes. Scottie used the time to desperately scan the surroundings for more carrots to dangle in front of her friends. As they passed a little courtyard within a cluster of gothic stone buildings, she saw one.

"Bella!" she cried. "Check out the yoga circle!"

A ring of about six crunchsters—wearing lots of earth tones and cowrie shells, but no shoes—were floating from one graceful pose to another.

"Actually, I think that's Tai Chi," Bella said, giving the group a dismissive glance before looking away.

"Oh," Scottie said. Then she squeezed Beck's hand—perhaps a little too hard—and added, "But I bet there's a great yoga scene here, huh? I mean, everyone knows Evanstonians are an earthy crowd."

"I guess," Beck shrugged. "Being about as flexible as a pretzel stick, I haven't really looked into it."

"And why does it matter anyway?" Amanda said, giving Scottie a suspicious look. "I mean, we're just *visiting*, Scottie. Since when are you all, 'Rah, Rah, Mountain Lions?'"

"Uh, the team is the Wildcats, actually," Beck said.

"Whatever," Amanda yawned. "The only animal I'm interested in at the moment is the Unicorn. If I don't get some cappuccino soon, I'm gonna keel."

"Fine," Scottie sighed. "I was just—"

What *was* she doing? Did she really think that looking at a few buildings was gonna make all the Chicks want to go to this school?

Dream on, she berated herself.

Suddenly, she felt her mood swing from giddy to squashy. Her coffee jones was zapped away, too. Instead of a caffeinated pick-me-up, she decided, she wanted some warm honey milk—something soothing that would help her forget that her silly Chicks-take-Northwestern idea had ever occurred to her.

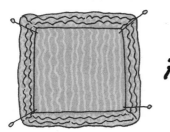

7 ✴ (Slip one stitch, knit one stitch)

The next day, Scottie was still feeling angsty. And whenever she felt angsty, she called Amanda.

She reached her on her cell, en route to a debutante luncheon with her parents and sounding harried.

"Okay, what's wrong?" Amanda said as soon as she heard Scottie's draggy greeting. "You sound all wallowy."

"I don't know." Scottie sighed. She was sitting on her bed surrounded by bundles of yarn, a bag of cookies, and CC. She plucked up a hank of melon-colored wool she'd bought a few weeks earlier and began winding it into a ball. "Maybe it's just the pressure of this whole year. You know, the college apps, the decision making, the planning."

"Are you kidding?" Amanda said. Scottie heard the telltale click of a makeup compact. Then Amanda began talking in a mush-mouthed drawl that made it clear she was putting on lipstick as she spoke. "That's the only thing that's getting me through this year."

"So the debbing is still beyond awful?" Scottie asked.

"Totally," Amanda said. "The other day at a dinner? I got trapped in a thirty-minute conversation about baguettes."

"About *bread?*" Scottie asked.

"Not *that* kind of baguette," Amanda said. "A Fendi baguette. You know, the fifteen-hundred-dollar purse?"

"Fifteen hundred dollars?!"

"The shocker to me," Amanda said, "is that *everybody* has to have one! Isn't fashion about being original? I mean, wait'll you see what I'm wearing to school tomorrow. I took some jeans—"

"Not your Paige jeans?!"

"Exactly my Paige jeans," Amanda retorted. "I cut them off at the calf and kinda frayed them, then I knitted in some gold thread so it kind of swags down to the ankles like a chandelier. I'm wearing it with a Michael Stars tank and tons of gold bangles."

"Sounds amazing," Scottie said, crunching into a chocolate chip cookie.

"Yeah," Amanda said with a sigh. *"So* much cooler than the boring suit I'm wearing right now. Speaking of which, I gotta go. We're here. Another deb luncheon, another poached salmon."

"Oh yeah, your life is *so* hard," Scottie laughed.

"So, are you okay?" Amanda said. "Or are you still wallowy?"

"Oh, I'm fine," Scottie said, pretty much meaning it. "I mean, the stuff I'm wallowing about is ages away, right? So why get in a wad about it now?"

Before Amanda could answer, Scottie's call waiting beeped in. It was Beck.

"Now I've gotta go, too," Scottie said. "Say hi to the Stepford Muffies for me."

"I hate you," Amanda said with a giggle in her voice. "See you at school tomorrow."

Scottie was laughing when she picked up Beck's call.

"Whatcha doin'?" Beck asked.

"Oh, you know," Scottie quipped, "strolling down Michigan Avenue, window shopping to kill time between my hot stone massage and my ladies' lunch."

"That's funny," Beck shot back, "since I called you on your *land* line.

I'm guessing you're actually sprawled on your bed in flannel jammies, socked in by yarn, a bag of Pepperidge Farm cookies, and a cat."

"You're *so* wrong," Scottie retorted. She pressed her half-wound melon yarn against her lips to keep from laughing.

"Oh, really?"

"It's a bag of Chips Ahoy, actually," Scottie said. "I'm feeling retro today."

"So why the ladies-who-lunch bit?" Beck wondered.

"Oh, I just wanted to remind you that I'm a big city girl to the end," Scottie said. "So don't let my little excursion to Evanston yesterday fool you."

"Don't worry," Beck said with a laugh. "In fact, I'm coming up with a ridiculously urban date for us for next weekend."

"That burlesque show with the absinthe and the hookahs that I saw in the Reader?" Scottie asked with mock earnestness. "*Very* cool."

"Okay, not *that* ridiculously urban," Beck said. "But it'll be good, I promise."

"I'm there," Scottie said. "Saturday?"

"I'll see you at the Factory," Beck said. "Now you better go. Aren't you late for your Botox shot?"

"No, silly," Scottie shot back. "Botox was last week. Today I'm having thigh fat injected into my lips."

Beck laughed so hard, he could barely choke out a good-bye. And Scottie hung up feeling like she'd finally exorcised the yuckiness of the previous day.

Which left her angst-free until, oh, the next morning. Because when she woke up for school and glanced at her day planner, she saw one thing—one *major* thing—scribbled on the day's page: Little Sib—first meeting.

As Scottie trudged down the hall, her stomach did a major flip-flop. Unlike Bella, who'd been able to begin her environmental activism from day one, so far Scottie's community service had been all about *preparing* to do community service.

Let's see, she ticked off on her sleepy fingers. *There was the orientation where I got my file on my little sib. Then there was the workshop about race and class sensitivity. Finally there was the two-day CPR certification* and *the test to make sure I know my way around Chicago.*

Scottie had made it through all her training. She'd even bought a special folder to store all her Big Sib paperwork. But now that she was poised to finally meet her little sib, her head felt like a panicked blank. All she knew at this fuzzy moment was that her sib, Nina, was twelve, that she was the oldest of five children, that she needed a little help with her reading comprehension, and that her single mom had emigrated from Poland nine years ago. Scottie had carefully written Nina's South Side address into her planner instead of scrawling it on an easy-to-lose scrap of paper the way she usually did. But other than that, she suddenly felt completely unprepared.

It didn't help matters that when she headed into the kitchen after her quick shower, she found her dad making pancakes. They were earnest, grainy, whole-wheat pancakes, but with enough syrup and bananas, they still counted as comfort food. Just the smell made Scottie want to blow off her whole day and curl up on the couch with CC and her latest quilt square. This one was going to be fringed in cotton candy angora to commemorate the previous Halloween when the Chicks had all worn pink wigs to school. Even Tay!

"Pancakes!" Scottie said, perching on one of the hard, Euro-sleek stools at the kitchen island. Even if her parents occasionally managed to turn a cozy meal out of it, the Shearer kitchen was anything but warm. To start with, it was carved out of a massive, old bread oven, with all-metal walls. To this, Scottie's parents had added so many stainless steel fixtures and gadgets that the whole place glinted.

Still, it was more appealing than a Monday at school.

"Good morning," Scottie's dad chirped as he plopped a short stack of cakes onto a plate and coasted it down the island counter toward her. Her mom shuffled into the kitchen a moment later. She was dressed for work in a pair of ancient linen capris and a paint-spattered tank top.

"How very Mr. Mom," her mom teased. She gave Scottie's dad an absentminded kiss as she passed him to head to the fridge. She took out a large bottle of pomegranate juice. But instead of pouring it into a glass like a *normal* person, she grabbed a paper towel, slapped it onto the island, and splashed the juice all over *that*. A big droplet of the stuff bounced up and hit Scottie squarely on the cheek.

"Mom!" she squealed, leaping up to get her own paper towel. "Do you know how much that stuff stains? People are gonna think I have the biggest zit on the planet."

She wet the towel and scrubbed at her cheek, checking her reflection in the chrome toaster.

"Sorry, honey," her mom said in the same out-of-it voice she'd used to greet her dad. "I wanted to see how the pigment in the juice diffuses on different weights of paper."

"Oh, I get it," Scottie said. She glanced at her dad and he nodded. Together they announced, "New painting phase."

"Why do you say it like that?" her mom pouted. "Like it's a bad thing?"

"Hey, I *love* getting takeout every night," Scottie said with a grin.

"And I love when you start a new series," her dad added. "So I guess this means I should schedule an opening at the gallery in, what, four months?"

"Don't rush me." Mom scowled, picking up the paper towel and holding the pomegranate stain up to the light. "I have a feeling this stuff is gonna be pretty volatile. But look at that *color*."

"First she paints with coffee," her dad said to Scottie. "Now pomegranate juice. All we need is some squid ink and maybe some saffron and we've got ourselves a pricy, gourmet meal."

"Speaking of," Scottie said, taking a big bite of her breakfast, "why the Sunday morning pancakes on Monday? Are we celebrating something?"

"Nah," her dad said, waving her off. "But I thought I should make up for yesterday. Your mother and I went out to brunch and left you here all alone."

Yeah, so I slept in, then feasted on a giant bowl of Lucky Charms like I do every Sunday morning, Scottie thought. *Why should this weekend have been any different?*

"So I didn't get a chance to talk to you about college visits," her dad went on. "You know, we should really plan some road trips if you want to check out a bunch of campuses before your applications are due."

Oh. That's why.

If Scottie had been feeling at all perked up by all the maple syrup in her system, the boost faded quickly. She retreated back into Monday morning droopiness.

"Well, what did you have in mind?" she asked, dropping her eyes to her plate and stabbing the final pancake morsel with her fork.

"Oh, it's not me who's looking for colleges," her dad said. "What do *you* have in mind?"

"It's a beautiful time to drive around New England," her mom suggested before Scottie had a chance to answer. "Amherst, Bennington, Wesleyan . . ."

Scottie swirled her forkful of pancake around and around in the puddle of syrup on her plate.

"Or if you're not thinking small, we could check out some Big Tens," her dad said. "You'd *love* Ann Arbor, sweetie."

Scottie's dad had gone to University of Michigan in Ann Arbor. Every year when the weather went crisp and cold, he got all nostalgic about having cider and doughnuts on football Saturdays. He'd reminisced to Scottie at least half a dozen times about studying in the dark and gothic law library. Ditto about denting his gold Cross pen during his senior finals because he'd gripped it so nervously. It all sounded very *Dead Poets Society*.

But not *very me*, Scottie thought. She slid off her stool, leaving her last soggy bite of pancake uneaten. She thunked her plate into the dishwasher and headed for the kitchen doorway.

"I'll have to think about it," she said, "and then I'll let you know."

"Good," her dad said. "We'll have a great time, honey. The first time *I* walked onto the campus at U of M, I tell ya—"

"I know, I know," Scottie cut him off. "It smelled like fall leaves and cigarette smoke and old books and you were *hooked*. I remember from the last time you told me, Dad."

"Your dad can't help it that he's rah-rah, Scottie," her mom said, peeling her eyes off her pomegranate stain to smirk at her husband. "He didn't become cool until he met *me*."

Oh God, Scottie groaned inwardly. Please *don't start in on* your *art school days. Yes, you pierced your ear in eight places and saw the Sex Pistols six times but, Mom? The edginess of all that has definitely passed its expiration date.*

But all she said out loud was, "You guys should play the Student Union. You'd *kill*. I wish I could stay for the rest of the comedy hour, but I've got school?"

"Oh, already?" her dad said, looking at the chrome clock on the wall in dismay. "Well, listen. Let's do this again soon. Waffles next time. And we can seriously hammer out some travel plans, okay?"

"Sure, Dad," Scottie said as she headed back to her room to grab her bag and bolt for school. "I'll work on my list."

Right after school, Scottie headed to Nina's neighborhood, Archer Heights. By the time she reached Nina's house, she was *seriously* craving some pirozhki. The avenue that ran between the L and Nina's street was lined with one lino-tiled bakery after another, all advertising the Polish turnovers, stuffed with meat, cabbage, or potato.

There were also more than a few dollar stores and fast food joints, not to mention a dusky-looking bar on every other corner, many with Polish names and each with a weathered OLD STYLE beer sign swinging over the door.

Nina's beige brick bungalow had the same shabby aura about it. The front lawn was neatly trimmed, but patchy, bisected by a cracked cement walk. The front porch was made out of cement, too.

The house's three front windows were all stocked with window boxes "planted" with a rainbow of plastic flowers—bright red, yellow, and orange gerbera daisies and tulips the color of Easter eggs.

Scottie smiled hesitantly at the window boxes. Were they tacky or cute?

On a Lincoln Park townhouse? Scottie thought. *Completely garish. But here?*

Scottie glanced up the street and spotted plenty of other candy-colored blooms brightening up the drab houses.

They're sweet, Scottie decided as she knocked on the front door.

They were also decidedly unfamiliar—which only made her more nervous. After all her Big Sib sensitivity training, Scottie was terrified that the first words out of her mouth would somehow be offensive.

Like, do I tell Nina I like the plastic flowers? Scottie debated. *Or would that sound condescending? Or is it condescending to even* think *that's condescending?*

As the doorknob began to turn, Scottie quickly decided to just leave the plastic flowers out of it. She pasted on a stiff smile as a woman opened the door. Her gray-blond hair was pulled into a tight ponytail and her hot-pink turtleneck brought out the rosiness in her cheeks. A very fat, gurgling baby was perched on her hip. He ducked his head and peeked shyly at Scottie, which made her smile harder.

"Ah, you must be Scott," the woman said in a thick, Polish accent. She motioned Scottie into the living room, which was crowded with two couches and a scattering of toys. "I'm Nina's mom, Zofia."

"It's Scottie, actually," Scottie said.

"Scottie?" Nina's mom said. "Such a strange name! You know, Nina has two Taylors in her class and one Ryan, and they are all girls! Maybe your mothers wanted boys?"

Scottie laughed, just as three tow-headed little girls ran into the living room and crowded around Zofia's legs. All of them grinned up at Scottie. Scottie smiled back—a real smile this time—as she reached out to touch the littlest girl's fine, blond hair.

"Nina!" Zofia called through a doorway that led into a narrow hallway. "Scottie is here."

Almost immediately, Nina appeared in the doorway. Her hair was a bit darker and thicker than her sisters' cornsilk, and her cheeks were narrow and elegant instead of chubby and rosy. She was wearing jeans that Scottie could tell were a close copy of Amanda's Paige jeans and purple suede sneakers that reminded Scottie of her favorite Pumas.

Scottie had the distinct impression that Nina had been hovering just out of sight, listening to Scottie talk to her mom. Scottie hoped Nina's shy smile and eager energy meant that she'd passed her first test.

"Hi," Nina said quietly. *Her* accent was all Chicago. "You made it."

"Of course I made it," Scottie said, a little too loudly. "So, what would you like to do? I have some ideas. . . ."

Ooh, I shouldn't have said that, Scottie cringed. She *probably has some ideas. At the training, they told me not to dominate too much—to let the little sib express herself.*

Nina almost ran to a pegboard next to the front door and snatched off her jacket.

"Wanna go?" she said.

"Oh, okay, sure," Scottie said, giving Zofia a questioning look.

"Have a good time," Zofia said before she spoke sharply to Nina. "Ninaleh, home by six, okay? I go to the nail shop in an hour. The babysitter will stay through dinner and help you get the littles to bed. I'll be home right after closing."

"Yeah, yeah, yeah. Okay, bye!" Nina said breathlessly, snatching the door open.

Before she and Scottie had even hit the front walk, Nina said, "So what are they?"

"What are . . ."

"Your ideas?" Nina said. A small smile—half-excited, half still-shy—was playing around her mouth.

"Oh, well," Scottie said, "we could stay around here. I did a Google on this European coffeehouse?"

"Webers? Or Racine Bakery?" Nina said quickly.

"Oh," Scottie said. "Well, yeah, of course you know them. Well, the ideas I *really* had were all on the North Side."

Scottie had carefully constructed a list of activities for Nina, from an after-school snack under the giant silver jelly bean in Millennium Park to a free chamber music concert at this church on Michigan Avenue. Not that Scottie really *liked* chamber music, but it seemed like the kind of thing you ought to do with your little sib. In fact, when Scottie had mentioned her plans to Lily—the earnest Big Sib/Little Sib coordinator who'd signed her up at the community service fair—Lily had clasped her hands and gotten all shiny.

"These are *perfect*," she'd said. "Educational, but not too structured. *And* they're activities that can really catalyze some healthy interfacing if Nina is at all retreating."

Scottie hadn't known exactly what Lily was talking about, but she'd carefully stored her ideas in her Big Sib folder.

"The North Side was *my* idea exactly," Nina said. Her shy smile went wider and bolder as she led the way back toward the L. "I never get to go there. My mom says it's too much hassle with the little kids, and she won't let me go by myself. I've been wanting to go to Ethel's Chocolate Lounge for ages. Cuz of course there are *no* chocolate lounges down here."

Nina sighed as they passed one of the countless bakeries on Archer

Avenue. A woman pushed through the door, bringing a gust of potato-scented steam with her.

"If I see one more pirozhki . . ." Nina muttered.

Scottie swallowed hard and steeled herself to play sympathetic ear to Nina's surly, disenchanted youth. But once the girls had ducked into the L station, Nina was all sweet smiles again.

"So, can we go to Ethel's?" she asked.

"Nina," Scottie said with a sly grin. "I happen to be quite the chocolate expert. And trust me when I tell you, we can do better."

"Nine dollars," Nina breathed. She and Scottie had just settled into their table at HotChocolate and were scanning their menus. "Nine dollars for a single dessert."

"But look at all you're getting," Scottie protested. She read aloud from the menu. "'Warm fudge brownie ala mode with salted caramel ice cream, unsweetened whipped cream, and caramel corn.'"

"Caramel corn!" Nina shrieked, before putting a hand over her mouth and looking around. The cafe was almost empty, it being the post-lunch and pre-dinner hour, but it still felt like the kind of cool, swank place where you didn't squeal about caramel corn.

"C'mon, Nina," Scottie coaxed. "I saw a blurb about this dessert in the *Reader* a few weeks ago and I've been dying to try it ever since. We'll split it—and it's my treat."

"Hey," Nina said, with another grin. "I never said I didn't want to try it."

When their waitress arrived, they ordered the brownie and, giggling, a couple mugs of hot chocolate for good measure.

And then, they stared at each other across the table in silence.

Okay, what do we talk about now? Scottie thought desperately. *I mean, what do we have in common besides the fact that we both love chocolate?*

Scottie looked into Nina's round blue eyes and saw the exact same terror flit across *her* face.

Which made Scottie laugh. "Oh man," she said. "This isn't exactly like hanging out with your girlfriends, is it?"

"No," Nina admitted. "But it's nice."

"And actually, this *is* the kind of thing I do with my girlfriends," Scottie said. "We're big snackers."

"My mom doesn't let me bring junk food for lunch," Nina said with an eye-roll. "She's all . . ." Nina adopted her mother's lilting Polish accent as she mimicked, "Ninaleh! How do you expect to *think* in school if you eat nothing but the Oreos. Now you'll *eat* my homemade pickles every day at lunch, and you will *like* it."

Scottie burst out laughing, which made Nina giggle, too.

"I guess it could be worse," Nina shrugged. "My friend Cynthia has never had a lunch bag without cabbage in it. *Some* kind of cabbage. Whoa, does it stink."

Scottie giggled some more. "But what about after school?" she asked. "Where do you guys hang out? Those coffeehouses in your neighborhood? Or what about Chinatown? That's pretty close to you."

Nina shrugged again.

"My mom works two jobs," she said. "Mornings she answers the phone at a realtor's office and then whenever she can get hours, she does nails at this salon. Sometimes she can get the babysitter, but when she can't, *I'm* the babysitter. Mostly, my friends come over to my house."

"That sounds hard," Scottie said.

"Katie's almost nine, so she can help with the littles," Nina said. "And Teddy—he's the baby—he's just this butterball who's happy to sit in his play yard."

Sounds familiar, Scottie thought dryly.

"But it's good," Nina said, and then Scottie saw *her* swallow hard, "to be able to get away."

At that moment, Scottie realized what this was all about. She wasn't here to rack up community service hours. She was here because Nina deserved a vacation from "the littles," and a little chocolate decadence, and someone who could focus on just *her* for a few hours a week.

And suddenly, Scottie felt up to the task. When she thought about spending two afternoons a week with Nina, she didn't see a bunch of contrived excursions to museums and parks and concerts. She saw them getting to know each other and talking. Really talking, not some Big-Sib-to-Little-Sib "interface."

Scottie could imagine something else, too. She pictured herself holding a skein of yarn up to Nina's cheek. It was a soft, brushed seafoam green, chunky-weight, maybe shot through with French blue or glinty, sunshine-yellow. It would be the perfect, but not-too-predictable, color for Nina's understated, blond prettiness.

Two years ago, Alice had done this for Scottie, thrusting a twist of coppery-brown yarn beneath Scottie's chin. It was yarn that had somehow conjured red highlights in her hair and a golden warmth in her pale skin. It had been a cozy companion as she'd made her first halting steps into her new knitty world, and it had sealed a deal between her and Alice. Scottie had known then that Alice would always be there for her. Not as a "mother figure" or some impossible attempt at a replacement for her late Aunt Roz. But as someone who was older than Scottie, but far from parental. Who was wiser than Scottie, but in no way a know-it-all.

She was basically, Scottie realized for the first time, *my big sib.*

And now it was Scottie's turn.

As the waitress plunked down the girls' mugs, which wafted an intoxicating chocolaty aroma into their faces, Scottie grinned.

"Nina," she said, thrusting out her cup to clink it against her little sib's, "have you ever heard of a place called Stockinette?"

8 ✦ (Double decrease)

Halo2Champ: Calling all chicks. R u there? I'm in exile and I gotta vent.

Scottie sat up in her desk chair so fast that CC, who was nestled in her lap, squawked in protest. Scottie gave the cat a placating pat with one hand and scrubbed at her sleepy eyes with the other.

And now, the moment we've been waiting for, she thought. *Time for a Tay tirade.*

Then she immediately felt guilty. It wasn't like she *wanted* Tay to be having a horrible time on her first weekend in Milwaukee. But Scottie was having a drag of a day. Sure, she was psyched about her date with Beck that night, but until then, Scottie had a stack of un-fun items on her agenda, from starting the ten-page beast of a paper she had to write for her AP English class to doing her history reading to finally blocking the memory quilt squares that had been lurking, wadded into balls, in her backpack for way too long.

A rant from Tay was the perfect way to break up her day. Scottie moused over to her IM window and started typing.

KnitChick17: I'm here! What's the happs in the wilds of Wisconsin?

HALO2CHAMP: Grooooaaan! He's driving me crazy.

Bella's screen name suddenly chimed into the window. Scottie knew not to expect Amanda to join in. Amanda wrote the occasional e-mail, but the whole IM thing? The thinking and rapid-fire typing, *at the same time?* It was basically her worst nightmare. To compensate, she had a cell phone plan without about a million minutes on it.

BELLISSIMA: Who's driving u crazy, yr dad? Hi, btw. i was just sending out an e-petition. Did u know the mountain gorillas of Rwanda have, like, no habitat left? It's terrible!

HALO2CHAMP: i know how they feel. U guys, I am a grl w/out a home.

KNITCHICK17: Oh man, does yr dad have u sleeping on the couch or something?

HALO2CHAMP: Nah. I have a bedroom. & a bathroom. Even my own shelf in the fridge.

BELLISSIMA: OK, I have to hide all my non-carob chocolate in a box under the bed, so I gotta say—that doesn't sound so bad.

HALO2CHAMP: Plz. I only have the shelf cuz the fridge is a barren wasteland. Nothin in it but takeout boxes & beer. Oh, & some half-drunk white wine. Guess he used that 2 entertain 1 of his "lady friends."

KNITCHICK17: Ew.

KNITCHICK17: Wait a minute. The lady friend. Yr dad doesn't have some secret stepmonster up there, does he? Was the whole job transfer thing a ruse? But in reality was he waiting 2 spring some secret love on you? Ohmigod—a love with a love child!!!!! DOES HE HAVE A WISCONSONIAN LOVE CHILD?!?!

HALO2CHAMP: Dude. U've been reading way 2 many bad novels.

HALO2CHAMP: B-sides, it's just the opposite. His swingin' single shtick's gotten worse.

BELLISSIMA: What could B worse than the COLOGNE?

KNITCHICK17: This coming from Miss Patchouli?

BELLISSIMA: Scuse me, but essential oils vs. Drakkar Noir? That's like comparing Godivas 2 my mom's carob soy-butter balls.

HALO2CHAMP: Whatev. It's not the cologne that's awful, it's the car.

KNITCHICK17: The Beamer?

HALO2CHAMP: Not anymore. He traded it in. 4 a PORSCHE!

BELLISSIMA: Ew!

KNITCHICK17: Ew!

HALO2CHAMP: It's a Boxster.

BELLISSIMA: What's that?

HALO2CHAMP: A convertible.

KNITCHICK17: Noooo!

HALO2CHAMP: Gets worse, dudes. So yesterday, he picks me up from the train station in the thing. It's red, of COURSE. So I just scooch down as far as I can in the seat and try not 2 make eye contact with anyone.

KNITCHICK17: Do u know anyone in Milwaukee?

HALO2CHAMP: No, but u can b humiliated in front of strangers. Remember that time a whole trainload of people made fun of u?

KNITCHICK17: Uh, I do now. Thanks for the happy memory.

BELLISSIMA: Don't worry, Scottie. I would've gotten hysterical 2 if the L had ripped my WIP right out of my hands and frogged the whole thing in 2 secs flat.

KNITCHICK17: OK, I think "hysterical" is overstating things JUST a bit, B. And anyway, we weren't talking about MY humiliation (4 a change). We were discussing TAY'S. Do go on, Tay.

HALO2CHAMP: Oh, u r just loving this, aren't u, Shearer.

KNITCHICK17: Course not. Now, what happened on the way home from the station?

HALO2CHAMP: Nothing. It was what happened last night. Dad wanted 2 go out 2 dinner, right?

KnitChick17: What, no takeout? No TV?

Halo2Champ: NO buffers at all! I swear, I thought abt bringing my iPod and just plugging in once we got 2 the restaurant. Or having "emergency" cell me. But Mr. A made me promise to make an effort. He said if I didn't, he was gonna call my dad 2 talk about family therapy AND make me knit him a pair of socks.

Bellissima: Um, is THREATENING really guidance counselor-like? That doesn't sound v. therapeutic.

KnitChick17: this is Tay we're talking abt. She doesn't respond 2, "How does that make you feel?" U have 2 wrestle her 2 the ground and force-feed her her mental health.

Halo2Champ: Hello, I'm still here!!!!

KnitChick17: Do u deny it?

Halo2Champ: Look, do u want to hear the rest of the story or not?

Bellissima: She didn't deny it. Y'know, I think you could BOTH use a little acupuncture from my mom.

KnitChick17: NO!

Halo2Champ: NO! Look, y don't we just talk when I get back—

KnitChick17: Don't u dare log off!!!!

Halo2Champ: No more needle talk?

Bellissima: Unless it's KNITTING needle talk. promise.

Halo2Champ: OK. So Dad insists on driving us 2 dinner. This time I was ready for the Porsche—wore a hat AND sunglasses.

KnitChick17: Camo. Good thinking.

Halo2Champ: Maybe 2 good. b/c when we get to the resto? Which, btw, was this dark and ferny steak house that couldn't BE more male—

Bellissima: that's a bad thing? Tay, u r the tomboyest girl i know!

Halo2Champ: Yeah, but cigar-smelly steak houses r male in a cheesy way. It's like peeing on yr property or roaring at rivals. It's just trying way 2 hard.

KnitChick17: Man, u r hard 2 please.

Bellissima: Way.

Halo2Champ: Not even the point! So Dad pulls up 2 the valet parking, rt? & he's gunning the motor and throwing his porschey weight around when up strolls this friend of his who's just come out of the restaurant. Talk about cheese. He's all paunchy & mustachey and his chin was greasy from his steak dinner. & then he gives me this LOOK.

Bellissima: What kind of look?

Halo2Champ: The kind of look a greasy-chinned old man gives 2 a girl in a Porsche. And then he kind of chuckles at my dad & gives him the thumbs up.

KnitChick17: Wait—WHAT?!?!?!?

Bellissima: Did he think u were— Wait—WHAT?!?!?

Halo2Champ: Yes, the disgusting thoughts u r thinking r CORRECT. This cheesehead thought that I was my dad's DATE.

KnitChick17: Ew, ew, ew!!!!!!!

Halo2Champ: Yeah, it's gross on too many levels to count. One of which is, if this guy thought I was my dad's date—

Bellissima: Urgle. Stop saying that.

Halo2Champ:—then that must mean my dad's been seen around town w/girls young enough 2 be his daughter. Why else would this guy think—

Bellissima: DON'T SAY IT.

KnitChick17: So what did u do?

Halo2Champ: Well, I refused 2 go in the restaurant, 4 1 thing. Dad tried 2 make me. Said he didn't know what i was so upset about. He tried 2 make me believe that the thumbs up was all in my head.

KnitChick17: R u sure it wasn't?

Halo2Champ: Scottie, plz.

BELLISSIMA: So did u leave?

HALO2CHAMP: Sort of.

HALO2CHAMP: I kinda refused 2 get back into the car, too.

KNITCHICK17: Wow, u threw a real hissy.

HALO2CHAMP: It was all the Porsche's fault! Riding around in a Porsche makes u seem like the kind of girl who would ride around in a Porsche.

BELLISSIMA: Well, u can't argue w/ that.

HALO2CHAMP: & I looked like the kind of girl who would ride around in a Porsche with a man old enough 2 be her dad.

KNITCHICK17: He IS yr father.

HALO2CHAMP: Nobody in Milwaukee knows that. Which means, no more me in the Porsche.

KNITCHICK17: So how'd you get home?

HALO2CHAMP: This isn't my home. Don't forget that. But anyway—taxi.

BELLISSIMA: They have cabs in Milwaukee?

HALO2CHAMP: I had 2 call 1. Reason #2,467 that Milwaukee sux. I thought abt taking the cab all the way back 2 Chicago, but I only had $16. I SO wanted 2 see John after all that.

Scottie raised her eyebrows. That was the second time Tay had revealed an inkling of gushy, girlfriendy feelings about John. Maybe Mr. A was getting through to Tay in more ways than one!

Before Scottie would ponder this possible transformation in her eternally thorny bud, her IM window chimed . . .

BELLISSIMA: Oh Tay. U poor thing.

HALO2CHAMP: Whatever. Let's talk abt something else.

KNITCHICK17: If it makes u feel any better, my dad is being a butt at the moment 2.

The words seemed to click onto Scottie's screen by their own volition. She honestly hadn't been thinking that at all, but now that she saw her sentence hovering at the end of the girls' IM stream, she realized that it was true.

Tay's reply burbled into the stream.

Halo2Champ: Gr8. I'd hate 2 think I'm the only 1 with a freak 4 a dad.

Scottie glanced at her stack of college applications. They were sitting on the corner of her desk—exactly where her dad had placed them weeks ago.

And what a coincidence, she thought. *There's the University of Michigan app right on top in all its yellow and blue glory.*

Huffing loudly, she swiped up the pile of glossy pamphlets and gave them a quick shuffle. Bryn Mawr landed on top.

"I don't even know where Bryn Mawr is," she muttered.

Again, she didn't *plan* to pull open her desk's file drawer—she just found herself doing it. Scottie wasn't much of a filer, not having much *to* file, so she'd always used the cavernous drawer to stash old stuff that she couldn't bear to part with. With a quick glance, she catalogued a musical jewelry box, a linty Wacky Wall Walker, a purple yo-yo she'd been obsessed with for about six months, and a pink felt box full of photos from her pre-digital-camera days. A ridiculous percentage of those snaps featured Amanda and Scottie in slumber party wear, laughing hysterically as they did headstands against the wall or piled each other's hair into towering, ultra-teased 'dos.

Scottie pushed the toys and boxes to the side and dumped the applications into the drawer. The slippery booklets fanned back into the drawer's recesses, covering the girly colors of her childhood with rah-rah shades of maize-and-blue, crimson, purple-and-white. She slammed the drawer shut and began typing again.

KNITCHICK17: Dad's all up in my Kool-Aid abt college!

HALO2CHAMP: Dude, how many times have i told u. That Kool-Aid riff? Not. Cool. Anyway, what's he doing?

KNITCHICK17: He's just after me. "Let's go visit some schools, Scottie. Why don't I drill u 4 your interviews, Scottie? How're those SATs? Why don't u go 2 Michigan, my dear ole alma mater?"

BELLISSIMA: I don't get it.

KNITCHICK17: I know! What's he thinking?

BELLISSIMA: No, I mean, I don't get what's wrong with what yr dad's doing.

KNITCHICK17: I told you, he's all up in my k—he's on my case, OK? Which is a new thing. I mean, for a long time it was totally the opposite. My parents were 2 busy being full-time artsy farts 2 notice me. & when they DID notice me, it was b/c they thought I was a fiber artist, made in their own image. But then we finally got into a groove. They let me live my life as a Chick w/ Sticks and I started 2 get my mom's paintings and tolerate their wacky art openings. They pretty much let me manage the school thing, since I kept my grades up and everything. But now they're trying 2 force-feed me apps to U of Michigan and Bryn Mawr.

BELLISSIMA: You know that Bryn Mawr is an all-girls school, don't you?

KNITCHICK17: What?!?!? See, that just proves it. Once again, my rents are trying 2 pigeonhole me as someone I'm NOT.

BELLISSIMA: My parents totally expect me 2 go 2 Oberlin or UC Berkeley.

KNITCHICK17: OK, how exactly is that a stretch?

BELLISSIMA: Well . . . OK, you have a point. So where do U want 2 go?

KNITCHICK17: If my dad would give me a little SPACE, maybe I could figure that out. Man, you'd think they'd be a LITTLE bummed that I'm leaving. I am their last kid, after all. But they just want 2 get rid of me!

HALO2CHAMP: Trust me, u've got it better than me. My mom actually asked me 2 teach her how 2 knit the other day.

BELLISSIMA: Aw, that's sweet!

HALO2CHAMP: Oh yeah, she has no life of her own so she has 2 start glomming onto mine. That's REAL cute.

BELLISSIMA: Well, what if u just HAPPEN 2 have the same interests as ur folks? Is that so bad? I mean, maybe I wouldn't be so into environmental activism if I didn't grow up in my parents' house. But now I'm way into it. I mean, those poor gorillas. . . .

KNITCHICK17: Wait a minute. The Save the Prairie Society is trying 2 help the Rwandan gorillas? That's kind of a stretch, isn't it?

BELLISSIMA: Oh, didn't I tell you? I'm working 4 GreenLeaves, now. I had 2 ditch the prairie people. They seemed way more interested in their annual fundraising ball than in actually hanging out on the prairie. I tried 2 organize a fact-gathering hike and the only people who came were—

The IM window went blank and there was a long pause.

HALO2CHAMP: Who, B?

BELLISSIMA: Oh, it doesn't matter.

KNITCHICK17: Hmm, do u have an eco-suitor? That would B news! U haven't gone out w/ anyone since Jaden.

Jaden was a beautiful knitter-boy that Bella had met at YarnCon Chicago the previous year. They'd dated for a few months, but Bella had put the kibosh on things when Jaden had gotten too serious about her.

"I'm too busy for a boyfriend," she'd declared at the time. "Jaden's a sweetie, and I *do* like the kissing, but he wants to be together *all* the time. I gotta have some solitude."

That's our indie Bella, Scottie thought with an incredulous head-shake.

Everybody at Stark is scrambling *for a significant other, so of course, she's anti-boyfriend.*

Scottie grinned and attacked her keyboard.

KNITCHICK17: Who was it, Bella? Tellustellustellus!

BELLISSIMA: It was . . . my parents!

KNITCHICK17: Oh.

KNITCHICK17: Well, why didn't you just say so? It's no biggie. U hang with ur rents all the time.

BELLISSIMA: Uh-huh. And u guys clearly think that's weird. Like I'm just doing the GreenLeaves thing to please them or something.

HALO2CHAMP: Plz! ME hanging with my parents is weird. But if u weren't meant 2 be a downward-dogging, feminist enviro-chick, you totally would have flipped out and joined the Young Republicans by now.

BELLISSIMA: Now THAT would be weird, right?

KNITCHICK17: I guess . . .

SHOPPRGRRRL: Scottie! Is ur ringer off or something?

KNITCHICK17: Amanda! We were just talking about how Bella's gonna save the world.

SHOPPRGRRRL: Forget the world. I've been trying 2 call u 4 half an hour. I need u 2 save ME!

A couple hours later, Scottie heard a *thump-thump-thump* on her front door. She tightened the belt on her bathrobe, ran her hands over her just-blown hair, and trudged to the front door. As she clacked open its locks and heaved it open, she announced, "I cannot believe I'm doing this."

When she beheld Amanda standing nervously in the doorway, her eyes widened.

"I can't believe *you're* doing this," Scottie screeched. "Where's your deb uni?!"

Amanda was wearing a dress, but it was as far from a debutante dress as you could get. It was mod and A-line and super-short and *red*. It was strapless, but for a spiderweb-like network of glinty lace that framed Amanda's collarbones perfectly and culminated in a halterneck.

"I told you," Amanda said, rushing past Scottie in a perfumey whoosh. "This isn't an 'official' deb party."

"So why don't you skip it?" Scottie asked. "I mean if it doesn't count?"

"Oh, believe me, I would," Amanda said with an eye roll. "But my mom heard about the party from Honor Gorham's mom and now she's pretty much forcing me to go."

"Ugh." Scottie grimaced. "So what happens at a non-official deb party?"

"See, that's what I'm worried about," Amanda said, wringing her hands. "*Nothing* happens. No curtsys. No formal introductions. No remembering the difference between the dessert spoon and the demi-tasse spoon. And no adults! It's just a mixer. All the debs and escorts are gonna just hang out, get to know each other, and 'have fun.'"

"No buffers." Scottie nodded, thinking about the IMarathon she'd just had about Tay and her dad.

"That's why I need you there," Amanda said simply.

"I got that," Scottie said, leading Amanda back to her room. "What I don't get is your get-up! Whatever happened to blending in with the country club wallpaper? To just coasting through your deb year unno-ticed?"

"Yeah," Amanda said. She glanced at her blaring reflection in Scot-tie's closet mirror and wrung her hands. "I don't know what happened, actually. I was all dressed to be drab. You know, the khaki mini-skirt, the cute little twin set, the ballet flats. I pulled my hair back in a pony-tail. I totally looked the part—but I felt like a big loser.

"After you agreed to come to the party with me," Amanda continued, slumping onto Scottie's bed and kicking off her teetery pumps, "I guess

I got a shot of bravery. All of a sudden, I was like, 'Hey, why am *I* changing for *them*?' Y'know?"

"So," Scottie said, motioning to Amanda's dress, "wardrobe change."

"Yeah," Amanda said, fingering her lacy halter shyly. "I just finished this. Do you like it?"

"You *made* that?" Scottie shrieked. "Wow, Amanda!"

"I *bought* the dress," Amanda corrected her. "At this cool vintage consignment shop. But I knitted up the halter myself. And Hannah helped me sew it on."

The previous year, Beck's mom had hired the Chicks to knit lace edging for her line of junior clothing. She'd even taken a black-and-white photo of the four girls working their sticks and put the image on the label. Of all the Chicks, Amanda had been the most inspired by the gig. Now she and Hannah talked regularly, lobbing design brainstorms back and forth like tennis balls.

"Well, it's awesome," Scottie declared, sitting next to Amanda to give the halter a closer inspection. "And it's very you. Which means, you're not gonna be invisible at this deb party. Totally the opposite, actually."

"I know," Amanda said, twisting a tendril of glossy dark hair around her finger nervously. "I guess I thought this dress would be a way to kind of say, 'Screw you,' to the whole deb scene. Bringing you would be the same thing."

"You mean 'bringing Jew,' don't you?" Scottie said with a mischievous smile.

"Scottie," Amanda scoffed, her cheeks flushing. "We live in Chicago. Being Jewish isn't exactly exotic."

"Not in Chicago," Scottie agreed. "But in Debland? I'm as exotic as a toucan."

"Scottie!" Amanda gasped while Scottie giggled.

"Come on," Scottie insisted. "Remember when I went to one of your debby things last year? When we had to give out goodie bags at that benefit?"

"Vaguely." Amanda rolled her eyes.

"Well, your *mother* sure remembers it," Scottie said. She grabbed an eyeliner and mascara tube out of the makeup caddy on her dresser and went to her closet mirror. "For six months after you dragged me to that thing, your mother had a little comment every time I saw her. 'Oh, Scottie. The van Aarps were so *curious* when they saw you at the benefit. They're not familiar with the Shearer name.'"

"And *you* told her, 'Nobody is. It's just the name my great-grandparents got stuck with at Ellis Island,'" Amanda said with a laugh. "I remember now. That was brilliant. I mean, my mom has this delusion that *everybody's* bloodline is traceable back to Plymouth Rock."

While Scottie giggled, Amanda asked, "So, what did Beck say about tonight?"

"Turns out he had a double feature all planned for us," Scottie said. "*Rushmore* and *The Royal Tenenbaums* are playing at that new revival theater on Fullerton. But since he's seen every Wes Anderson movie, oh, about two dozen times, he agreed to meet us at your little sock hop instead."

"You guys are the best," Amanda said, hopping off the bed and burrowing into Scottie's closet. She began flipping through the hangers, searching for an outfit for Scottie to wear to the party.

Scottie smiled as she selected a pair of earrings from her jewelry box.

"You know Beck," she said. "He loves to watch *movies* about neurotic people, but *he's* ridiculously reasonable."

"Opposites attract, huh?" Amanda joked as she squinted at a brown corduroy skirt, then shook her head and stuffed it back into the closet.

"Okay," Scottie countered with a dry smile, "I'm going to choose not to point out that *you're* the one in the middle of a pre-party freak-out."

"Touché," Amanda said. "Thanks for doing this with me, especially given, y'know, how you are when it comes to stuff like this."

Scottie paused, one earring poised before her lobe.

•• Chicks with Sticks

"What do you mean?" she said. "How *am* I?"

"*You* know," Amanda said, helping herself to a squirt of some sparkly body lotion on Scottie's dresser. "You don't like new things."

"Excuse me?" Scottie balked. "Who's always dragging the Chicks to new things, like yarn-spinning classes or designing for Hannah? Me!"

"Well, yeah," Amanda shrugged, "but come on, yarn-based outings don't count. That's totally your comfort zone. And come to think of it, stuff you do with the Chicks—or Beck, for that matter—shouldn't really count either. I mean, it's not so hard to risk falling on your butt if there's more than one butt involved."

Amanda paused.

"Okay, that came out sounding weird, but you know what I mean."

Scottie blinked at her. Annoyingly, she *did* know what Amanda meant. But it would have been even more annoying—not to mention a pre-party buzzkill—to admit it. So instead, she reached past Amanda into her closet and pulled out a V-necked top with flowy, split sleeves and a yellow-and-orange plaid miniskirt.

"How about this?" she offered.

"Perfect," Amanda said.

"The Stepford Muffies will approve?" Scottie asked as she pulled out a pair of black suede boots to go with the outfit.

"As long as you remember your place," Amanda winked, "and don't go making eyes at any van Aarps."

"Oh," Scottie simpered as she quickly shimmied into the skirt. "But a hook-up with a van Aarp would make your mother so *proud.*"

Amanda snorted loudly and Scottie—feeling lighthearted again—giggled too. Amanda swiped her tiny red purse off of Scottie's bed. It was time to go.

Scottie found her own cute little party-purse amongst the sneakers and boots on her closet floor. As she fished her wallet, lip gloss, and Altoids out of her backpack to slip into it, she found herself gazing longingly at her latest quilt square-in-progress. It was made from the

Midnight Pine scraps of the first sweater Tay had ever knitted—and then frogged completely. She had a sudden urge to stuff it into her purse so she could have it to work on if the party turned out to be awful. But she quickly shook the impulse off.

Amanda's so right, she thought with a head-shake. *I'm seventeen years old and I want to bring a security blanket—or at least a fragment of one—to a party just because it's a new scene.*

Squaring her shoulders, Scottie stuffed the half-finished square back into her pack and clicked the purse shut.

But, as she followed Amanda out of her room, she couldn't help noting the consolation for leaving her knitting behind: *I'd be willing to bet that I'm gonna find more material for my memory quilt tonight.*

9 * (Change to double-pointed needles)

The party was in the Gold Coast, where most of the debutante crowd lived. But unlike Amanda's high-rise condo on Michigan Avenue, the party pad was a Victorian graystone. Along with an imposing block of other mansions, the house watched over a pretty courtyard dominated by the Newberry Library. Every time Scottie visited this part of town, she gazed at the houses and imagined she was pale and corseted, glooming around one of the Edith Wharton novels she'd read for her American lit class. She'd always wondered who could possibly have the guts—not to mention the money—to live in one of those monstrous homes.

Now she knew. They were people like the party's host, Kelsey Mac-Laren. According to Amanda, Kelsey's family were paper magnates.

"Toilet paper," she explained as she and Scottie climbed the long, stone staircase that led to the ornately carved front door. "And tissue and paper towels and stuff like that. I heard my dad say once that they make those little sheets of waxed paper that you use to grab your cookies at the bakery and that stuff alone nets the company like ninety million dollars a year."

"Get out!" Scottie breathed.

She was prepared for a palace when they walked through the ornately carved front door. What she found was room after room of antique chairs and couches upholstered in various flowery and striped fabrics that somehow all matched. The partiers standing in clusters around all this furniture matched, too. They all seemed to have perfectly symmetrical faces and straight hair ranging from buttery blond to honey brown.

"I call them R & R's," Amanda whispered as she watched Scottie take in the crowd. "Reese-and-Ryans—pre-divorce, of course. They're America's sweethearts."

Scottie popped her mouth open and pointed a finger toward the back of her throat.

"Exactly," Amanda sighed. "Let's go get something to drink."

They made their way to a giant, black-and-white kitchen. It looked to Scottie like the kind of room where half a dozen servants should be rushing around getting dinner ready. Instead, the marble countertop was scattered with sodas, a spread of nuts, cheeses, and other salty snacks, and a scattering of frosty bottles containing vodka, gin, and white wine.

"I'm thinking the bar's theme is Mumsy's upholstery," Scottie said, pointing out the booze to Amanda. "Spill all you want and they won't stain."

Amanda rolled her eyes and reached for a bottle of Perrier.

"Maybe they're hoping the alcohol will make them more interesting," she whispered.

A sextet of boys—all of them indeed as generically handsome as Ryan Phillippe—sat at the vast kitchen table, flipping quarters into shot glasses and guffawing between drinks. A few girls stood behind their chairs, overseeing the action with the same doting smiles Scottie usually associated with soccer moms. They swayed a bit to some muffled hip-hop playing in a distant room.

Okay, Amanda wasn't kidding, Scottie thought as she grabbed a Red Bull for herself. *These folks all look like they could star in Neutrogena commercials.*

Right down to their sweet smiles. One of the girls spotted Amanda and waved at her.

"Wow, check out that dress!" the girl said. "Is that how they do it at Olivia Stark?"

"Just like *that's* how they do it at Latin," Amanda said, pointing at the girl's preppy pink sweater, skinny black pants, and the tiny, silver kidney bean hanging from her neck. The Latin School was just a few blocks away. Most Gold Coast kids went there.

Unless they're fashion-forward freaks like Amanda, Scottie thought with an affectionate grin. *Then they go to Stark.*

"Whoa, Amanda," one of the boys said, glancing up as he passed a vodka-slick quarter to his buddy. "You look hot."

"Doesn't she?" the girl in pink said. "Amanda, you're so brave. I barely recognize you."

"That's the whole point, Honor," Amanda said with a plastic smile.

Honor smiled back, just as widely. But through it, Scottie could see confusion in her pretty, pale-blue eyes. Honor didn't get Amanda's joke or her attitude. But, Scottie realized, years of socialite-training meant she was going to be gamely gracious anyway.

"Isn't it cool that Kelsey threw this party?" Honor went on, fiddling with her Tiffany necklace. "It's so nice to be able to forget about all the curtsying and waltzing for, like, a minute. And look!"

Honor pointed a manicured finger at the snack spread.

"No mushroom puffs to be found!"

"There might as well be," Amanda said, looking bored as she took a sip of Perrier. "When you all grow up and make your kids go through this, you'll serve mushroom puffs at your parties, too, right? Mushroom puffs and poached salmon."

Scottie raised her eyebrows. Where was Amanda going with this?

"I suppose," Honor agreed with an indulgent laugh. "It's just what you do. And I gotta admit, I like the mushroom puffs, even if I'm a little sick of them at the moment."

"It's just what you do," Amanda repeated, squinting at Honor. "That's why we're all here. Because it's just what you do. Unless you decide it *isn't* just what you do. I, for one, plan to stop the vicious cycle some day. If I have a daughter, I'm not letting her get *near* a long white dress until she gets married. And maybe not even then."

Honor's lips were pursed and she was fiddling madly with her necklace now. Her smile faded, ever so slightly.

"If you hate this so much, why are you here?" she asked stiffly.

"Because my parents are making me be here," Amanda spat. "Aren't yours?"

"Well . . . no," Honor said. "I mean, I didn't exactly *ask* to deb. But they never exactly told me to do it either. It was just . . . well, I just always knew I would. It's kind of like graduating from high school, y'know? It's just—

"—what you do," Amanda filled in. "Yup. Heard ya the first time."

"Um, I think we better go look for Beck," Scottie said, grabbing Amanda by the elbow and pulling her toward the kitchen door. "He should be here by now."

"Right, Beck. Another impostor!" Amanda said, widening her eyes and putting a hand over her open mouth. *"Quelle scandal!"*

Scottie shot an embarrassed smile back at the quarters crowd, who stared after them with perplexed, wide eyes. Then she yanked Amanda through the door.

"What was that?" she asked, steering Amanda back into the sprawling living room. "You totally went *Gossip Girl* on that deb."

"Honor," Amanda said with a curled lip. "Her name is Honor Gorham. The name was way popular with the pilgrims."

Scottie shrugged. It wasn't like Honor gave *herself* her snooty name. "Well, I don't know why you had to harsh on her that much," Scottie said. "She seemed nice enough. Kinda clueless, but nice."

"See, you don't get it," Amanda said. "She *seems* nice. But underneath, the true debness always comes out."

"Well, that hasn't happened to you," Scottie countered. "So why do you assume it'll happen to all the others?"

"Do you see anyone else here who's dressed like me?" Amanda whispered, motioning to all the khaki and cardigans in the room. "Or anyone who's as miserable as I am?"

Scottie looked around the room. A couple of girls were seated artfully on a couch, flirting with a couple of guys who were perched on the couch arms. A set designer couldn't have placed them better. Another boy was bounding down the curving staircase with the practiced grace of a gazelle. At the bottom of the steps, he slid a good five feet across the polished parquet floor, landing suavely in front of a willowy blond. He handed her a small silver box that he'd obviously fetched for her from upstairs. She smiled slyly, pulled a cigarette out of the box and held it to her lips while the guy whipped out a Zippo to light it.

Everybody else in the room seemed to be shellacked in a veneer of perfection, too. Scottie felt like she'd been time-warped back into a John Hughes movie. She was Molly Ringwald surrounded by an army of Blaines. Even if Amanda was as rich and pedigreed as these folks (well, except for toilet paper boy over there), Scottie knew she felt the same way.

And suddenly, Scottie felt like she and Amanda were on the same page again. Instead of being passionately Parsons-bound vs. stymied by senior year, they were two misfit peas in a pod, rebelling together against good breeding and blond hair.

"I guess you're right," Scottie said, giving Amanda a wink. "There's a definite stench in here."

She giggled and sniffed the air. "Smells like, hmmm, a combo of smugness and horses."

Amanda snorted and started to respond with a zinger of her own when a voice—a male voice—bubbled into their conversation.

"I'd say it's more like silver polish and poached salmon. You know debs. They *loves* them some poached salmon."

Amanda and Scottie both froze. Together they turned and saw that a boy was slouched deep into the flowery sofa behind them. His feet were crossed at the ankle and planted neatly between a couple gold-filigreed candy dishes on the coffee table. In one hand, he swirled a glass of seltzer, the ice cubes clinking against crystal. He gazed up at Amanda with a wry smile and one eyebrow cocked.

"And in answer to your question," he added, "there *is* someone here who's as miserable as you are. You're looking at him."

Amanda glanced at Scottie and sniffed. Scottie could tell just what she was thinking. Of all the Ryans in the room, this guy looked like the Ryanest. His chin was chiseled and cleft, his eyes were blue and charmingly squinty, his hair was sandy blond and tousled just so. His clothes were on the original side—some nicely distressed jeans and a sporty, vintage-looking bowling shirt—but everything else about him screamed *establishment*.

"You look pretty comfortable to me," Amanda challenged.

"Well, you can submit to The Season kicking and screaming," the guy said, unfurling himself from the couch, "or you can cruise under the radar. Y'know, stealthy scorn. Personally, I prefer the latter."

Amanda was taken aback.

"Me too, actually," she defended herself. "I mean, it's not like you've ever noticed me before, right?"

"Oh, yes I have," the boy said. He gazed into his glass, swirled the ice cubes again, then gave Amanda a sidelong look. "But I thought you were on board with all this. In fact, you seemed just like all the others. Oh sure, maybe you were a little less . . . blond. But other than that, you were completely compliant, always there, partying politely and curtsying with the best of 'em."

Scottie watched Amanda catch her breath and square her shoulders indignantly.

Let the withering begin, Scottie thought, looking expectantly at Amanda.

** *Chicks with Sticks*

If she had felt a twinge of sympathy for Honor, she had none for this guy. He was smug squared!

"What you saw was me flying under the radar right along with you," Amanda said.

"But not anymore, I see," the boy said, nodding at Amanda's outfit. "So you're saying you're *not* a model deb? And now you've outed yourself?"

"I think the proper terminology," Amanda retorted with a dry smile, "is 'compromised.'"

"Oh, a little spy speak," the boy said. "So do you have a code name?"

"Oh, I suppose you can call me by my real name, Amanda," Amanda quipped. "Y'know, since I'm already compromised."

Scottie glanced at Amanda, feeling incredulous.

Okay, she is so not deflating this guy, she observed. *In fact, it sorta sounds like she's . . . flirting with him? What's going on here?*

"Jamison," the boy introduced himself, giving his drink another glassy rattle. Then he turned his smile—which Scottie couldn't help noticing was extra-sparkly—on her.

"I'm Scottie," she said.

"Like F. Scott Fitzgerald?"

Scottie sighed. "I'd say *you're* more like F. Scott Fitzgerald than I am," she said. "Didn't he hang out with lots of debutantes, too?"

Scottie felt Amanda's surprised eyes on her.

Well, someone's *gotta pick up the slack around here,* Scottie said to Amanda in her head. *Since your put-down powers seem to have evaporated.*

Jamison didn't seem put down, though. In fact, he looked delighted.

"You guys *are* different from the other debs," he said. "Explanation, please?"

"I'm not revealing my secrets to *you*," Amanda burst out. "How do I know you're not a mole?"

Okay, that was definitely flirting, Scottie thought, squinting at Amanda and Jamison. *Which does not compute. Amanda only likes Toby clones, and this dude is so far from Toby, they're like two different species.*

Scottie tried to beam *what the hell* vibes in Amanda's direction but, for once, their best friend telepathy didn't work. Amanda was too busy grinning at Jamison to even be aware of Scottie.

And a moment later, a distraction arrived for Scottie as well.

"Hey, can I get the next waltz?"

At the sound of Beck's voice, so close to her ear that she could feel his breath, Scottie spun around.

"Hey!" she whispered, grabbing both his hands and giving them a squeeze. She was thrilled to see him. Not only did he smell fabulous— like warm cotton and shampoo and his own sweet, Beckish scent—but he was also the perfect dish-mate for this scene.

"Sorry it took me so long to find you," Beck whispered. "I ran into the guy who lives here. Kelsey?"

"The toilet paper prince himself?" Scottie whispered with a grin. "What an honor."

"If you say so," Beck murmured, giving Scottie a quick kiss on the lips. "So, um, why are we whispering?"

"Because," Scottie breathed, "something very weird is happening with Amanda right now."

She motioned slightly with her head at Amanda, who was giggling now—giggling!—at something Jamison had just said.

"The dress?" Beck said, angling his head. "Well, I don't think we're gonna be seeing it in WASP Wear Daily, but I wouldn't call it weird."

"Not the dress," Scottie hissed. "The guy! I think there's, like, *sparkage* going on between her and that guy."

Beck had to eavesdrop on Amanda and Jamison for only about thirty seconds before he agreed.

"Oh yeah," he said. "There's enough electricity there to light up—"

He looked around the mammoth room.

"—well, not *this* house, but definitely a couple rooms in it."

"Exactly!" Scottie said. "But Jamison's not her type at all. He's all blond and perfect and his name is *Jamison*. She likes boys who are scruffy and nerdy/cool."

"Like the guy she broke up with?" Beck said. He took her Red Bull out of her hand and helped himself to a sip. "Well, Scottie, she *did* break up with him. Maybe that's not her type anymore."

"No," Scottie insisted. "Even if she's done with Toby clones, *this* guy? This guy is her worst night—"

"Oh good, Beck's here!"

Amanda, with Jamison right behind her, had just scooted up to them. Amanda's cheeks looked a little pinker than usual. Her skin kind of glowed, in fact.

Maybe that's because of all the tasteful, low-light lamps in here, Scottie speculated. *The same goes for her eyes looking all dewy and lashy. But as for that goofy smile? That I can't explain—*

"So Jamison just told me about this underground party that a friend of his is having," Amanda said brightly. "Wanna go? He said there's gonna be an amazing DJ. And he can get us in, even if it's gonna be mostly college kids there."

Scottie looked from Amanda to Beck—who seemed supremely amused—then back to Amanda.

"Really," Scottie said flatly. "And you want to go to this thing?"

"Well, it's better than hanging out with all these R & R's, isn't it?" Jamison volunteered with a rakish smile.

Scottie stifled a gasp, then ducked her head toward Amanda's.

"I thought you weren't gonna reveal your secrets!" she hissed.

"Well, not to the R & R's themselves." Amanda giggled. "But, if you can believe it, I think I've found someone who hates this scene as much as I do. Maybe even more!"

"No way," Scottie said. "Amanda, *look* at him."

"I am!" Amanda said, sounding breathy. "In particular, I'm looking at those blue eyes and that jaw. You could slice cheese on it!"

"Exactly!" Scottie squeaked. "He's as Ryan as they get!"

"No, he's different," Amanda said assuredly. "Like you said, not *all* of us have to be infected by the Curtsy Curse."

Scottie shook her head, confused. "When did I say—?"

But Amanda was barely listening to her. She was too busy sneaking glances at Jamison. Scottie hadn't seen her crash into a crush this hard since she'd met Toby.

"C'mon," Amanda said. "It'll be fun."

"OhmiGod," Scottie said. She was getting incredibly frustrated—and she didn't quite know why. "I can't believe you really want to hang with debby boy over there."

Amanda smiled a bit giddily.

"I told you," she said. "He's different."

"You met him literally a minute ago," Scottie protested.

"I can just tell," Amanda said. "And hey, even if the party's a bust, it's better than hanging out with Kelsey and Co. I did my duty and put in my face time. Now, we can go have some fun."

"I don't know." Scottie bit her lip and glanced at Beck. His hands were shoved in his pockets and he was eyeing the glossy clusters of partiers with a mixture of horror and morbid fascination. She was sure he wouldn't want to go to yet another party.

"Listen," Amanda said. "Like I said before, you were awesome to hold my hand through this stupid mixer, but now you're off the hook. If you guys don't want to go to the party, you can go see that Mount Rushmore movie. You know that's what you wanted to do anyway."

"It's just *Rushmore*," Scottie said. "And yeah, you're right. We'll go to the movie while you and Jamison go do your glamour thing."

Amanda laughed and hugged Scottie good-bye.

Scottie waved and smiled as Amanda and Jamison practically skipped through the ornate front door. But then, her shoulders sagged. Yes, she wanted to flee this scene as much as Amanda had. And yeah, she *had* been looking forward to one of Beck's cozy movie nights. He always brought a surprise grab bag of candy, held her hand, and whispered little witticisms in her ear, no matter how absorbed he was in the flick. Yet Scottie still felt deflated. In ten minutes, she'd gone from being Amanda's savior—the only person who could get her through this tedious night—to being her third wheel; completely expendable.

At least I'm going to a Wes Anderson movie, Scottie bright-sided as she plunked her near-empty Red Bull can onto the coffee table and turned toward Beck. *I mean it's kind of hard to feel lame when you're comparing yourself to Max Fischer and Herman Blume.*

"Okay," she said to Beck. "I guess we're going back to Plan A. I don't suppose you brought any candy, did you?"

"Naw," Beck said. He glanced at his watch. "What's more, *Rushmore* started twenty minutes ago."

"Oh, man!" Scottie said, kicking at the Persian rug with her boot toe. "I ruined our whole night."

"No, you didn't," Beck said. He grinned devilishly. "Only half of it. We just need to kill a couple hours and then we can catch *The Royal Tenenbaums.*"

"Okay," Scottie said. "What should we do?"

Beck gazed down at her. His eyes crinkled into a sweet smile and his full lips went puckery.

Well! Scottie thought mischievously. *Looks like Beck wants to kill time with a little necking. No prob—*

"Wait right here!" Beck said. Then he turned on his heel and dashed away.

O-kay, never mind then, Scottie thought. Her cheeks flamed as she glanced around. She noticed that someone had turned off the hip-hop and put on some lame Latin tunes. *So, I've been ditched by my best friend* and *my boyfriend, and now I have to fend for myself among the Reeses and Ryans and their bad music.*

Scottie spotted a trio of girls chatting nearby, shrugged, and headed over to them.

"Hi," she said with faux brightness.

She braced herself as three sets of blue eyes looked her up and down.

Okay, here's the part where they sense my lack of pedigree, Scottie thought, *then slap a scarlet ND (as in Non-Deb) on my chest.*

"Hi," said the tallest girl, waving a graceful hand at Scottie. "Are you as bored as we are?"

Scottie blinked. The girl actually seemed . . . nice.

"And, what's with all the gin?" said her friend, the one with the sparkly diamond earrings. "What are we, seventy? I would kill for some Starbucks."

"Or at least some less painful music," said the third girl as she pulled a compact out of her purse and smoothed on some pale pink lip gloss. Scottie laughed and nodded in agreement.

They're nice and . . . normal, Scottie realized. *I can't wait to tell Aman—*

"Hey everybody!"

Scottie jumped as Honor Gorham's voice trilled out behind her. Scottie turned to see Honor sashaying into the room with a crowd of party people behind her. She was waving what looked like a broomstick.

"It's time to lim-bo!" Honor sang.

Scottie raised one eyebrow.

Oh my God, the limbo? she scoffed in her head. *How very Saturday-night-at-the-country-club!*

She turned back to her new pals, ready to share her jibe. But when she saw the girls' faces, she gulped it back.

Diamond Earring Girl's eyes had become as sparkly as her jewelry. The tall girl was already bobbing her shoulders to the goofy beat. And Lip Gloss Girl was looping her arm through Scottie's.

"Oh! That's why they're playing that goofy music. It's the limbo!" she cried excitedly. "Come on!"

"Um, that's okay," Scottie said, trying to extricate herself from the girl's grip.

"Oh, you've *got* to!" Lip Gloss Girl said tugging at her. "The limbo is *so fun*."

Scottie scrambled for an excuse. "My boyfriend'll be back in a second," she squeaked. But when she craned her neck to look for Beck, he was nowhere to be seen.

"No worries," Lip Gloss Girl said. "We'll keep you entertained until he comes back."

This is not *happening,* Scottie thought as the girl dragged her into the crowd trailing Honor. They all formed a circle in the foyer. In the middle of the circle, Honor held one end of the broomstick. A grinning Ryan grabbed the other. They lowered the pole to hip level and beckoned to the party kids to start scooching beneath it.

"Whoo hoo!" Diamond Earring girl squealed as she tilted backward and shuffled beneath the stick.

"Me next!" called the tall girl. She fluttered her fingers and grinned as she skimmed under the limbo pole.

"Now you!" Lip Gloss Girl said to Scottie.

"Oh, no," Scottie protested shiftily. "That's okay. *You* go."

"I know!" Lip Gloss Girl shouted, grabbing Scottie's hand. "We'll go together!"

Oh, God, no!

Scottie tried to make her escape, but Lip Gloss Girl had her hand in an iron grip.

"Whoo!" the girl hooted, bending backward.

There was nothing Scottie could do but tilt back as well and sidle, mortified, toward the limbo stick.

"Lower, lower, lower!" chanted the kids in the circle.

"Ooooooo-kay!" Honor agreed with a giggle.

She and the Ryan lowered the limbo pole. Lip Gloss Girl hooted again and dexterously bent herself farther.

Scottie gritted her teeth and tried to do the same. But she'd *never* been the most flexible person, and the next thing she knew . . .

"Noooo!" Scottie shrieked.

With her free hand, Scottie reached instinctively for the limbo pole.

Which only meant that when she splatted flat on her back? She pulled Honor and the Ryan down on top of her! And they, of course, took Lip Gloss Girl down with them.

And that's how Scottie found herself flattened beneath a stack of debutantes in the home of Chicago's toilet paper prince.

Amanda never said anything about the limbo, Scottie raged in her head. *She is in* so *much trouble.*

After what seemed like a *very* long, giggly pause, Honor, the Ryan, and Lip Gloss Girl finally got up so Scottie could lurch to her feet. Gasping and red-faced, she began to slink toward the edge of the room. That's when someone *else* grabbed her hand.

"Oh, come *on,*" she sputtered, pulling her hand away impatiently.

"Scottie?"

She looked up in surprise. "Beck!" she cried. "Where have you been? More important, how much of that did you just see?"

"Enough to know that you should never, ever go on a cruise," Beck said with a sympathetic smile. "Are you okay?"

"Physically? Yes," Scottie said. "But socially? I'm feeling pretty humiliated."

She leaned against Beck while he laughed and patted her head.

"Hey," Scottie joked wanly, "at least I found a way to kill some time before we head to the movie theater."

"Actually, there's been a change of plans," Beck said as he guided Scottie up the stairs and down a hallway.

"Where are we going?" Scottie said. The horrible limbo music grew fainter as they padded down a long hallway. Finally, they turned a corner and Beck opened a door.

Behind it was a cozy den filled with smushy leather couches, a coffee table laden with snacks, and a large-screen television. Beck pointed

• • Chicks with Sticks

Scottie toward the central couch and strode over to a cabinet next to the TV. He opened it and began flipping through the DVDs inside.

"Um, Beck?" Scottie said. As Beck pulled out a disc, she glanced at the door in alarm. "What are you doing?"

"It turns out that Kelsey?" Beck said, hitting a button on the DVD player. "He's a film geek, too. And he gave me permission to . . ."

Suddenly, the TV screen flickered to life and Scottie saw the familiar opening credits of *Rushmore*.

"Beck!" she squealed.

Beck plopped down on the couch next to Scottie. She kicked off her high-heeled boots, tucked her legs beneath her, and cuddled up next to him.

"This *is* just what I wanted," she cooed in his ear before kissing his cheek.

"But you get an A for effort down there," Beck said.

"Yeah, right," Scottie joked as she nestled into that favorite nook beneath Beck's arm. "The next time I propose a party, please just whisper one word in my ear: limbo. I'll totally remember where I prefer to be. At the movies. With you."

"Or the Chicks," Beck teased.

"Except," Scottie said slyly, "when I want to do this."

She leaned in and planted a kiss on Beck's sweet, smiling mouth.

10 ✴ (Leave stitches on holder)

At noon on Monday, Scottie strode into the school cafeteria feeling ravenous. But not for the seitan joes on the menu.

Definitely *not for the seitan joes*, Scottie thought, sticking her tongue out and grimacing.

Seitan joes, aka sloppy joes made out of wheat gluten, aka Satan Burgers, were the brain child of Principal Heath, she of the cleansing breaths. They were on the cafeteria blackboard every third day, alternating with tofurkey loaf and soy dogs. All three were pretty disgusting, but seitan joes were definitely the grossest.

They were also, in Scottie's opinion, total overkill. Even before Dr. Heath's arrival, Stark had been ridiculously progressive. There was a multi-culti mural in just about every hallway. Dissection of fetal pigs, frogs, and even roundworms had been abolished after vociferous protests by the student body. And the classrooms on the top floor were all heated and cooled by solar energy.

Which would be great, Scottie thought, *if not for the fact that we live in* Chicago *and between November and April, the sun pretty much goes into hibernation. I have two classes on the top floor this year and I'm already knitting up fingerless gloves and nose-warmers to get me through them without freezing to death.*

Now, the Stark students had to deal with a daily diet of soy and seitan, too.

If the cold doesn't kill us, Scottie thought with a rueful laugh, *all the meat-substitute-based methane might!*

If lunchtime wasn't the food-fest that it used to be, it was still prime time for gossip. And *that's* what Scottie was hungry for today. She and Amanda had played phone tag all day on Sunday so Scottie still hadn't heard about Jamison's party.

She also had some dirt of her own to dish.

When she got to the Chicks' regular table, only Tay and John were there. Lunch seemed to interest John as little as it did Scottie. He only had a taste for Tay's *neck.*

Scottie loudly scraped her chair out from under the table and cleared her throat several times. Tay sprang away from her neck-nuzzling boyfriend and glanced at Scottie sheepishly. As a rule, Tay never blushed, but right now she definitely looked a little pink.

"Holy PDA, you guys!" Scottie squawked with a big grin.

Tay glowered at her. "Like you haven't done worse," she grumbled.

"It's my fault," John blurted, his grin even bigger than Scottie's. "I couldn't help myself. This is the first time I've seen Tay-Tay since she got back from Milwaukee."

"I told you not to say the M-word," Tay complained.

"And," John added, ignoring Tay's protest, "she just smells so *good.* Smell her, Scottie!"

"No way!" Tay and Scottie yelled simultaneously.

While Tay rearranged her shirt collar to make her neck a little less accessible to her swoony b.f., Scottie pulled her knitting and a carton of leftover Kung Pao chicken out of her backpack.

"So I guess the rest of the weekend wasn't so great either?" she asked Tay.

"Let's just say I broke my promise to Mr. A," Tay said, slumping down in her chair. "My iPod buds stayed in my ears all day Sunday—even after the battery died."

"Ouch," Scottie said.

"New subject," Tay ordered, waving away Scottie's sympathy. "Until I have to go back up there, I'm just going to forget Milwaukee *and* my dad exist."

"Oh, *that's* healthy!"

That was Bella, who had just arrived at their table with a cafeteria tray clutched in her hands. She was looking indignantly at Tay.

Tay eyed the roast beef sandwich and Fritos resting on her brown bag. John's lunch was even more junky—a slab of deep-dish pizza and a twin-pack of Twinkies. Tay shrugged.

"Bella," she sighed, "I know you love the Satan burgers, but I've told you a hundred times—I don't eat meat made of wheat. You're just gonna have to learn to live with my ugly habit of eating food that tastes *good*."

"I wasn't talking about that," Bella said, fluttering into the chair next to Scottie and clunking down her tray—and its musty-smelling mound of seitan.

"Tay," she began to lecture, "avoiding your dad isn't going to help you guys heal. I mean, yes, the whole Porsche episode was yucky, but you could also see it as an opportunity to really talk about your relationship."

"Hello?" John said. "Tay and I swap spit daily and *we* don't talk about our relationship. You really think she's gonna get all chatty with her *dad?*"

"*And that's* TMI twice in five minutes," Tay said. She covered John's mouth with her hand and shook her head at him. "Don't *make* me send you over to sit with your basketball buddies."

John just grabbed Tay's hand away and laughed. He didn't, Scottie noticed, let Tay's hand go when the moment was over.

This made Scottie smiley and wistful all at once. John and Tay were In Love—not in like, like Scottie and Beck, not obsessed with each other and not merely hot for each other, but truly, sweetly, in-for-the-long-haul in love.

Scottie wished she could ask Tay about the whole Love thing. What did it feel like? How had Tay known when she'd officially fallen? How often did they say it to each other?

But she knew Tay would take to *that* conversation as enthusiastically as she was going to go to Milwaukee twice a month. So Scottie decided to focus on the opposite-of-love: war.

"So," she said as she flipped open her Chinese food carton and pulled a pair of disposable chopsticks out of her lunch sack, "*guess* who I saw at Joe yesterday?"

Scottie had gone to the coffeehouse for the afternoon to do her homework away from her dad's constant college questions.

"David Schwimmer again?" Tay said with a yawn. "Scottie, you've spotted him like half a dozen times. Face it. The guy's from Chicago and he's chronically unemployed, so of *course* he's always hanging out in coffee shops here. As celebrity sightings go, he's a dud."

"Not him," Scottie said. "It was a *them*. Four of them, to be exact. The Babes with Batting!"

"The quilters?" Bella said between bites of seitan joe. "Who are they? Did you say hi?"

"Did I say *hi?*" Scottie blustered. "Bella, those girls don't want to exchange *pleasantries* with us! They want to replace us! Now that I know who they are, I'm even more sure of that. It's Emma Duncan, Grier D'abruzzo, and Lissie Goldblatt. You know them. Each one is snootier than the last. And then there's Ilana Cross. I'm pretty sure she's the ringleader. *She's* hated me ever since the fourth grade."

"Why?" Bella squeaked.

"Oh it's so dumb," Scottie scoffed. "We were at some slumber party and I kinda outed Ilana as the one who farted during the séance."

"And she's still holding a grudge?" John guffawed. "Man, if guys got all huffy every time one of us cut one, we'd have no friends left."

"Especially now that you're all eating Satan burgers," Tay riffed.

"Ew," Scottie said with a giggle. "Anyway, Ilana and Co. were sitting in *our* spots on the couch near the fireplace. They were stitching on this quilt spread across all of their laps and gossiping so hard, I seriously thought they were gonna start spitting acid."

"Oh, like *you're* above gossiping," Tay said. "You're doing it right now!"

"Not like this," Scottie insisted. "They were making a list of all the Stark girls they suspect of having boob jobs. Then came the ones with nose jobs. *Then* they started speculating about *dyed hair.* Since when is that even notable, much less gossip-worthy?"

"Especially coming from Lissie Goldblatt," Tay said, "who clearly has a chin implant."

Scottie almost choked on her Kung Pao she laughed so hard. But she sobered up quickly when she said, "The thing is, before the 'babes' got on the subject of surgery? I'm *sure* they were talking about us. The minute I sat down near them, they did that thing where they all looked over at me then started shushing each other. Then Grier was all, 'Better change the subject, you guys!' I mean, how obvious can you get?"

"I guess that depends on how overactive your imagination is," Tay said, raising one eyebrow.

"What are you saying?" Scottie said.

"I'm just not so sure the Babes with Batting are out to get us," Tay said. "Don't you think you're being just a *leetle* bit paranoid?"

"What?!" Scottie squeaked. She spun to face Bella.

"Do you think that, too?"

Bella cringed through her mouthful of seitan joe.

"Well," she wheedled, "I've never heard of *quilters* being so, y'know, combative."

Scottie was about to retort when Amanda flounced up.

"Hi guys," she said, plopping a white paper bag onto the table. Her hair looked windblown and her cheeks were rosy, which made her look more stunning than ever.

Or maybe, Scottie mused, *Amanda looks pretty because of that gleam in her eye. That* crushy *gleam.*

Amanda sat down and pulled her bag open hungrily.

"I was having a major falafel craving so I dashed down the street," she explained. She pulled a foil-wrapped pita out of the bag, along with a paper pouch of curly fries.

A fully deep-fried lunch? Scottie observed. *Well, that clinches it. When Amanda's single, she's a salad bar girl. But being in like makes her crave all things full-fat—yet* still *lose weight from all the adrenaline coursing through her veins.*

"So," Scottie announced, "clearly things went well after you left the party with Mister . . . hey, what is Jamison's last name?"

Amanda paused, chewed her lip for a moment, then mumbled something.

"What was that?" Tay said.

"I said Steele," Amanda blurted, giving Scottie a defensive look. "His last name is Steele."

"Jamison Steele?" Scottie hooted. "You've got to be kidding. Wait a minute, don't tell me he's heir to a romance novel empire."

"No," Amanda pouted. Then her voice dropped again and she rasped, "It's a chalk empire."

"Chalk?" Bella said, looking utterly confused.

Amanda blew a wisp of dark hair out of her eyes and blurted, "His family owns a company that sells chalk to basically every school in the country, okay?"

"That's a lot of chalk," Scottie said, trying not to laugh. "The Steeles—chalk kings of Chicago."

"Hey, chalk is cooler than toilet paper," Amanda grumbled.

"That *is* true," Scottie said. Then she angled her head and looked hard at Amanda's flushed face; at the way she was breaking her French fries into little pieces but not eating them; at the slightly unfocused, dreamy cast in her eyes.

"Wow," she said quietly. "So you really like him, huh?"

Amanda looked at her sheepishly. "Yeah," she admitted. "I know it makes me look like a total hypocrite, crushing on one of *them*. But Scottie, I was right. Jamison *is* different."

"So tell us about the party!" Bella said. "Scottie IM'd me and Tay about it yesterday."

"Oh my God," Amanda gushed, unwrapping her falafel. "It was *such* a scene. I felt like I was already in New York! I mean, everybody was dressed in these amazing DIY duds, or they were wearing dresses by really cool local designers. And the DJ *was* amazing. I'd never heard of half the bands he played. Jamison and I danced for *hours*. And when we weren't dancing, we were talking to the wildest people—and dissing the deb thing the whole time. Jamison had some WASP jokes that made *me* blush. I mean, I thought *I* hated debbing. . . ."

"Well, I don't know why."

Scottie jumped as a chilly voice floated into the Chicks' midst.

"Being a debutante," the girl lurking behind Scottie went on, "is no more lame than, say, *knitting*."

Scottie turned to find herself gazing up at the surgically altered chin of Lissie Goldblatt. Ilana Cross was at her side and behind them stood Emma and Grier, each posing like a supermodel. All of them wore the same sour, condescending smiles.

Once they had the Chicks' attention, Ilana turned to Lissie and announced, "I *knew* I smelled something barnyardy. I thought it was the Satan burgers, but now I realize it was all that wool."

"Whew," Emma said eagerly, waving a hand in front of her face and wrinkling her nose.

"Well, you would know a lot about gross smells, wouldn't you Ilana?" Tay said, fixing Ilana with a wide smile.

Scottie slapped a hand over her mouth to keep from shrieking with laughter, a move that Ilana caught. Ilana blanched for a split second— before getting surlier than ever.

"I know some other things, too," she said, "like that you might get a little surprise when you show up for your so-called 'stitch 'n bitch' tomorrow."

Tay's face went from light to dark in an instant.

"What do you mean?" she growled.

"Here's the thing," Grier blurted, stepping to the front of the quilters' pack. She shifted her wad of gum to her cheek and started prattling, ticking her items of business off on her fingers as she went.

"I just got a major part in Stark's production of *The Vagina Monologues*, which means I have rehearsals on Wednesdays and Fridays. On Thursdays, Lissie has a standing appointment at Nail Bar and Emma has her SAT class because she totally bombed the PSATS."

"Okay, *that's* not the point, *Grier*," Emma said, huffing impatiently.

Grier covered her mouth with a limp hand.

"Whoops, I forgot. That was supposed to be a secret, wasn't it?"

She cocked her head, shot Emma a faux-apologetic smile, then turned back to the Chicks.

"So where was I?" she said, gazing at the ceiling and giving her gum a chomp.

"Monday," Ilana said.

"Oh, right," Grier said. She snapped her gum again and went on. "On *Mondays,* I have to take my sister to her Suzuki class, Lissie has private skiing lessons to prep for Christmas in Steamboat, and Ilana goes shopping with her mom."

"You go shopping *every* Monday?" Amanda demanded of Ilana, her mouth hanging open.

Ilana straightened her pleated miniskirt, then smoothed down the waistband of her sparkly, jersey T-shirt.

"*I* don't make my own clothes," she said. "Some of us aren't that, y'know, *homespun.*"

Bella fingered the fuzzy, bell-shaped sleeve of her hand-knitted sweater and frowned. But Amanda merely rolled her eyes and said, "Here's what I really want to know. Why on *earth* should we care about your schedules?"

"Because," Ilana said, examining one of her polished fingernails distractedly, "of Tuesdays."

"What's happening on Tuesdays?" Scottie wondered.

"Nothing," Ilana declared. "That's the point. It's the only day all four of us are free. Which means the Babes with Batting will be switching our bees at Joe from Wednesdays to Tuesdays."

Ilana dragged her eyes lazily from her hand to Scottie's burning face.

"Starting tomorrow," she added.

"Oh, no you *won't!*" Scottie yelled. She completely forgot to assume the tone of casual weariness all of them had been using for this little face-off. "Never Mind the Frogs has been meeting on Tuesdays for *two years*. That's our day and you know it."

"Um, *excuse* me, but I don't believe I ever saw an official roster at Joe," Lissie said, grinning catlike at her friends. "I mean, are you *allowed* to just claim a day there?"

"No," Grier said, playing along. She chomped her gum with extra vigor and smiled at the Chicks malevolently. "I don't think you are."

"Whatever," Tay scoffed. "Frogs has as many as twenty people knitting every Tuesday now. There'll be no room for you and your little, *tiny* needles. End of story."

"Or it'll be the other way around," Ilana said calmly. "I mean, it's first come, first served, right? And we have at least a dozen quilters who have study periods for their last class. Which means we can get to Joe a full hour before school ends. So . . . if there's no room for you *frogs* when you get there? Oh well!"

Scottie gasped and looked at her friends in outrage. "No way," she whispered. "They can't do that, can they?"

For the first time, Tay looked alarmed. "What're we gonna do?" she whispered back. "Pick 'em up and throw them out?"

• Chicks with Sticks

Scottie gripped the edge of the table, at a complete loss for a clever comeback for the Babes. Finally, after an embarrassingly long pause, she stuck out her chin and glared up at Ilana.

"Here's the thing about knitters," she said. "We have way more tricks up our sleeves than you can ever imagine."

"Oh, like knit *two*, purl *two* instead of knit one, purl one?" Ilana replied, sarcasm making her voice brittle. "Whoa, that's impressive! What other tricks have you got— knit, knit, purl, purl? Or the ever-popular purl, purl, knit, knit?"

Scottie's cheeks flamed. Clearly, she didn't have Ilana's talent for making mean. *Which I guess I should feel good about?* she thought woefully.

With nothing else to say, Scottie made a desperate attempt at sneery body language. She clamped her mouth shut, twisted in her seat, and turned her stiff, straight back to the Babes. Then she scooped up her chopsticks and began poking around in her Chinese food carton with intense interest. The other Chicks used the same "just ignore them" tactic.

After a long moment of disdainful silence, the Babes finally skulked away, exchanging cackles and high-fives as they went. When they were out of ear shot, Scottie exhaled loudly and slumped over the table, her head in her hands.

"This is horrible," she groaned. *"Horrible!* It's a coup!"

"Well, maybe it's not *quite* as serious as overthrowing a government," Bella suggested gently.

"But it *is* pretty aggressive," Tay had to admit. "Those Babes are evil."

"Yeah," John agreed. "Man, it's hard being a girl. Guys just throw a punch and get it over with. The way girls do things is much more subversive. Underhanded. Dangerous, even! Which is a kind of a turn-on, now that I think about it. . . ."

He laughed and gave Tay's waist a pinch.

"You are *so* weird," Tay said. "Why don't you go knit or something?"

"Don't mind if I do," John said. He popped the last of his Twinkie into his mouth, then pulled a burgundy-and-blue striped cap-in-progress out of his messenger bag. He spaced his stitches neatly around his circular needle and began knitting with a swift, jerky rhythm. John had been knitting for about a year and he was actually getting pretty good at it.

"Well, I think John is wrong," Amanda announced, taking a big chomp out of her pita. "The Babes would be dangerous if they could actually pull this off, but I don't believe they can for a minute. They're totally bluffing."

"Really?" Scottie squeaked.

"Really," Amanda declared confidently. "And if they *do* make some weak attempt to infiltrate Frogs, we'll just keep ignoring them."

"Yeah," Bella piped. "We definitely shouldn't engage them. Why should we compete over whether quilting is better than knitting?"

"Right," Tay said. "We *know* knitting's better."

"Yeah-huh!" Scottie cried, pumping her fist.

"You guys," Amanda said. "This isn't a game of Go to the Head of the Craft. This is a meaningless turf war, pure and simple. And like Scottie said—we've had Tuesdays at Joe for two years now and we're gonna keep on having Tuesdays at Joe. This is a blip."

Amanda sounded so confident that Scottie was almost convinced. She decided not to panic—yet. She even attempted some bravado.

"Those girls *so* went about this the wrong way," she said. "If they'd just *asked* us to switch days instead of poaching, maybe we would have considered it. I mean, I'd love to bring Nina to Frogs, since I've totally infected her with the knitting bug. But I only see her on Wednesdays and Fridays."

"And I rarely have deb duty on Fridays," Amanda piped up, "so that day would work for me, too."

"But now," Scottie glowered, "they're *never* getting our Tuesdays."

"Damn straight," John agreed. He held up his hand, inviting Scottie to high-five him. Scottie looked around sheepishly, then shrugged and gave his hand a slap. High fives weren't really the Chicks' thing, but John was sweet for trying.

"Hey," Bella said, "if you guys are looking for something to do with your Fridays, you should come paint the French fry bus with me!"

"Um, I don't think Amanda needs any more French fries," Tay joked, swiping a curly fry from Amanda's lunch and popping it into her mouth.

"Oh, that's just my nickname for it," Bella said. "It's this bus that's going to travel across the country to let the world know about the importance of alternative fuels! The thing's gonna run on nothing but leftover French fry oil from fast food restaurants! Isn't that cool?!"

"Wow, Bella," Scottie said, shooting Amanda and Tay sidelong glances. "I had no idea you were so . . . passionate about alternative fuels. So GreenLeaves is branching out from endangered species and stuff?"

"Oh, GreenLeaves," Bella scoffed. "I got really disenchanted with them. I mean, it seems like everybody who worked there smoked clove cigarettes! *When* they weren't composing beat poetry about whales and stuff. It was like being environmental activists was just one little part of their hipster identities. And smoking cloves? How is *that* good for the environment? No, the Alternative Fuel Consortium is much more me. Not only do they *not* pollute the air, but the exhaust from the French fry bus smells really yummy! Kinda like hush puppies."

Scottie guffawed. "Bella, you're going crazy!" she said. "How many different service projects are you gonna rack up before graduation?"

"I'm just looking for the right fit," Bella defended herself. She'd finished her seitan joe and was moving on to her dessert, another Dr. Heath creation called Granougat, an *extremely* chewy granola bar. "Not everybody can be as lucky as you, Scottie. Sounds like things are going great with Nina."

"They are, amazing as it sounds," Scottie said with a happy shrug.

"Just dumb luck, I guess. *And* the fact that Nina's an amazing kid. She's so sweet, but she's cool, too. And she totally gets the knitting thing. She's already almost finished her first scarf. She says it's a fabulous way to block out the racket of her little sisters and brother."

She turned to Bella, who was working very hard to sink her teeth into her Granougat.

"Don't worry," she assured her. "I'm sure a Bella-ready project is out there for you. Maybe the French fry bus will be a match."

"And if it isn't," Bella shrugged between gnaws on her dessert, "at least it'll look good on my college apps. Schools love to see that you're well-rounded and up for trying lots of different things."

Scottie froze. She felt like she'd been kicked in the stomach.

And here I thought it was good *that things are going so well with Nina,* she brooded. *Turns out, it just makes me a one-note Jane.*

Scottie shook her head hard. She didn't want to think about that. Not when there was so much else to occupy her mind, from the new development in Amanda's love life, to battling the Babes with Batting, to her next activity with Nina.

Which, hello, I'm doing for her, Scottie reminded herself with just a hint of self-righteousness. *Not for the sake of some application. I can't imagine what could be wrong about that.*

Scottie cast a shifty glance at Bella, who'd finally given up on her Granougat and begun knitting and studying her notes for her next class. Scottie wondered what Bella would say if she voiced her skepticism out loud.

But the bell was just a couple minutes away.

What's more, Scottie thought with a shrug, *college applications are* months *away.*

So she filed the question away for another day, some time—Scottie didn't know exactly when—in the future.

11 * (Pick up stitches along edge)

As Scottie left the Chinatown L station, she sighed. It was Friday—a week and a half after Jamison Steele and the Babes with Batting had entered the Chicks' orbit—and she was feeling a bit weary.

Amanda had been right: the Chicks had maintained their grip on Tuesdays at Joe—but not without a fight. The day after Ilana and her gang confronted them in the cafeteria, they'd indeed beat the Chicks to Joe with half a dozen other quilters in tow. By the time the Chicks arrived with their usual crowd of yarnheads—from Maryn and Tiff, who were collaborating on some lace gloves for the senior prom, to Regan and Polly, Amanda's freeforming buds from University of Chicago—the Babes had taken over. They'd sprawled out in front of the flickering fireplace, bits of fabric and spools of thread strewn about so that every surface on which the Chicks might have sat was conveniently occupied.

Amanda and Scottie, at the front of their pack of knitters, looked at each other in dismay. Scottie felt squashiness begin to build around her mouth and eyes. But before she could say anything to the infiltrators, Amanda grabbed her elbow and squeezed hard. Then she looked into Scottie's eyes, raising her eyebrows and pursing her lips. After years of silent communication across Stark school classrooms, Scottie could easily read Amanda's meaning.

Let me handle it. I've got a plan.

Scottie nodded subtly. Then Amanda rearranged her face into a sun-shiney smile and turned to the Babes.

"You made it!" she exclaimed, practically skipping up to Ilana, Emma, Grier, and Lissie. They were nested elbow-to-elbow on the Chicks' favorite shabby couch, draped in their half-stitched crazy quilt.

"Ooh," Amanda cried, squeezing in between Ilana and Emma. "Lemme see!"

She bent over to examine the quilt top, fingering the irregular slices of fabric and the neat white stitches that linked them all together.

"Awesome," she said. As she motioned to the growing pack of knitters gathering behind Scottie, she said to Ilana, "I hope you have enough needles and thread for all of us."

"What?" Ilana sneered.

"Well the flyer said you'd provide supplies, didn't it?" Amanda said. "And it also pointed out that knitting is, like, *so* over. So, duh, we're switching to quilting!"

Scottie pressed her knuckles into her lips to keep from howling with laughter. She could tell what Amanda was up to, and it was brilliant.

"So how do you *do* the actual quilting part?" Amanda pressed on. "I mean is there a trick to it?"

"Nah," Grier said, chomping her gum between sips of latte. "You just do a running stitch with white thread. It's pretty simple."

Ilana squinted at Grier for a long, uncomfortable moment before she turned to speak to Amanda.

"Our flyer was simple *too*," she pointed out. "But somehow you got it wrong. It said that *you* bring your own needle and thread and *we'd* provide the treats."

She motioned to a plate of chocolate-covered graham crackers on the graffiti-covered coffee table.

"Ohhhhh!" Amanda said, slapping her forehead. Then she smiled

• • Chicks with Sticks

sweetly and said, "You know me and my LD. I must have misread your flyer."

"Well . . ." Ilana said. She reached for a bag at her feet and tucked the top closed.

Probably to hide the scads of extra needles she has in there, Scottie realized with a giggle.

"Sorry you can't join us," Ilana said, looking pained by her own politeness.

One of the Babes' pals—whom Scottie couldn't help but notice didn't seem very interested in working on the quilt, not when there were mochas to nurse and texts to thumb into their PDAs—leaned forward.

"Wait a minute, Ilana," she stage-whispered. "I thought you said this group was gonna be exclusive. You're gonna let those weird knitting chicks in?"

Amanda pretended she hadn't heard. Instead she clasped her hands beneath her chin and zapped Ilana with another 100-watt smile.

"You are so sweeeeet," she cooed. Ilana squirmed visibly but Amanda ignored that, too. "I guess we'll just have to knit today. But *next* week, we'll definitely BYO the quilting supplies. You'll still be here on Tuesdays, right?"

"Um, right," Ilana mumbled.

"Great!" Amanda said. She scooped up a couple chocolate graham crackers and took a big bite out of one of them. "See you then!"

She flounced perkily back to the Froggers and said loudly, "Oh well, we'll be knitting today, you guys. Let's sit up front. I see some booths available. It'll be a fun change of pace!"

Regan, never known for her tact, plunked her hands on her round hips and yelped, "We're sitting in the *booths*?! What the hell—"

"—o Kitty backpack pattern?" Scottie blurted over Regan's outrage. "Why yes, I *did* remember to bring it for you. But it's really complicated, so it'll be great to have a table to spread it out on. Let's go!"

Regan was still in protest mode, but she let Scottie yank her toward the front of the coffeehouse. The rest of the Froggers followed. When they'd settled themselves into a cluster of booths and tables, Amanda grinned.

"My prediction?" she whispered. "By next week, most of those so-called 'quilters' are gonna be history. And when *we* decide we like sitting up here even more than we liked the back lounge, the *Babes* are gonna decide the lounge is lame. Or they'll just give up Tuesdays entirely to avoid seeing us every week."

"Do you really think they're gonna respond to reverse psychology?" Tay sputtered. "They're not toddlers, Amanda."

"Let's not forget that this is all about a grade school grudge," Amanda pointed out.

"Yeah, maturity isn't really Ilana's strong suit," Scottie said. The rubber band of nerves that had been gripping her chest ever since lunch the previous day started to loosen.

"And besides," she added, "even if these girls are actually interested in quilting, which I doubt, it won't last. They didn't pick it because it spoke to them, the way we chose knitting. To them, it's just one more trend. This month it's quilting. Next month, it'll be cultivating bushy eyebrows or photo collaging or something."

"I hope you're right," Bella said, already squirming in the hard, wooden seat of their booth. "Because I don't have as much knitty mojo when I'm not sitting in my favorite bean bag. A sense of place is very important to the spiritual aspect of knitting, you know."

"Trust me," Amanda said.

The Froggers trusted her. And the following Tuesday? The quilters definitely thinned out. The four Babes had only two buddies with them; two buddies who barely pretended to be passionate about quilting. That had left enough room in the lounge for the Froggers to crowd in around them and ask a million faux-interested questions about quilting. By the time they'd all trooped out of Joe at dinner time, the Babes had looked exhausted.

◆ ◆ Chicks with Sticks

Something tells me, Scottie thought to herself now with a victorious smile, *they might peter out as early as next week.*

And that was a good thing, because Never Mind the Frogs was about the only place all four Chicks had been able to get together lately. Amanda, for one, had been triple-shifting. When she wasn't pulling deb duty at curtsy classes and a stultifying string of parties, she'd been hanging out with Jamison so they could debrief each other about the lameness of said parties. And when she wasn't debbing *or* with Jamison, she'd been obsessing over her Parsons application, poring over her port-folio and weighing every word of her essays.

Bella was spending more time than ever on her community service work.

And Tay seemed to be making up for time lost to her Milwaukee weekends by spending every spare minute in Chicago with John.

The only person Scottie had been seeing on a regular basis was Nina. She was on her way to meet Nina this very minute, in fact. They were after-school-snacking in Chinatown before meeting Bella and the other folks in the Alternative Fuel Consortium at a nearby playlot, where they were going to help paint the French fry bus.

But we're doing it because it sounds cool and fun and good for the earth, Scottie reminded herself happily, *not because we need to—what was it that Lily at Big Sibs/Little Sibs said?—to "catalyze some healthy interfacing."*

Since meeting Nina, Scottie had barely looked at the exhaustive list of Big Sib/Little Sib activities she'd dreamed up during her training. The awkwardness of their first hour together had melted away as fast as they could devour their salted caramel ice cream at HotChocolate. Now, there was no need for time fillers. They were often as content to hang out over coffee and yarn as they were to embark on an Activity with a capital A.

She and Nina were bridging the tween-to-teen divide, Scottie sus-pected, because their relationship wasn't nearly as one-sided as she'd thought it would be. Sure, Scottie *was* the older one, which meant she could fill Nina in on many secrets of post-twelve life. She told her all about the treacheries of high school, for instance, and let her know that it *was* possible to recover from actually being sweet sixteen and never been kissed. (Scottie knew from experience.) She told Nina that yes, her boobs would probably get bigger, but no, it wasn't likely that her period would ever get less annoying.

But Nina had things to teach Scottie, too. She explained her South Side neighborhood, for instance, outlining the cultures that seemed to shift every few blocks. She talked about what it was like being both daughter and something of a co-parent in her house. And she told Scottie how to stomach a Polish dinner of blood sausage and sauerkraut without getting a stomachache. (It took a complex combination of Pepto and parsley oil.)

For Scottie, the friendship was something completely new and sweetly familiar at the same time. She often found herself recreating with Nina things she'd done with the Chicks once upon a time.

Before everybody got so busy, Scottie thought as she walked through the giant, Pagoda-style arch at Chinatown's entrance.

It was a short trek down the main drag to Double Happiness, her favorite shop in the neighborhood. It made Scottie smile just to swing through the front door. The place was a sort of soda fountain, candy shop, and general store all crammed into one big, linoleum-tiled room. Scottie breezed down the central aisle, casting a creeped-out peek at the withered-looking herbs displayed on the left wall, and a greedy glance at the bins of fruity candy to her right. When she reached the bubble-tea counter in the back, she found Nina, perched on an aqua high-boy chair, already waiting for her.

"Hey!" Scottie said, hopping onto the chair next to her. "I'm glad you're here already. We have exactly one hour to while away before we get all painty at the French fry bus."

"I'm one step ahead of ya," Nina said, flicking her single blond braid over her shoulder. "I already ordered us our bubble teas. I got lychee for you and triple-berry for me."

"Fab," Scottie said just as a girl with spiky black hair popped through a swinging door behind the counter. She plopped a couple of tall, plastic cups before them. Simultaneously, Nina and Scottie grabbed their drinks' wide-mouthed plastic straws and sucked up a few beads of black, gummy tapioca along with mouthfuls of tart, fruity tea.

"Bubble tea is sorta like sushi," Scottie observed as she felt one of the squishy pearls slither down her throat. "The first bite is always a little scary, but once you realize how yummy it is, you get over the weirdness."

"No way," Nina insisted. "Raw fish is way creepier than tapioca."

"For a long time, I felt that way, too." Scottie nodded sagely. "My parents were sushi freaks and I wouldn't touch the stuff. At every other one of their art openings, *there* would be the waiters passing around little mounds of orange fish eggs and slabs of red, raw tuna. And all of it was wrapped in seaweed that smelled like just that—green stuff that had washed up on the beach. Nausea! And *then*, the leftovers would land in our fridge and haunt me for days."

"Your parents have *waiters* at their parties?" Nina said.

"Oh! Well . . . " Scottie squirmed, kicking herself. "The servers are usually starving art students. And my parents only hire them for gallery parties. It's kind of a business thing."

"Oh," Nina said. As she often did, she nodded matter-of-factly and moved on. Scottie had found that Nina was as straightforwardly cheerful as she herself was broody. "So what made you start liking sushi?"

"Oh, Amanda played a trick on me," Scottie said. Nina hadn't met Amanda yet, but she'd heard all about her. "It was at one of our Sacred Sleepovers at her place. She pulled out these little dumplings that she'd gotten at Trader Joe's. It was 'fusion' cuisine, she told us, but she wouldn't tell us what and *what* had been fused in there. Still, I never met a dumpling I didn't like, so I tried one. Inside a spring roll wrapper, I could taste rice and something kind of sweet and sour, and something salty, and it had this texture that was creamy and poppy all at once. I loved it! I ate three of 'em before Amanda told me what was really inside the dumpling."

"And it was sushi?!" Nina squealed.

"Yellowtail, roe, *and* seaweed," Scottie confirmed. "I gagged for about five minutes before I realized, I was gonna be bummed if I never tasted that stuff again. So I became a sushi eater. It's still a mental leap every time I sit down to some, but trust me, it's worth it."

"No way," Nina said, shaking her head as she slurped up a string of tapioca pearls. "You'll never catch me eating raw fish. I won't even eat golabki, so I'm sure not eating anything wrapped in seaweed."

"Golabki?" Scottie said.

"You know," Nina said, sliding off her chair. "Stuffed cabbage leaves. Cabbage—yich!"

She shuddered, then peered down the closest aisle of treats. "Hey, do you want to get some candy to-go?"

"Are you kidding?" Scottie said. "Where else can I find myself a . . ."

Hopping out of her own seat, Scottie snatched a weird-looking lollipop out of a nearby bin and squinted at it. ". . . a lime T-rex head covered with 'gummi flesh?' On a stick, no less!"

Nina laughed and disappeared down the first cramped and dusty candy aisle. Scottie followed her and they began treasure hunting.

"Ooh, have you ever had these?" Nina said, pointing at a cardboard box of tiny plastic domes sealed with foil lids. "They're little fruits, like lychee nuts or Japanese raspberries, floating in some sort of Jello stuff. *Very* weird."

"Not as weird as this!" Scottie said, pulling out a bag of gummy lightning bugs that glowed when you plucked them up with a flashlight/tweezer.

"Ewwww!" Nina said, sticking her tongue out at the yellow and red bugs.

Still nursing their teas, Scottie and Nina each assembled a stash of jiggly candies and headed for the cash register up front. Just before they reached it though, Scottie saw one of the random delights that made Chinatown one of her favorite places on earth.

"Press-on nails!" she exclaimed. She rushed over to a rickety, wire rack and snatched a plastic-wrapped card off the display. Mounted on the card were ten long pointy plastic fingernails, each airbrushed with a teensy-tiny sunset-over-the-beach scene. They were as cheesy as you could get.

"Amanda and I used to *love* these," Scottie squealed. "We'd put 'em on Friday afternoon and wear them all weekend until our moms made us peel them off on Monday morning. Not only did they look *so* cool . . ."

Scottie smiled sarcastically. ". . . but they were so long that it was impossible to help with household chores while you were wearing them."

"Oh yeah," Nina scoffed. *"That'd* go over in my house."

"Let's get some!" Scottie blurted.

"Are you serious?" Nina said. Her eyes were wide and protesting, but when Scottie looked closer, she could see a gleam in them as well.

"We don't have to wear them all weekend," Scottie said. "Let's just put 'em on now and wear them til they get unbearable. You can't have much more fun than this for ninety-nine cents!"

"When you put it that way," Nina said with a giggle.

"Which do you want?" Scottie said, scanning the rack. "The ocean sunset nails? The jungle scene? Or the urban skyline?"

"Oh, definitely the ocean," Nina said. "Then I can pretend I've been to the beach."

"Yeah, if only," Scottie laughed. She plucked another set of sunset nails off the rack and headed to the cash register. She paid for their nails, candy, and her tea, but when Nina insisted, Scottie let her pay for her own bubble tea. She knew Nina was a little self-conscious about having less spending money than Scottie did, so Scottie made sure not to make a big deal out of paying for *everything* the girls did together. She could see the pride Nina took in pulling out her funky sock monkey wallet and counting out the money her mom gave her for these outings.

"Okay," Scottie said when they'd walked out of the shop with two paper bags full of loot. "If we put on our nails on the L, we should be there right on time."

Nina laughed some more and ran-walked to the station. Scottie hustled to keep up with her, laughing breathlessly herself.

It felt good to be pulling this goofy fake nail stunt again. It felt even better to be introducing Nina to such frivolous fun.

If only we were the same age, Scottie thought, *this relationship could last more than a year.*

Or *it could keep on going,* Scottie realized suddenly, *if I stayed in Chicago!*

As she tromped down the sidewalk next to Nina, who was waxing on about how much her baby sisters would love her press-on nails, Scottie's breath quickened a bit.

So, the whole Chicks-with-Sticks-take-on-Northwestern plan bombed, she thought. *That doesn't mean that I can't go there on my own. Maybe it's lame to go to school in Chicago when I've lived here my entire life, but it would be a cool thing to keep on being there for Nina, wouldn't it? Not to mention Beck and Tay.*

As she pulled out her L card and followed Nina through the train station turnstile, Scottie listed all the stellar schools in Chicago.

Okay, she allowed, *DePaul is too close to home, seeing as I can walk there from my loft. But Loyola is kind of a hike. And Northwestern is a great school, even if it would make me feel a bit Felicity-like to follow my b.f. to his college. I could try to get into University of Chicago. So what if I've always found Hyde Park to be depressing and I don't have a burning desire to win a MacArthur genius grant like every other kid at U of C? I'd get an incredible education.*

By the time she and Nina tumbled into their seats on the red line, a happy, if vague, sense of hope had begun bubbling up inside of Scottie.

Maybe, she told herself, *just maybe, moving on in life doesn't have to mean giving my entire life* up.

Before she could consider any other logistics for her plan, Nina tore the cellophane off the press-on nail kits and squealed, "I'll put yours on you, then you do me."

Scottie nodded and splayed her fingers so Nina could stick the fake nails onto her real ones. She felt a warm sense of well-being flow through her. Sure, these wacky props took her back. But now she also had a plan—okay, a plannish sense of direction—that would take her forward.

What happened next only boosted Scottie's confidence, but first it threw her for a loop.

Scottie and Nina found their way to the address Bella had given them. When they arrived at the playlot—a rubber-floored jungle-gym-and-swing-set area for little kids fronted by a basketball court for big ones—the place was already milling with people, most of them dressed in natural fibers and wielding a Bella-style aura of crunch. They were prepping a long, white school bus as if it were a hospital patient. Several people were organizing paint cans by color on a long tarp and a few others were putting finishing touches on the elaborate design that had been sketched onto the bus. In the outline, Scottie could see great sprays of corn, bundles of sugar beets, an undulating river, and other sources of alternative fuel.

Still other Consortium folks were lining up at a rickety table, presumably to get their painting assignments. It was there that Scottie spotted Bella.

"Hey!" Scottie called, waving wildly. She grabbed Nina's hand to lead her over to Bella but only succeeded in gouging one of her pointy nails straight into Nina's palm. This, of course, made them both dissolve into punchy giggles. They were still snorting and holding their sides when they reached Bella.

"You must be Nina!" Bella said, enfolding Nina into a feathery embrace.

"Otherwise known," Scottie said, waggling her faux nails at Bella, "as my mani twin!"

"Oh!" Bella said, looking at Scottie and Nina's hands, a confused smile wavering on her lips. "Did you *just* have those done?"

"Yeah," Scottie laughed. "But don't worry. They're just press-ons. I won't be showing up at Stark on Monday with 'em on. Your earthy cred is safe with me."

"I wasn't thinking about that," Bella said. "I was thinking about this!"

She motioned with her own short-nailed hand at the blue tape, paint cans, and carpet cutters piled on the tarps—art supplies that would be pretty hard to handle with inch-long plastic nails.

"Oh my God," Scottie moaned through a laugh. "I didn't even think of that."

She began popping the nails off, leaving her real ones gummy with fresh adhesive.

"Listen, Nina," Scottie said, "if you want to keep yours on, I'm sure we can find a job for you that won't ruin them."

"Yeah . . ." Bella said with a bit of uncertainty. "Let's go ask the coordinator."

Nina shook her head and looked sheepish.

"They were just a game," she said. She began to pull at one of the sunset-painted talons. "I thought it'd be funny to show them to the littles, but I don't want to bother the coordinator about it."

"It's no bother," Bella said. She smiled at Nina and put a delicate hand on her back to guide her toward the collapsible table. "You need to talk to him anyway to get your job assignment for the afternoon."

Scottie smiled gratefully at Bella.

Of course, Bellissima doesn't need Big Sib training to see that Nina doesn't want to give up her wacky nails just yet.

Scottie fell into the short line with Bella and Nina. After a gray-haired couple in matching Earth shoes had gotten their instructions, Scottie and Nina bellied up to the table. They waited as the coordinator jotted some notes on a clipboard. As he wrote, he rested his forehead on his left palm and twined his fingers through his thick, matted curls. Finally, he finished writing, using a stabbing motion to make the final period, and looked up at Scottie and Nina.

"Hi there. We can stay for the next three hours," Scottie began, "and we'd really appreciate it if you could give Nina here something kinda low-impact because . . ."

Scottie's voice trailed off as she gazed at the coordinator's face. Those world-weary dark eyes. That down-turned lush mouth. The matte-brown curls that looked like they'd been slept on half-a-dozen times since their last washing. She knew this guy!

"Hey," she exclaimed, "you're the barista from Joe! Reuben!"

"Yeah," he said. His voice took on the tone of impatience and contempt Scottie was accustomed to. "What of it? Do you not *approve* of my day job? I'll have you know, I refuse—*refuse*—to handle any coffee beans whose harvest threatens wild songbirds."

"Oh, I wasn't—" Scottie stuttered. "I was just surprised."

"What, that a lowly *barista* might have beliefs?" the man sneered. "Beliefs that I *act* upon, not just talk about like most of the poseurs who hang at Joe?"

Then he cast a softened glance at Bella. "Not talking about you, Bella," he said.

"Oh, I know, Reuben," Bella said.

"I didn't mean to offend you," Scottie said. "I was just surprised to see you out of context is all. I guess I figured you were going to college when you weren't working at Joe."

"Yeah, well . . ." Reuben cast a loving glance toward the bus. "I'm taking a little deferral on the whole college thing. I figured I could learn a lot more by founding this Consortium and driving our good ol' bus across the country than I could ever learn from some old guys in elbow patches."

"Cool!" Scottie said. She cocked her head as she looked at Reuben. She was seeing his surliness in a whole new light now. He wasn't just a grouch for the sake of it. He was an angry young man hell bent on saving the earth for future generations. With French fry oil!

"Yeah," Bella said enthusiastically. "European kids do that all the time. They go out and experience the real world before they head to college. That way, when they start their education, they *really* have their feet on the ground and some serious goals."

"Yeah, well, we'll see about that whole college thing," Reuben said, looking hazily into the distance now. "I mean, if I can get some serious publicity with our Alt Fuel Bus, who knows how far we can take our message."

"*Tscha!*" Scottie said, nodding vigorously. She glanced at Nina, who was staring at Reuben like he was a rock star. Which was pretty much how he was carrying himself. The slouchy, sullen barista Scottie knew from Joe had all but disappeared. Now, Reuben seemed so sure of himself that Scottie found herself wondering if he had a point.

You know, she realized, racking up another epiphany for the day, *Reuben's totally right. Who says you* have *to go to college to make a contribution in the world? He's learning from* life. *Even my mom says that art school was just the beginning of her training; that she didn't* really *begin to paint until she'd lived a little.*

It appeared that Bella hadn't considered this either.

"But—" Bella blurted, "don't you think you could take your message that much further if you had, y'know, a degree? Or even two? I mean, if you got a master's in environmental science, you'd have major credentials behind your ideas. You could get published, even."

"That's so elitist, man," Reuben said, even though he said it in the same sweet tone he always used for Bella. "I don't need some meaningless letters after my name to have an opinion."

"Yeah, but you need them if anyone's gonna listen to you!" Bella almost-snapped. "And they're not meaningless!"

Scottie's mouth popped open. As she stared at Bella, her mind buzzed.

Wait a minute, she thought. *Have Bella and I pulled a Freaky Friday? She's the one who's supposed to be all about peace and love and accepting people as they are, no matter how different. And I'm the one who "doesn't like new things." But now she's cross-examining Reuben the Barista . . .*

Scottie watched as Bella marched over to the stack of art supplies and grabbed a paint can, ready to put her nose to the grindstone. Then she glanced at Reuben, whose surly slouch suddenly looked purposeful.

. . . and I'm the one who wants to hop onto the French fry bus!

12 *(Make selvage)

Clearly, Reuben had found one of Bella's rare exposed nerves and tweaked it. Over the next few weeks, she attacked her college applications with a fervor that Scottie had never seen in her mellow bud. Given the fact that Bella was—beneath her Pollyanna smiles and wobbly yoga poses—quietly brilliant, Scottie had assumed she would breeze her way into whatever college she wanted without breaking a sweat.

But clearly, Bella was leaving nothing to chance. By the time the Chicks gathered at Tay's house for a Sacred Sleepover on a bitter Saturday in early December, her half-dozen applications had been stocked with polished essays, glowing letters of recommendation, and carefully culled resumes, then sent off to their admissions offices, priority mail.

Amanda was even deeper into her application process. She'd sent an early admissions app to Parsons in November. And for the past week, she'd been waking up every morning in a cold sweat, then dashing in her pajamas to her lobby to check the mailbox for an acceptance letter. So far, no letter had surfaced and she was getting edgier by the day.

Scottie was right there with her on the edgy part, but not because she was waiting for an acceptance. It was because she still hadn't sent in a single application—or even decided on one school she wanted to consider!

Every time she tried to rifle through her stack of college brochures, she felt her eyes glaze over. When she tried to whittle down her list by earmarking the schools she *didn't* want to go to, she found herself tossing them *all* out. And when she took the opposite tack and tried to pick a college she *would* want to go to, all of the schools began to look identically, blandly acceptable, and thus, just as impossible to choose among.

She knew that taking her dad up on his offer to tour colleges might help her make a decision. Then again, it was hard to imagine her overeager parents being able to help steer her toward the school of her dreams. The same went for some boosterish student host squiring her around a campus with a bunch of other befuddled seniors.

So, the college applications were still in their file drawer—and still blank.

But there's still time before they're due, Scottie reminded herself. Before the deadlines hit, she assumed, *something* would happen to boot her out of her indecision. What that something might be, she had no clue. But if she sweated it too much, she felt certain it would never surface.

That's how it works when you're looking for love, right? she thought with a shrug. *If you look too hard for it, it'll never come. So why should it be any different when it comes to choosing the path that could alter your life forever? You can't just . . .* pick *it. You have to be inspired. The timing has to be right. You have to feel it in your bones.*

Until Scottie's bones started telling her whether she wanted to move to Madison or Ann Arbor, Ithaca or Durham, she was doing her best to put the whole business out of her mind and have faith that clarity was just around the corner.

The distraction of the Sacred Sleepover helped. Well, it helped Scottie, at least. For Tay, the presence of a fifth wheel at the SSO seemed to be *adding* angst. Twice already, Tay's mom, Laura, had crept into the living room where the Chicks were hanging out, a hesitant smile playing around her tiny, bow-shaped mouth, her soft, brown eyes looking hopeful behind her round glasses. There was something a bit sad about her slightly squished, curly hair and the crease-marks in the lap of her long, purple skirt.

The first time she'd peeked in, she'd offered to make up beds for Amanda, Bella, and Scottie on Tay's bedroom floor, an offer that Tay had brusquely dismissed.

The second time, Laura had clutched a bag of tortilla chips in each of her hands.

"I brought you more chips," she offered to the girls. They were lazing around the living room, only moving out of their grooves in the loveseat and chairs to sample from the snacks on the coffee table.

"Bella," Laura said, motioning with one of the bags at a vat of green dip, "it was so nice of your mom to make all that guacamole for you girls. She must have used ten avocadoes!"

"Yeah, my mom doesn't exactly know how to cook for a small crowd, even though there're just three of us at home," Bella said, grinning at Laura over the mohair caplet she was knitting. "She has this policy of always having extra, just in case, you know, a family of eight drops in for dinner."

"So, tell me which you'd prefer," Laura said, squinting at the chip bags. "Let's see, we have hot 'n spicy red corn chips, or restaurant style with lime."

"Just leave 'em both, Mom," Tay sighed. She'd been working some yarn, knitting herself some super-chunky black socks. But she'd stopped when her mother came in. Now she just plucked at her ball of yarn restlessly, all her knitty steam seemingly gone. "Not that we need 'em."

She pointed at a speckled pottery bowl brimming with blue corn chips.

"I *am* capable of getting my friends more grub if we need it," Tay said without meeting her mother's eyes.

"I know that, sweetie," Laura said. The "sweetie" made Tay flinch, but she didn't otherwise react. Instead, she clamped her lips shut and studiously refused to make eye contact with her mom. Laura strained to catch Tay's gaze for a few seconds before she sagged visibly and gave up.

"I was just trying to help," she murmured.

"Thanks, Laura," Scottie said quietly. She bit her lip. She knew if the Chicks had been hanging out at *her* loft, she'd be just as irritated by the parental intrusion as Tay was. But here, she couldn't help but feel sorry for Laura, who was clearly torn between beating a timid retreat and try-trying again to make Tay like her—or even look at her.

Of course, you only had to look at how out-of-place Tay seemed in her mother's home to know that Laura's efforts were futile. Tay was like a minimalist painting. Her spiky hair, her scuffed-up boots, her cargo pants and crew neck sweater wardrobe—all were thick slashes of black.

Meanwhile, Laura's decorating scheme felt like a desert landscape, all soft edges and earthy colors. Half the space in the bookshelves was taken up by the undulating, speckled vessels Laura had made in her pottery class, or, as Tay put it, "the Divorcées Mud Club." The bathtub was rimmed in scented candles and the kitchen was stocked with a million flavors of herbal tea. Every piece of furniture cradled you like a grandmother's lap.

Needless to say, the apartment made Tay itch, even if, when pressed, she *might* admit that the squishy furniture did make for pretty comfort-able seating during Halo 2 marathons. The only room that had Tay's stamp, or lack of one, was her bedroom. She'd covered over her mother's rust orange paint job with funky black and white stripes and carelessly taped posters of Shaun White and Tony Hawk. The room had one soft touch, a blanket Tay had knitted herself.

Of course, Scottie admitted, *the blanket's primary-colored with thick black borders, but it* is *soft.*

When Laura slunk back out of the living room, having placed the chip bags on the corner of the coffee table, she left behind a silence that could have been awkward, were it not for item #27 on Amanda's long list of debutante duties: always be ready to gracefully fill a gap in the conversation.

"So," she chirped, lifting her head from its loungey position on the arm of her chair, "you would not believe what I had to do for—" She made exaggerated quote symbols in the air. "—'community service' the other day."

"Let me guess," Tay said, clearly grateful to exorcise the Laura-vibes from the room. She picked up her sock and began working it again. "You had to test diamond jewelry for a focus group? Or, hey, were you one of those ceremonial ping-pong ball girls on TV? You know, the ones who choose the winning Lotto numbers?"

"Tay, Tay, Tay," Amanda scolded in mock horror. "A door prize at a fundraiser is deb, but the Lotto? That's very *un*-deb. If you don't learn these things, I'm afraid you'll never make it in high society."

"No!" Tay cried, flinging her forearm over her eyes. "Say it ain't so!"

"Say it *isn't* so, my dear," Bella said, adopting the prim diction of an etiquette instructor. Then she turned to the giggling Amanda. "So what *did* you have to do?"

"I was a flower girl at a tennis exhibition," Amanda said, pretending to gag. "I had to wear a suit and high heels and hand these ginormous bouquets of flowers to the tennis players. The women get the flowers before they even walk onto the court, and the men get them only if they win. Doesn't that strike you as sexist?"

"Wow," Bella said. She'd been lounging on the floor, but now she straightened up to stare at Amanda. *"How* is that community service?"

"I don't know," Amanda sighed. "Maybe it's a service to give Roger Federer something nice to smell after he got all sweaty winning his game? The guy *was* pretty rank."

"You gave flowers to *Roger Federer?"* Tay yelled.

"Yessss," Amanda sighed. "I know, it's totally frivolous and embarrassing."

· · Chicks with Sticks

"You met Roger Federer," Tay said flatly, "and all you care about is how smelly he was. When John hears this, he's gonna die."

"Yeah, Jamison was kind of outraged, too," Amanda said. She reached down from her cushy perch to put a hand on Bella's shoulder.

"Do you totally hate me?" she whined. "I mean, here you are out there saving the gorillas . . . or was it the prairies?"

"Actually, she's pumping alternative fuels," Scottie provided gently.

"Oh, don't worry about it," Bella said quickly, waving Scottie off. "You know, saving the world is saving the world, right? Does it really matter *exactly* how we do it?"

"Then we shouldn't criticize Amanda for being a flower girl, right?" Tay said, reaching a long leg across the coffee table to give Bella a teasing poke with her toe. "I mean, *she* saved the world from the stank of a post-game Roger Federer."

"Maybe I should have put it that way to Jamison," Amanda laughed. "He was *all* up on his proletariat high horse about the tennis thing."

"Well, you don't disagree with him, do you?" Scottie asked.

Amanda's face furrowed into an expression that was half vexation, half confusion. "Noooo," she said hesitantly. "I might have, somehow, started playing devil's advocate, though. I mean, Jamison is *so* neg about our little deb world, sometimes I find myself saying, 'Oh, it's not *that* bad.' Isn't that weird?"

"Yeah!" Tay, Scottie, and Bella said together.

"Okay, don't be *too* quick to make me feel like a traitor," Amanda said.

"Amanda!" Scottie exclaimed. "For literally *years* you've been ranting to us about the whole society thing. About how it's exclusive and elitist. About how you'd rather eat a loaf of Wonder Bread than have to spend five minutes talking to the Honor Gorhams of the world. Now, just because you've met your match, you're changing your tune?"

"My match . . ." Amanda said dreamily. "You really think so?"

"Amanda!" Scottie squealed. "What's going on with you?"

"I guess," Amanda said, a guilty smile on her face, "I'm starting to think that something that brought me and Jamison together can't be that bad. I mean, one reason we get along so well is we're both from the same world—and hating it, yeah. But that's the whole point of being a debutante in the first place isn't it? To bring people together. I mean, maybe in a sick, warped way, those country club elders know what they're doing."

"Oh. My. God," Scottie cackled. "I have seen it *all.*"

"Oh no, you haven't," Tay said, leaning over the coffee table and scooching aside a tub of wasabi peas to dig out a couple DVDs. "As you know, SSO rules dictate that the host picks the movie and *I* have gotten something sick and twisted."

"Tay, I told you," Bella shrieked in protest, "I *cannot* watch any more horror movies. *Evil Spawn* gave me nightmares for a month."

"These are scary in a different way," Tay said, holding up the discs. "I got a couple Russ Meyer flicks about girls who ride motorcycles and get into fistfights and stuff. Camp-o-rama."

"Did you go to Beck for movie recommendations?" Scottie accused with a squinty grin. "These flicks sound suspiciously film geekish."

"My sources are confidential," Tay insisted.

"Hey, at least it's not *Ghost World* again," Amanda muttered. "I really can't take any more disaffected Thora Birch movies."

"Hey, if we're gonna start the movie," Scottie said, "I need new snackage." She roused herself from the deep recesses of her couch cushion and began sifting through the munchies on the coffee table. She skimmed over the three kinds of tortilla chips, the cookies, and the wasabi peas. She was even uninspired by the red-and-green candy corn she herself had brought.

"I'm feeling like sugar," Scottie mused, "but not *these* kinds of sugar. Hmmm."

As if she'd been outside the door, waiting for an entrance, Laura suddenly appeared. She looked both sheepish and proud as she carried a tray of big, blocky Rice Krispie treats before her.

"I know you girls have plenty of snacks," she began, "but I forgot that I'd made these marshmallow squares for you this morning. Do you have room for them?"

Scottie's eyes lit up. She was just about to say "Perfect!" when Tay spoke up first.

"Mom," she said, her voice dripping with disdain. *"Marshmallow squares? What do you think we are, little kids?"*

Scottie caught her breath as she watched Laura begin to wilt. First her mouth turned downward. Then her shoulders sagged. Finally her back slumped so much that she seemed to shrink before the girls' very eyes.

Scottie cast a shifty glance around the room. Tay was still glaring at her mother with twin laser beams of anger. Bella chewed on a cuticle and cast worried glances at Tay. And Amanda gazed at the ceiling, probably wracking the debutante's handbook in her head for a way to extricate them all from the mother-daughter clash.

Scottie held her breath.

Laura will leave in a minute, she told herself, *and then maybe we can talk to Tay about what's happening between them. Which she'll just* love.

Scottie rolled her eyes and waited.

The only problem was, Laura didn't leave. She seemed so deflated by Tay's scorn that she couldn't find the energy to move.

Scottie squirmed. It was very clear that Tay was winning this battle—brutally so. And before Scottie could think it through, she found herself speaking up for the underdog.

"I'd like a marshmallow square," she announced, hopping to her feet. She felt Tay's laser beams turn on her, but she didn't—or couldn't—meet her eyes. Instead, she took the plate from Laura, who smiled gratefully. Then she gave the rest of the girls a little wave, which was probably meant to look more breezy than it actually did.

"Enjoy," she said as she turned to head out of the room. "Just let me know if you need anything else."

Still feeling Tay's gaze on her, Scottie nervously plucked one of the sticky blocks off the plate and crunched into it.

"Mmmm, I love these things," she said. "Hey, Amanda, remember when we tried to make these at your house once and we ruined some expensive copper pot? Your maid was *mad*."

Tay snorted, shook her head, and muttered something.

Finally, Scottie couldn't avoid it anymore. She put the plate of treats on the coffee table and looked at Tay.

"What was that you said?" she asked.

Tay burrowed farther into her loveseat and crossed her arms over her chest. Then she flung both legs over the arm and gazed at the ceiling.

"Nothing," she said. "Forget it."

Scottie felt herself droop a little, just like Laura. She was hardly ever phased by Tay's bluntness—not since the first days of their friendship when Scottie hadn't known what to make of Tay's sarcasm, her sullen barbs, her tendency to call Scottie on her every goofy gaffe. By now, Tay's quills were just one of the things Scottie loved about her, as normal and familiar as Bella's unrelenting sweetness.

But this wasn't just Tay's usual surliness. This was different, Scottie realized, because Scottie had aided and abetted the enemy. Even if she didn't know exactly *why* Laura was the enemy, it had clearly been the wrong choice to make.

"No, let's not forget it," Scottie pressed on. She found herself making a couple finger-shaped dents in her marshmallow square as she challenged Tay. "I know you're mad at me so you might as well just have it out and be done with it."

"Okay then," Tay said, returning her laser beams to Scottie. "Do you want to know what I said? I said, 'The memory quilt strikes again.'"

She thrust out her chin and returned her gaze to the ceiling.

"Um, okay," Scottie said carefully. She perched on the arm of one of the chairs. "What does that mean, exactly?"

"It means," Tay said with a weary whoosh of air, "that you'll do anything—even getting all warm and fuzzy with *my mom*—to bring back the past."

"I didn't get warm and fuzzy with your mom," Scottie scoffed. "Is it so wrong to love Rice Krispie treats?"

"It's not wrong," Tay retorted. "It's just twelve, is what it is."

"Oh, because I eat a certain kind of snack, I'm immature?" Scottie retorted, feeling her cheeks flame into two pink splotches.

"No, it's because you're living in the past," Tay said calmly. "You're always looking backward, Scottie. It's like, you don't even *want* to grow up. Meanwhile, I'd give anything to be in your place—a senior with one foot out the door."

Scottie huffed and tried to fling her marshmallow square onto a paper plate on the coffee table. Unfortunately, it was so melty by now that it stuck to her thumb. She had to flick her hand back and forth several times before it let go and landed on the plate with a plop.

This sort of made it hard for Scottie to be all indignant, but she did her best.

"You're just taking your angst out on me," she said. "I'm sorry if your life sucks right now, but being pissed off at all the people in it isn't gonna make it any better."

"Oh, did you learn that thera-speak from your Big Sib training?" Tay said. "Or maybe you and Mr. A have been talking?"

Now Scottie felt feverish with a combo of anger and anxiety. What had begun as a spat between her and Tay, something they could brush past with a few jokey jabs and a quick apology, was escalating into something ugly.

"C'mon," Scottie said, forcing a smile. She tossed a paper napkin on top of the stack of marshmallow treats and grabbed one of the DVDs.

Peering at it, she snorted. *"Beyond the Valley of the Dolls?* What *is* this? And, oh my God! Did you see the credits? Roger Ebert wrote it. *Ebert."*

"See, that's just what I'm talking about," Tay said, jumping to her feet. "You don't want to deal with anything so you literally sweep it under the rug!"

She pointed at the Rice Krispie treats, now under cover. "If that's not immature," Tay accused, "I don't know what is."

"Oh, like it's grown-up to treat your mom like dirt when she's just trying to be nice to you?" Scottie blurted back.

Tay clenched her fists together and glared at the floor because, Scottie assumed, she was too mad to look at her. "You *so* don't get it," Tay said. Her voice was so low it rumbled. "You, who've lived in the same place *forever*, whose parents are always all happy-happy, jokey-jokey together. You, who doesn't even *want* to leave. Me? I don't even want to stay in this room!"

Tay popped to her feet and stomped off to her bedroom, leaving Scottie, Amanda, and Bella behind, stunned and speechless.

At least, until Scottie finally said, "What do we do now?"

"We've gotta talk to her," Bella said simply. "She's upset."

"Well, so am I!" Scottie cried. "She basically accused me of being a big Peter Pan."

She saw Amanda and Bella exchange a furtive look.

"What, you think I'm immature, too?" Scottie cried.

"No," Amanda sighed. "But Tay might have a point about you not liking—"

"—new things," Scottie said dryly. "Yeah, I've heard that one before."

"Well, maybe we're wrong," Bella said. "I mean, just because you don't *talk* about where you want to go to college and stuff doesn't mean you're not thinking about it. Cuz, of course, you're making plans, just like all of us."

"Yeah," Scottie sulked. "I'm just not, you know, *obsessed* with next year. I mean, next year is next year. It's a long way away."

"Well," Bella squirmed, "that's true, I guess."

"Listen," Amanda said, unfurling herself from her seat. "We could get existential about the rest of our lives and all, but Tay is fuming in the room next door. Yes, she flew off the handle. But she's also right about us not getting it. I mean, Scottie, we've both been misunderstood by our parents, but at least we haven't been through the whole hairy divorce thing."

"And the joint custody thing," Bella added with a little shiver. "That's like the worst of both worlds."

"You're right," Scottie said sadly.

"So lemme just go talk to her," Amanda said. "I mean, you guys got all in a wad about a *marshmallow square*, for God's sake. I'll smooth Tay's feathers and then you two can do your mutual noogie thing and get over it, okay?"

"Yeah," Bella said, a sly smile starting, "because noogies aren't immature at all."

Scottie smiled back at her, shakily. And she felt grateful as she watched Amanda head for Tay's bedroom. That was the best thing about there being four Chicks—when two of them clashed, there were two more of them who could help make things better.

Except . . . this time, getting that help didn't feel right.

"Wait!" Scottie cried.

Amanda paused and glanced over her shoulder.

"Let me talk to her," Scottie declared, wiping the melted marshmallow off her fingers and getting to her feet. "I need to be the one to make this better."

"Now *that's* mature," Bella said, hopping to her feet to give Scottie a hug. "We'll be here when you get back, watching *Beyond the Valley of the Dolls.*"

Scottie gave Bella a tremulous smile and headed for the hallway. She passed Laura's closed bedroom door, and crossed through the kitchen to reach Tay's room at the back of the flat. Tay's door, clearly flung shut in a hurry, was cracked a bit. Scottie heaved a deep breath and got ready to knock. But just before she could, she heard Tay murmuring behind the door. Her voice was soft, reedy, and yearning—downright *feminine*.

And the things she was *saying?* They made Scottie's face go hot again. Tay was clearly talking to John on the phone.

Once upon a time, when Scottie had stumbled upon Tay's secret blog, she'd had to wrestle with herself about whether or not to read it. But now, there was no question about what to do. She backed away from the door quickly, sliding in her socks across the kitchen floor to avoid any telltale creaks. Then she sat at the kitchen table to wait for her friend.

Tay emerged five minutes later, her frown melted away, her shoulders unhunched. She eyed Scottie for a moment, one eyebrow raised. Then she said, "The thing is, I kind of like marshmallow squares, too."

"I know," Scottie said quietly. "But I'm sorry I butted into you and your mom's business."

"I'm sorry I accused you of being a Lost Boy," Tay said.

"You were kinda right though," Scottie said, with a sheepish smile.

"And so were you," Tay said, sitting across from Scottie. She folded her hands on the table and stared at them intently. "Things would be better if I would just cut my mom some slack. The only problem is, every time I try to be nice to her, her static cling gets even worse. And then I get even more mad than before."

"You just haven't figured out yet how to forgive her," Scottie said. "You will. Trust me, I have some experience in this area."

Tay shot Scottie a knowing glance. "I know you do," she said. She was silent for a minute. "So it can get better? With the 'rents?"

"Definitely," Scottie nodded. "When you're ready for it. Having friends who get what you're going through helps. And Tay? I actually do, even if my family might be more happy-happy, jokey-jokey than yours."

Tay swallowed hard and nodded. After another minute of silence, Scottie offered, "Want to give me a noogie?"

Tay barked out a laugh and shook her head. "I want a Rice Krispie treat, though," she said. "C'mon, let's go gorge."

Scottie laughed as she followed Tay back to the living room. When they arrived, they found Amanda and Bella crouched in front of the TV. They'd turned it on, and now they were struggling to decipher the DVD player. Over the blare of the local news, they were arguing over which button would magically cue up the movie.

"You are such *girls*," Tay joked. After uncovering the marshmallow treats and grabbing one, she joined Amanda and Bella at the TV. Amanda shot Scottie a glance over Tay's head. Scottie smiled and nodded at her.

As Amanda grinned back, something on the television caught Scottie's eye.

At the same time, Tay grabbed the remote.

"All you do to make it go to the DVD," she said, "is press this—"

"Wait!" Scottie yelled. "Don't press that button. Look at the news. Isn't that—?"

Scottie couldn't go on. She simply pointed at the screen, her mouth hanging open. On the news was a generic press conference by one of Chicago's countless aldermen. It was the kind of sound byte Scottie saw in passing all the time, never paying it any attention. Usually the alderman vowed to close down a bar that was too close to a school or investigate a zoning ordinance or something like that. Snooze-ville.

But at *this* press conference, Scottie spotted someone in the row of staffers standing behind the alderman. Someone who made her stop, hold her breath, and squint at the screen. It was a teenage girl clutching a clipboard and looking serious, her honey-colored hair pulled back into a big, fluffy bun and her lean, lanky body straitjacketed into a suit.

"Bella!" Scottie gasped. "What are you doing on TV?"

13 • (Knit the knit stitches and purl the purl stitches)

Bella bounced up to Scottie's locker Monday morning before the first bell. She was nibbling on a crumbly-looking brown lump that was nestled in wax paper. Like all the baked goods that Bella brought to school, it smelled strongly of wheat germ or steel-cut oats or *something* grainily good for you.

"Want some apple-groat bar?" Bella offered. "My dad and I made 'em yesterday. They're so moist, you barely even know the groats are there."

"Uh-huh," Scottie said dubiously. "Seeing as I have a luscious two-pack of Pop Tarts in my locker, I think I'll pass."

"Oh really?!" Bella said brightly. *Too* brightly. "Junk food, sweet junk food! What flavor?"

Scottie scrutinized Bella, from her over-wide smile to her just-this-side-of-desperate eyes.

"You didn't tell them, did you?" she accused.

"Didn't tell who what?" Bella asked, already looking guilty.

"You didn't tell your parents about your fifteen minutes on the local news Saturday night!"

"No, I didn't!" Bella wailed, crushing her lump of health food in her fist and hanging her head. "How can I? I mean, how exactly do I tell them that their daughter has become The Man? *How* do I go about breaking their leftie hearts?"

"Bella," Scottie laughed. "So you bagged the eco-stunts to work for an alderman. Why is that so horrible?"

"Well, *I* don't think it's horrible, obviously," Bella said. "I think it's pretty cool. I mean, Chris Sawyer is all about the people. Someone can come to him and tell him their street isn't safe and needs speed bumps, or that they're being scammed by their landlord, or that their building's been assessed for way too much money, and Chris will totally help them."

"Ooh, the power," Scottie joked, "I've got chills."

"Yeah, it's not very glamorous," Bella admitted. "He's about as grass roots as you can get. But *that's* why his work matters. He's making a difference for individual people!"

"So what's the problem?" Scottie wondered. She waved hello to a few Froggers as they passed by, then pulled some books out of her backpack and plunked them into her locker. "I'd say all that stuff totally falls into the Brearley family mission statement. Y'know, do unto others, make the world a better place, all with a side of organic groats."

"Well, that's the thing," Bella said, slumping against Amanda's locker (Amanda hadn't arrived yet). "The alderman's office? It's kind of anti-crunch. People there keep insane hours, never stopping to even do a quick stretch and cleansing breath, much less an hour of yoga. They totally subsist on doughnuts and coffee, even though I keep bringing in groat muffins and herbal tea bags. And talk about aggressive energy. Constituents are constantly coming in with some beef for the alderman and it's we volunteers and staffers who have to intercept them. Sometimes they really get in your face!"

"You mean the staffers' faces, right?" Scottie said. She pulled two half-knitted quilt squares out of her backpack and frowned at them, trying to decide which one she wanted to work on at lunch. "I mean, you're there answering phones and stuffing envelopes and stuff like that, right? You're not having fights with constituents!"

Bella fluttered one hand to her mouth to hide a devilish grin.

"No way!" Scottie cried. She forgot the quilt squares and turned her full attention on Bella. "Tell me everything."

"Well," Bella began, "these two next-door neighbors came in, right? And one of them wanted to get a survey done because he was sure the neighbor's fence was three inches too far into his backyard."

"Three inches!" Scottie guffawed.

"That's what I said," Bella said. "I mean, where's the common sense in that? So the guy starts screaming at me. I mean, *screaming*."

"Really?!" Scottie said.

"Yeah," Bella chirped. "Then his neighbor started screaming at *him*. So I started yelling at *both* of them about wasting taxpayers' money over three inches of backyard."

"No way!" Scottie screeched again.

"And that's not all," Bella admitted, her face full of pride. "I *also* lectured them about citizenship and karma and anger management and the gorillas of Rwanda."

"Uh, I'm not getting that last one," Scottie said.

"You know, loss of habitat? Backyard borders?" Bella said. Off Scottie's shrug, she said, "It made sense at the time. I mean, I had a whole *thesis* going. I felt like I was in a movie playing a trial lawyer and it was *fun*. And guess what? It worked. The neighbors acted totally sorry. They dropped their complaints and shook hands, and after they left, I saw them go into the bar across the street together. Not that beer is the healthiest way to bond, but hey, I'll take it."

Scottie stared at Bella for a long, shocked moment before she blurted, "And you don't think your parents would be totally proud of that? Bella, you're like the Ban Ki-moon of the forty-fourth ward!"

"Yeah, but Ban Ki-moon's still a politician," Bella pointed out. "As in *the* establishment. And as you know, my parents are about as *anti*-establishment as you can get."

"Well, sweetie," Scottie said, "you're probably gonna have to tell them at *some* point. I mean, one of these days, they're gonna find the business suits in the back of your closet. Or the BlackBerry in your underwear drawer. Next thing you know, they'll be giving you surprise political awareness tests, and taking you to the guidance counselor's office wailing, 'Why couldn't she just be smoking pot like *we* were!'"

Bella gave Scottie a playful shove as she dissolved into giggles. When she recovered, Bella shook her head in wonder. "The *real* reason I have to tell them is, I kinda see myself doing this as, like, a career," she admitted. "I even decided to apply to a couple colleges just because they had strong poli sci programs. After thinking all these years that I would end up as an English professor or lay midwife or professional crafter or something like that! It's crazy, isn't it? What this whole college application process tells you about yourself?"

Before Scottie could even try to come up with an answer for that one, she heard something behind her: Sobs. Heartbroken, impossible-to-hold back sobs—ones that Scottie recognized.

"Amanda?" Scottie called. She turned toward the sound of the crying and peered through the crowd of students heading to their homerooms. Amanda, who always stood out in a crowd, who was pretty much the girl you were talking about when you said "larger than life," was slumped against the hallway wall, looking as tiny and vulnerable as Scottie had ever seen her. Her hand was pressed over her mouth in a vain attempt to stifle her cries and mascara was running down her cheeks in two black streaks.

Scottie and Bella ran to her. Only when Bella snatched up Amanda's free hand and squeezed it, did Amanda look up. She gazed into Scottie's eyes and choked, "I didn't get in."

She didn't have to explain anything else. Scottie and Bella looked at each other with wide, stricken eyes.

"Parsons," Scottie whispered.

Scottie and Amanda didn't have any morning classes together, so Scottie had to wait three hours before she could properly shower Amanda with sympathy over lunch.

That might have been a blessing. Scottie needed the time to get over her own shock.

If Amanda *could get rejected from fashion design school, what does that say about the world?* Scottie thought in outrage. A tiny voice in the back of her head added, *What does that say about* my *prospects?*

If she'd really wanted to know, she probably could have asked Bella. By the time Scottie arrived at lunch, Bella was already sitting next to Amanda, her laptop open on the table.

"See!" Bella said, pointing at the screen. "I e-mailed Mr. Adrian in first period and he just got back to me. He says sixty-nine percent of Stark kids who don't get early acceptance *do* go on to be admitted to their first-choice schools with the rest of the applicants. So just because you didn't make the super-early cut does *not* mean you're not getting in."

Amanda had calmed down by now, but her mascara-free eyes were still a little puffy. Even worse, they looked hopeless. She shook her head. "That's no guarantee," she said. "I could still get rejected completely. And now, that's all I'm gonna be able to think about until *spring.*"

Scottie sat on Amanda's other side and put an arm around her shoulders. "I know," she whispered. "It sucks. But you just have to have faith that everything's gonna be okay."

"Faith?" Amanda said with a curled lip. "Like that's good for anything. *Faith* isn't gonna get me into Parsons. Being a better designer than the *hundreds* of other kids who want to go there will. And I bet you none of *them* have learning disabilities."

As Scottie squeezed Amanda's shoulders harder, Tay and John arrived at their table, hand in hand. Tay quickly jumped into the fray. "So you think that's what did it?" she asked, tossing her brown bag onto the table. "Your LD?"

"Who knows?" Amanda said with a sigh.

"Well *I* know that if that's why they rejected you," Bella said fiercely, "you have grounds for a lawsuit. There's this little thing they might not have heard of called the Americans with Disabilities Act!"

"Whoa, get a load of you, aldergirl," Tay said, gaping across the table. "You go from peacenik to prosecutor in sixty seconds. Just please tell me you're not gonna start dressing like Hillary Clinton."

"Har, har," Bella said.

The Chicks had had a million lunchtime moments like this—when somebody's angst was eased by a round of affectionate sparring. But Amanda couldn't seem to pull herself out of her fear and self-loathing to join in. Neither could Scottie.

If anyone could come close to understanding how it felt to be Amanda, it was Scottie. Amanda's every school day was filled with roadblocks. Being asked to, say, read out loud in class or complete a math quiz in a mere fifty minutes could ruin her entire day. She was so talented as a knitter, so frustrated as a student. And over the years, Scottie had shared this roller coaster with her.

So now, Scottie felt the pain of Amanda's rejection, too. If she couldn't summon up collegiate passion for herself, she *could* feel it on behalf of her friend.

She turned and stared into Amanda's sad eyes. "Okay, so maybe you don't have faith in yourself," Scottie declared. "I'll have it for you. I *know* you're gonna get in, Amanda. And not because of Mr. A's statistics. It's because—"

Scottie was surprised to feel a lump rise in her throat. "—it's because you deserve it!" she choked out. "Out of all of us, you *deserve* this. Someday I'm gonna see your stuff in the window at Mortally Wounded. I know it. And I know you're gonna get into Parsons, too. You have to, Amanda. You just *have* to."

In Amanda's eyes, which had welled up again, Scottie thought she saw a flicker of hope. But then, Amanda's cell phone rang in her purse and the flicker went dead. Amanda broke Scottie's gaze to pull out her cell. When she looked at the caller ID, she hesitated for a moment. Then she sighed and flipped the phone open. Her "hello" was flat and low. After a moment, she shook her head.

"Yeaaaah," she said into the phone, "I don't know if I can make it today."

After another pause, she snapped, "I *know*, Jamison, but I don't really *care* if I get a stupid 'deb demerit.' We both know that you don't either, so why are you giving me crap about it?"

While Amanda listened to Jamison's response, she rolled her eyes. "So this is all about *you*," she said. "You just don't want to be bored without me there."

Scottie exchanged a wide-eyed look with Tay and Bella. When had Jamison morphed into a major irritant? At the SSO on Saturday, Amanda had brought up at least half a dozen Jamison stories. During each one, she'd gotten, as Tay put it, "mushy as an overripe banana."

"Well, I'm *sorry*," Amanda was saying now, "but it's not my job to keep you entertained. I have a life of my own, you know."

While Amanda listened to Jamison's retort, she slammed her hand down on her lunch bag.

"No, this isn't about something else," Amanda spat. "This is about *you*, Jamison, just *expecting* that I'll always be there to be your fun, little, deb-dissing comrade. You're already taking me for granted and we've only known each other for, like, a minute. But what else should I expect from the Chalk Prince of Chicago? Entitled much?"

Now Scottie could hear Jamison's voice coming from Amanda's cell. The words were blurry, but his tone was loud and clear. He was bewildered and stung.

"So that's how you react the first time I'm not at your beck and call," Amanda sneered. "Well, it's good to know the truth about you,

•• Chicks with Sticks

Jamison—you're not nearly as different from the rest of our crowd as I thought."

"Oooh," Scottie whispered to Bella. *"That's* below the belt for these two."

"Whatever," Amanda continued tartly. "I've gotta go. I've only got fifteen minutes left in lunch and unlike the other deborexics, *I* actually eat."

Amanda snapped her phone closed and glared at it for a second. But by the time she looked up at her friends, her anger seemed to have evaporated. She just looked weary.

"Okay, you can tell *us* the truth," Tay said. *"Was* that really about Jamison or are you just pissed at the world, by way of Parsons?"

"Both, I guess," Amanda said. She poked desultorily at her lunch bag, but didn't open it, despite what she'd said to Jamison. "I suppose Jamison didn't *really* do anything wrong. He was just being . . . him. No matter how different he is, I think, deep down, he still expects girls to act a certain way."

"What kind of way?" Scottie said.

"Like a *debutante!*" Amanda sneered. "Like the kind of girl who'd do anything to bag the Chalk Prince of Chicago. Like the kind of girl I'm supposed to be, but really, *really* didn't want to be."

"You don't have to be her," Bella declared. "You *aren't* her. You're Amanda Scott, knitter grrrrl!"

"Well, maybe I'm not!" Amanda said. Her face was a pale mask of worry. She ripped a strip of brown paper off of her lunch bag and nervously began to tear it into little bits. "I didn't get into Parsons, did I? So what does that leave me with? A white gown, some opera-length gloves, and a parade of prospects. Maybe this rejection is a sign that that's really what I'm meant to do—to just get married to some Jamison-type and give tea parties for the rest of my life."

"Amanda!" Scottie protested. "That's ridiculous. You would never in a million years!"

"I guess," Amanda sighed. "Unless that's my fate, right Bella? You're always talking about fate."

"Yes . . ." Bella said uncomfortably. "That's true but . . . but I think you can also make your own fate. Like with us. I mean, I believe we were fated to be friends, but *we* had to take that fate and run with it, right? There've definitely been times when one of us, or *all* of us, could have given up on each other. But we didn't. You're not just tossed around by fate. You have power there, too."

Whoa, Tay was right, Scottie thought, taking a bite of her sandwich and looking admiringly at Bella. *Bella really is a natural politician. She spun that fate thing but* good.

Which wasn't to say that Scottie didn't agree. Believing in fate and totally *giving in* to fate were two very different things.

"You just *did* take your fate into your own hands," Scottie reminded Amanda. "You're ditching deb duty this afternoon, aren't you?"

Amanda shrugged. "That just kind of popped out when Jamison called," she admitted. "I actually hadn't planned to blow it off. And now I'm wondering if I should just suck it up and go."

"Of course you shouldn't go!" Scottie said. "If you skip, you'll be saying you're not *really* debutante material."

"I guess," Amanda drawled. Then she gave her friends a beseeching look. "Are *you* guys free after school? Maybe we could hang out."

Bella hesitated, then pulled out her BlackBerry, while across the table, Tay slumped. Because, of course, Scottie realized, they were probably both booked up with extracurriculars. Scottie, too, had a ton to do. Since she was seeing Nina two afternoons a week, she was slammed with studying on the days that remained.

But a Chick in crisis *so* outranked homework.

"I'm free this afternoon," Scottie declared. "Since you're clearly not eating that lunch, I think we should go out to eat. You wouldn't want anyone to think you're deborexic."

"That sounds cool," Amanda said tremulously. "I have loads of yarn in my bag, too. I was prepared, after all, for a long, boring afternoon at Curtsy Class."

"Perfect," Scottie said. "It's a date."

"Or is it fate?" Bella said with a wide grin. She was looking at her BlackBerry's screen. "I just got a text from the alderman's office. One of the other high school volunteers wants to switch shifts with me this afternoon. So I'm free!"

"Aw, man . . ." Tay said. She thumped the cafeteria table in frustration. "Of course, this afternoon, I've got the *one* thing I can't blow off."

"Mr. A," Bella, Scottie, and Amanda droned.

"Yup," Tay sighed.

"Wait a minute," John protested. "What if you'd had plans with *me*? *Me* you could blow off?"

"Oh, honey," Amanda said, shaking her head at Tay's b.f. "You guys have been together all this time and you *still* don't know about the BBB Code of Honor?"

"Man, you guys love your acronyms," John said (to which Tay harrumphed). "So what's BBB?"

"Boyfriend on the Back Burner," Bella told him earnestly. "It's what you do when you have a girlfriend in crisis."

"Oh," John said with a sullen shrug. "Well, I guess that's fair enough. Although I still think I should outrank Mr. Adrian."

"If I don't show up at Mr. A's," Tay said matter-of-factly, "he'll open up a can of academic whoop-ass on me. Whereas *you* would just keep me up late with an extended phone date."

"True enough," John said.

"Anyway, you guys should take your relative mental health," Tay said to Amanda, Scottie, and Bella, "and go without me."

"We'll miss you," Amanda said, giving Tay a grateful smile.

Tay squirmed, no doubt fighting off the urge to say something equally mushy in response. She was saved by the end-of-lunch bell. Scottie laughed as Tay shot out of her chair, gave the Chicks a wave, and made a beeline for the door.

Scottie, meanwhile, went to her next class with a lightness in her step—the cleansed feeling she always had after working through an intense moment with her friends.

She knew taking Amanda out to soothe her Parsons-broken heart wouldn't change her situation. *But at least it lets her know,* Scottie thought, *she doesn't have to suffer through her wait alone.*

# 14 ✴ (Pick up stitches)

After school, Scottie proposed a diner. Not some new-fangled chrome-and-neon joint, but a true-blue greasy spoon, shaped like a railroad car, redolent of fried meat, and perched on a busy corner in Wrigleyville.

Amanda's eyes widened as the waitress slapped a groaning plate of cheese fries and a chocolate shake with three straws onto the girls' table. The she gaped at Bella.

"I can't believe you authorized this, Miss Groat," she said.

"Groats are a lot of good things," Bella said, "but they're *not* comfort food. And that's what we're here for, isn't it? Salty, greasy comfort—preferably followed by apple pie."

Scottie guffawed.

"I don't think Tay could have said it better," she said.

Amanda nibbled a fry and said, "I wish she was here."

"Yeah," Scottie said. "You know Tay. She'd be all, 'Parsons doesn't want ya? So screw 'em and get on with your life.'"

"She *does* have that warm, sensitive touch," Amanda said, clasping her hands beneath her chin with faux sincerity. Then she took a slurp of milkshake.

"Oh, man, that is good," she breathed. "It tastes even better when I think about what I *would* be eating if I were in Curtsy Class right now. Today's lesson is about, I kid you not, how to eat soup. Apparently, a cream soup requires a different spooning technique than say, a consommé."

"You have *got* to be joking," Scottie said.

"I'm not," Amanda said, shaking her head. "Poor Jamison. I can't believe I'm making him go through that alone. And the things I said!"

"I'm sure he'll forgive you," Scottie said, "if you just explain."

"You're right," Amanda said, nodding hard. "I'll call him to apologize." She grinned. "And, of course," she added, "to get his soup notes."

"Wow, it really *is* a good thing Tay isn't here," Bella said, taking a sip of the milkshake. "You *know* all that bourgie stuff makes her want to vomit."

"Bella!" Scottie cried, dropping her cheese fry back on the plate with a curled lip. "You used the V word! Ugh, I can't eat anymore."

"Sorry!" Bella cried. "I forgot."

"Oh, it's okay," Scottie said, waving Bella off. "I wasn't really that hungry anyway."

"Yeah," Amanda said, poking at the mountain of fries, then licking bright orange cheese sauce off her finger. "Gorging on junk food just isn't as fun without Tay around. Not that I gorge, mind you."

"And let's be honest," Scottie said. "Tay needs some cheering up, too. I mean, these Milwaukee weekends?"

"They suck," Amanda said.

"They *hugely* suck," Bella said. "It just makes my heart hurt to think about her brooding around that bachelor pad. You know, she won't even take any of her stuff up there? Nothing that won't fit in her suitcase. The walls of her room are *bare*."

A sudden brainstorm made Scottie grip the edge of the formica table. "We need to get Tay a bachelor pad-warming gift," she declared. "Something to brighten her dreary, Wisconsinian existence."

"You're so right!" Amanda said.

"How about some new yarn?" Bella suggested. "She's got lots of knitting time up there."

"Yeah, but she can travel with knitting gear," Scottie said.

"I know," Amanda said with an evil grin. "We'll get her some stuff to decorate her room. If we twist her arm enough, I bet you she'll actually put it up. She'll pretend to hate it, but secretly? She'll love it."

"Ooh, and how about a second skateboard?" Bella said. "I know she doesn't take her Chicago board to Milwaukee with her. If she had one up there, it would give her an escape."

"Perfect!" Scottie said. She was so psyched, she forgot that she was nauseous and shoved a cheese fry into her mouth. "So when should we go shopping? This weekend?"

"How about now?" Amanda said.

Scottie and Bella glanced at each other.

"But sweetie," Scottie said to Amanda, "this afternoon is supposed to be all about *you*, helping you lick your wounds . . ."

". . . and slurp your milkshake," Bella said. To illustrate, she took another noisy sip of Amanda's chocolate shake.

"You know what?" Amanda said. For the first time that day, her smile was wide and genuine. "I'd love to do a little Tay-shopping. It'll help me get out of my head. Come on, there's nothing more feel-good than helping a fellow Chick. But then again . . ."

She flashed Scottie and Bella a grateful smile. ". . . you guys know that."

A half-hour later, the girls hopped off a bus in front of a double-wide storefront in Wicker Park—but not the tidied-up, yuppified part of neighborhood. This was a stretch of the Wicker Park that used to be—grungy and badass, with biker bars instead of Starbucks and bare-bones taquerias instead of sushi spots.

"So this is Tay's favorite store?" Bella said, gazing at the window mannequins arranged in attitudinal slouches and draped in baggy skatewear.

"Stockpile," Scottie said, reading the sign above their heads. "Yup, she's mentioned this place to me more than once. It's kind of a skaters' department store. They sell gear, but also gifts and clothes and other fun stuff."

"Let's go!" Amanda said. She pushed through the Stockpile door with Bella and Scottie behind her. Never mind that, in her wedge-heeled boots, empire-waisted coat, and giant sunglasses, Amanda looked like she belonged in a skater shop as much as Paris Hilton belonged in a Motel 6. When she walked into any store, she owned it.

"Halt!"

Amanda gasped and skidded to a stop.

Unless, Scottie thought with a cringe, *that store happens to be Stockpile.*

The three girls turned toward the surly voice that had stopped them in their tracks. Looming behind a raised counter was a slight—and surly—young woman. Her hair was cut into a wispy shag and dyed blue. On her tight T-shirt was a snarling pig that Scottie could only assume was some cool skater logo. Her face was pale, makeup-free, and sneering.

"Bags," the girl barked, holding out a hand with tattooed knuckles.

"Excuse me?" Bella squeaked.

"Either I'll take your bags," the girl said impatiently, "or *you'll* take your bags—and leave."

"Oh!" Scottie said. "It's so we won't shoplift, right?"

"Ding, ding, ding," the girl said impatiently.

"Oh," Bella cried, "but we would never—"

"Oh my *God,*" the girl said. "Do I have to come down there and pry your little hemp backpack out of your hands, Ani DiFranco?"

Meekly, Bella handed her bag up to the girl and got a grubby plastic troll in exchange. Bella turned to Scottie. "I'm starting to get why this is Tay's favorite store," she whispered.

As Amanda traded her bag for an old Smurf, Scottie said, "Just be glad it's not a baguette."

Amanda laughed dryly and said, "Let's shop."

After Scottie exchanged her backpack for a vintage Gumby, the girls began to wend their way through the store.

"It looks like just clothes over there," Scottie said, pointing to the left side of the big, boxy store. "Let's skip that."

"Hey," Amanda said, pointing at the right side. "Check out those things!"

Scattered on the wall like candy-colored bubbles were big, shiny vinyl dots. They reminded Scottie of the Colorforms she used to play with when she was a kid.

"Those are perfect for Tay's room!" Scottie said. "She can slap 'em on and peel 'em off at will, so she won't really feel like she's committing to her bedroom—"

"—*but*," Bella said, "she'll still get a decorative zing out of 'em."

Excitedly, Amanda called out to Bag Girl, "Um, those dots on the wall? They're for sale, aren't they? They're not just store decorations?"

"Oh, nooo," Bag Girl simpered, puckering her lips with exaggerated poutiness. "We don't want to sell our big, shiny dots. That would wreck our feng shui!"

Then she squinted at Bella and added, sarcastically, "Right, Ani?"

Before Bella could say anything, Bag Girl snapped, "Of *course* the dots are for sale. That's the whole idea behind a store, get it? Exchange of cash for goods?"

She pointed at Amanda. "That's a concept I can see *you're* familiar with, princess."

"O-kay," Amanda said, widening her eyes at Scottie. "Remind me how much I love Tay?"

"Much," Scottie said simply. "Tell ya what, let's put the dots on our to-buy list and head to the back of the store. I see a bunch of skateboards on the wall there. Maybe by the time we go to pay, Bag Girl will be on her break."

"Excellent thinking," Amanda said. She shot Bag Girl a sneer before stalking toward the back wall.

"You do realize, don't you," Scottie said as she followed her, "that when you give Bag Girl the evil eye, she probably thinks you want to be her BFF?"

Amanda snorted. "Almost forgot," she said. "Must think like a Tay."

Next to Scottie, Bella froze. Then she pointed.

"I don't know about *a* Tay," she said, "but *our* Tay has *got* to have that skateboard."

Scottie followed Bella's gaze to the wall of skateboards. Most of the decks were emblazoned with slashy designs or growling cartoon characters, but the one Bella was looking at was sleek and mod. The tip of the board was decorated with a small, dark gray female figure—the universal, skirted stick figure you see on traffic signs and the doors of women's restrooms.

Behind this was a duplicate stick girl—but larger than the first and shaded with a lighter gray. Behind *that* girl was another. And then another.

"There are four of them," Amanda whispered.

Scottie darted over to the wall to take a closer look at the deck.

"The brand is called Girl!" she exclaimed. "And it's on sale!"

"We'll take it, we'll take it!" Bella squealed, jumping up and down.

"Uh, not so fast, Ani."

Bella landed with a thump, then slowly peered over her shoulder. Bag Girl was right behind them, her arms crossed over her chest.

"A sale board," Bag Girl said imperiously, "means you buy it as is. No wheel-swapping and no new trucks or bushings."

"Um, considering we have no idea what trucks or bushings are," Scottie said, "I think that'll be just fine."

"And," Bag Girl went on, ignoring Scottie, "you gotta try it to buy it."

"Um, what?" Bella said.

"It's a liability thing," Bag Girl said with a shrug. "So you can't come back and tell us we sold you an off-balance, bargain board."

"But we wouldn't—" Scottie started to say. "I mean how could we do that when we don't even know—"

"Dude," Bag Girl cut in. "I don't *really* need to hear about the extent of your ignorance? I trust ya. I do. Nevertheless, store policy stands. You gotta try it to buy it."

Scottie's mouth popped open. She glanced indignantly from Amanda to Bella, then back to Bag Girl.

"Okay," she blurted. "Fine! I'll do it."

"Excellent," Bag Girl said with a snarky smile.

As she went to pull the Girl board off the wall, Amanda gaped at Scottie.

"Have you ever *been* on a skateboard?"

"Noooo," Scottie said. Then she planted her fists on her hips and declared angrily, "Oh my God. I'm gonna die, aren't I?"

"It's not worth it," Amanda said. "We can find the board somewhere else."

"But it's so perfect," Bella protested. "And with those four girls on it? It's fa—"

"Fate," Scottie finished for her. To Amanda she said, "She's right. This is *the* board for us to get for Tay."

"Well then," Amanda said, rolling up her sleeves, "we'll test drive it together. What's that saying, 'United we fall?'"

"Okay, a) that's *not* the most optimistic misquote," Scottie said. "And b) have you forgotten Bella's whole balance issue? She can barely stand on one leg when she's *not* on wheels."

"Still," Amanda insisted, "we can't let you do this alone."

"She's right," Bella said. In the next instant, her face brightened.

"Hey, I know!" she said. "Scottie, you stand on the skateboard and Amanda and I will stay on the floor on either side of you. We'll roll you along and make sure you don't fall."

"I don't know," Scottie whispered nervously. "Do you think Bag Girl will buy it?"

"Oh, sure I will!"

Bag Girl was standing next to the huddled Chicks, a big grin on her face. "No problem," she went on jovially. "The only requirement is . . ."

Bag Girl motioned to the Chicks to follow her as she stomped up to a gray, metal door and flung it open. ". . . you have to ride on that."

Scottie, Amanda, and Bella peered through the door and unleashed a collective gasp. In the cement lot behind the store was a structure that looked like a giant bowl, its steep sides shored up by wooden beams.

"The half-pipe," Bag Girl announced with a smug smile.

Scottie rolled her eyes.

"Well," she said, "at least when we *all* die, we'll go out in a blaze of glory."

Bella squeaked in terror—until Amanda glimpsed a ray of hope.

"Look," she pointed out. "One side of the pipe is half the height of the other. It's only, like, six feet tall. Bella and I can stand at the bottom and hang on to your hands while you go down the side."

"Really?!" Scottie said. "Do you think you guys are strong enough to catch me?"

"Please," Amanda scoffed. "We're the Chicks with Sticks. We can do anything."

Next to them, Bag Girl guffawed. "The Chicks with Sticks?" she shouted. "What the hell is *that?*"

Bella smiled and said, "It's about kni—"

Scottie slapped a hand over Bella's mouth. "You know," she whispered, "something tells me Bag Girl is *not* going to get it."

Then she turned to the girl with a scowl, grabbed the skateboard from her, and began to tromp up the rickety wooden staircase that led to the shorter side of the half-pipe. Bella, Amanda, and Bag Girl followed.

When they reached the platform at the lip of the pipe, Amanda glared at the girl. "Is there anybody *else* who can supervise this fiasco?" she said. "Don't you need to be harassing shoplifters up front?"

"Oh, don't you worry your pretty little head," Bag Girl said. "I got Meat to take the front desk for me."

Bella turned to Scottie and asked, "Did she just say *Meat?*"

"Cute nickname," Scottie said. "What's it short for?"

"Now I *really* get why this is Tay's favorite store," Bella muttered.

"Quit stallin'," Bag Girl said. She plucked a helmet off a row of hooks near the stairs and handed it to Scottie. "And start skating."

Scottie buckled on the helmet with trembling hands while Amanda and Bella slid gingerly to the bottom of the half-pipe. Scottie stepped onto the super-wobbly board and reached down toward her friends.

"We'll catch you!" Bella cried. "We prom-ISE!"

Her promise ended with a shriek, because Scottie had lost her balance and tipped over the edge of the pipe. She was hurtling downward! Above her, she heard Bag Girl laughing. And then, Scottie didn't hear anything at all—because she herself was screaming.

"*Aiiiiiighhh!*" she screeched as she careened down the pipe. She felt four hands grappling for her, but only one of them—Amanda's, Scottie thought—connected. She gripped Scottie's hand so tightly, it hurt. But, even as Scottie's descent gained momentum, she didn't let go. Which meant that, instead of swooping up the other side of the half-pipe, Scottie rolled in a semicircle around Amanda—and began to shoot back up the short side!

"*Aieeeeeeee!*" Scottie screamed as she went vertical.

The next thing she knew, she was airborne!

And then, she collided with something sort of soft and sort of bony. Bag Girl! She broke Scottie's fall to the platform.

Miraculously, Scottie realized that, not only was she alive, she was unhurt!

And Bag Girl?

She was no longer laughing.

Scottie scrambled to her feet, grabbed the Girl board and waved it over her head! "We'll take it, we'll take it!" she yelled triumphantly.

Amanda and Bella quickly scrambled up to join Scottie on the platform. Together they jumped up and down, laughing and shrieking.

Next to them, Bag Girl groaned.

"Ohhhh." Bella stopped jumping and looked down at her.

Here we go, Scottie thought. *Our sweet Bella is gonna be totally compassionate with mean old Bag Girl.*

"Are you all right?" Bella asked.

See?

"Yeah," Bag Girl moaned. "I think I've got some nasty bruises, but I'll make it."

"Good," Bella said. Then she shot Bag Girl a devilish grin. "Karma's a bitch, isn't it?"

"Bella!" Scottie gasped. Then she began to shriek with laughter.

Meanwhile, Amanda handed Bag Girl her Smurf.

"I'm going to need my purse back," she said. "Do you take American Express?"

15 ✦ (Pick up dropped stitches)

And that wasn't the only adventure of the week.

Alice's book was finally published that Thursday, and her husband was throwing her an oh-so-Alice fondue party to launch it.

Scottie arrived at Alice and Elliott's funky little bungalow in Edgewater a few minutes after five. She twirled the old-fashioned doorbell mounted in the door but nobody answered. Scottie could hear people inside, chattering above a Blossom Dearie song, so, after another brief wait, she shrugged and tried the doorknob.

I should have known, she realized when the door swung open. *Alice and Elliott aren't exactly lock-your-door types.*

On first look, it didn't seem like there was much in the house worth stealing anyway. You had to know Alice—and remember her old yarn shop—to understand the appeal of her home.

At KnitWit, you'd find knitting needles planted in flower pots, crockery yarn bowls that looked like they'd been broken and reglued multiple times, and antique knitting magazines catalogued inside kitchen cabinets.

Alice's house had the same shabby charm. The living room ceiling was strung with white lights and the dining room was set up like a little cafe, with three small tables that could be pushed together for dinner parties or kept apart for intimate knitting klatches. The kitchen was overgrown with tendrilly hanging plants, and each bedroom was painted the color of a different flavor sorbet. A collection of old type-writers inhabited one of the nonworking fireplaces, and a kitchen wall was covered with vintage potato mashers, noodle cutters, and meat tenderizers, turquoise paint chipping off their wooden handles. All the bits and pieces seemed totally random, but put together, the house was the essence of Alice and her husband in all their quirky glory.

Needless to say, Scottie loved it there—both as a refugee from her parents' painfully hip loft and as someone who adored Alice.

Tonight, two of the dining room tables were laden with cheese and chocolate bubbling in pots over little blue flames. The bread and fruit dippers for the fondue were skewered on knitting needles.

The third table was stacked high with copies of Alice's book. The volumes were small and thick—the perfect size for stashing in your knitting bag. The image on the cover brought a nostalgic lump to Scottie's throat. It was KnitWit's front door, the one with the purple glass door-knob and the chronically dusty blackboard. The board was chalked simply with PURLICUE, BY ALICE BIERMAN. A drawing of a little skein of blue yarn hovered beneath the title. The words on the yarn's label were, A KNITTY MEMOIR.

As Scottie stared at the book cover, memories washing over her, Bella crept up behind her.

"I know," she said softly, "it got to me, too."

"Sometimes I still can't believe KnitWit's gone," Scottie said. "That we only had it for a few months. It didn't take very long for it to totally change our lives, did it."

"Scottie, it was *us* who changed our lives," Bella corrected her. "I meant it when I told Amanda that you make your own fate. I wasn't just trying to cheer her up."

"I know," Scottie allowed, "but let's face it. Alice definitely helped. Not to mention our sticks. Speaking of, you brought the present, didn't you?"

• • Chicks with Sticks

"Tscha," Bella whispered. She held up a gift bag tied with a bundle of mismatched yarn. Inside was a Knit-On (and on and on) Friendship Scarf. Scottie had started the congratulatory gift over a year earlier, way back when Alice had first gotten her book deal. After knitting up about a foot of the scarf out of fuzzy cashmere scraps, she'd strung a length of holding yarn through the loops and passed it on to Amanda. *She'd* added a panel dotted with flowers and given it to Tay. And so on and so on . . . When the scarf was long enough to wrap Alice's entire body, let alone her neck, the girls had finally bound it off, fringed it, and stashed it away for publication day.

Now that the day was finally here, Scottie was almost as excited to give Alice her gift as she was to read her book.

"Let's track Alice down as soon as Amanda and Tay get here," Scottie said, gazing into the living room. Alice was nowhere to be seen. She was probably in the kitchen, helping to whip up some other yummies for the party. Because that was the kind of thing Alice did. She wasn't the sort to sit around and be feted. She was, always, a host.

Scottie did spot quite a few other people she recognized—KnitWit regulars that she hadn't seen for ages.

"Hey, there's Greenie!" Scottie whispered to Bella, pointing at the first person she'd ever met at KnitWit. Back then, Greenie had had hair the color of mint-chocolate chip ice cream. Now it was peppermint pink.

"And ooh," Scottie added, "look at Jane's baby! So cute!"

Jane had been pregnant when the girls had first met her in Alice's knitting class. The Chicks had knitted booties for her baby shower. Now her roly-poly daughter was old enough for actual shoes. She was toddling around the living room, mushing strawberries in each of her fists, looking adorable in a hand-knitted dress.

Scottie was just getting ready to say hello to Becca, another old classmate, when through the crowd, she spotted Amanda. It was impossible to miss her—not with the giant, poofy garment bag she had slung over her shoulder.

Tay was behind her, gazing at the party the way she always did—with a combination of anticipation (of party snacks) and dread (of party chat).

Scottie clasped her hands, pretending to be a proud mama. "Our little debutante and her escort have arrived," she cooed to Bella.

"Get ready to curtsy," Bella giggled back.

Together, they lifted their right hands, pinkies carefully arched, and headed over to their friends.

"Mademoiselle," Scottie said, dipping clunkily to the floor. "I didn't know you were on duty later. So what is it tonight? A benefit? Some debby dinner?"

"I don't have anything," Amanda blurted. For the first time, Scottie saw that her skin was pale and her eyes were darting wildly. "Except an emergency! "

Within a few minutes, the Chicks were gathered in Alice and Elliott's bedroom, staring at Amanda's debutante gown.

Or what was left of it.

Amanda had been forced to compile a huge wardrobe of super-conservative clothes for her debut season, from nubbly suits for teas to silk sweater sets for brunches to swingy little party dresses for evening functions. But none of these outfits mattered half as much as the gown Amanda would wear at her coming-out ball. It had been custom made for her out of snowy silk satin, with a sweetheart neckline, a drop-waist bodice, and a skirt poofed out with layers and layers of tulle. Amanda had suffered through four different fittings for this dress. Her mother had given her a three-generations-old string of pearls to wear with it. The hair and makeup that would accompany The Dress were already plotted out.

Everything was in place.

Except . . . that the dress was in shreds.

"Whoa," Tay said, looking at the bodice, which was detached from

• *Chicks with Sticks*

the skirt and sliced into several pieces. "And I thought my little hissy in Milwaukee was bad. Amanda, when *you* get mad, you slash and burn!"

"I wasn't mad!" Amanda wailed, picking up a swatch of frayed satin and crumpling it in her fist. "At least, not in the *angry* sense of the word. Mad as in crazy? Yes. I was definitely insane to think I could do this."

"Do what? Get out of debbing?" Scottie said. "Well, yeah. I mean there's still time to get another dress, right? If you'd *really* wanted to sabotage it all, you should have waited until the night before the ball to break out the scissors."

"No!" Amanda cried. "You don't get it. I *didn't* want to get out of debbing. Yeah, I freaked on Monday, but before that I'd finally gotten sort of okay with it. Especially if Jamison could be my escort."

"So why kill the dress?" Scottie said, running a wistful hand over the creamy, decapitated skirt. "I have to admit, I kinda liked it. It reminded me of a Beautiful Bride Barbie doll I had when I was little."

"Okay, I'm gonna pretend I didn't hear that," Amanda growled, "only because I'm freaking here. What *happened* was, I thought I'd do a little doctoring. Like what I've been doing with my everyday clothes."

She motioned at the jeans she was wearing. She'd lopped off the cuffs and replaced them with a couple hand-knitted leg warmers bunched artfully around her ankles.

"I wanted to keep the skirt," Amanda explained, "and do some yarny deconstruction/reconstruction on the bodice. I had it all planned out in my head."

"That sounds fabulous," Bella said. "So what happened?"

"Well, I got started on Sunday night, y'know, with the deconstruction part. . . ." Amanda began. She began picking the polish off an already chipped fingernail while her face crunched into her own version of squashiness.

"And," Scottie finished for her gently, "Monday morning you heard from Parsons."

(Knitwise)

"Yeah," Amanda sighed. "I was so upset, I just shoved the whole thing in my closet. I didn't want to face debbing, much less designing."

"But then we cheered you up," Bella said, stooping a bit to put her head onto Amanda's shoulder.

"Yeah," Amanda said, smiling gratefully. "And I wanted to *stay* cheered up. So . . ."

"You kept the dress tucked away in the closet," Tay said with a knowing nod. "Big time denial. Yeah, Mr. A loves it when I do that. It's truly annoying."

"So what happened?" Scottie asked, a little more breathlessly than she would have liked. "What made you pull the dress out of the closet?"

"What choice did I have?" Amanda shrugged. "I mean, the big Debut is *gonna* happen. And I've gotta have something to wear. So finally, I looked at it this afternoon."

"And then you freaked," Tay said matter-of-factly.

"I don't know what I was thinking!" Amanda cried. "I mean, if I can't even get into design *school*, what made me think I could design a ball gown?!"

"You haven't gotten in *yet*," Bella reminded Amanda. "Yet."

"And you *can* do it," Scottie declared. "You've *done* it. You've done it to Chanel suits and three-hundred-dollar jeans, so why is this dress any different?"

"Because it is," Amanda insisted, her lower lip trembling. "And because it's now—post-Parsons. Every time I look at all this stuff—" Amanda slapped at a filmy swatch of tulle. "—*that's* what I think of. I *know* I had all these ideas before, but now, my mind's just blank. All I can see is that rejection letter."

"Maybe it'd help if you pictured your mom's face," Tay said. "You know, after she finds out you cut up a ball gown that costs as much as a car."

"Bwahhhh!" Amanda wailed, breaking out into full-on sobs now.

"Tay!" Scottie and Bella squawked, gaping at her.

"Hey, desperate times," Tay shrugged.

"She's riiiight," Amanda screeched. She sank onto the bed. Billows of silk satin and stalks of bodice boning poked up around her, making her look like a baby bird, abandoned in a cushy nest. "I am desperate! I'm a desperate debutante with nowhere to go to college next year. I'm pa-*the*-tiiiiiic."

"That is so not true," Scottie declared. "And we are going to fix this."

"With what?" Amanda wailed. "A magic wand?"

Scottie didn't have a wand. She did, however, have a couple of fairy godmothers.

"Hannah!" she blurted, sighing with relief when the vision of Beck's crazy-talented mother popped into her head. She turned to Amanda. "Hannah can sew this dress back together for you. I bet your mom won't even know it was ruined!"

"Ruined," Amanda said flatly. She patted her satin nest idly, almost as if she was apologizing to the dissected dress.

Or maybe, Scottie realized, *she's remembering why she cut it up—to make it into something much better than her perfect dress; to make it into an Amanda original.*

Which made "ruined" a *really* bad choice of words.

"I mean—" Scottie stuttered. "See, I was just thinking, y'know, if you wanted to go back to where you started—"

"—which was my party, wasn't it, girls?"

Scottie spun around.

"Alice!" she cried. "Hi!"

"Congratulations," Bella sing-songed. Amanda clamped her lips down on her sobs and gave Alice a limp wave.

"Amanda's having a little *moment*," Tay explained, crossing her arms over her chest and locking eyes with Alice. Scottie could read Tay's thoughts in her indulgent head-shake: *You know how girls are. Dra-ma.*

"Uh-oh," Alice said. She sat next to Amanda on the white satin as if it were the most normal thing in the world for someone to bring an imploded ball gown to your book launch party. "Tell me what happened."

"Noth-nothing," Amanda said, through a hiccup. She tried to smile through the tears coursing down her face. "I don't want to distract you from your party. It's your big night. We made you a pre-present and everything."

Bella held out the gift bag she was still clutching.

"I can't wait to see it," Alice said sweetly. She took the bag and put it on the floor next to the bed. Then she turned her attention back to Amanda.

"Amanda," she said. She smiled kindly as she tried to catch Amanda's pink-rimmed eyes.

"Alice," Amanda said back. This time her smile wasn't just a product of good etiquette—it was real. Scottie knew just how Amanda must have felt. When Alice looked you in the eye and let you know that she understood, you felt safer. You felt like the ground beneath your feet had suddenly grown more solid, like you couldn't fall because Alice's arms were holding you in place.

"Tell me," Alice said.

So Amanda did. She told her about the Parsons rejection and the debutante dress and Jamison and her tear-clothes-up-then-knit-them-back-to-life design dreams.

"I love that idea!" Alice said. She pointed at Amanda's jeans and added, "You know what that is, don't you? It's freeforming but taking it to the next level—freeforming within the guidelines of existing garments, which is even more interesting and challenging than doing it with no limitations at all."

Amanda started crying again. This time, it seemed, with gratitude.

"Seeeee," she said. "You get what I'm trying to do. But my mother would *never* understand." Amanda sniffled, wiped her nose with the back of her hand, and glanced at Scottie.

•• *Chicks with Sticks*

"Which I guess is why I'm gonna take the dress to Hannah," she decided. "She'll help me put it back together. I can do my little break-it-down-build-it-up thing with other clothes. It's not like debbing is my thing anyway. I'm only doing it for my parents. So I might as well do it in a dress they like."

"Really?" Alice said. She frowned and slid off the bed. She took Amanda's hand and pulled her to her feet, too. Then she gazed at the bits-of-dress arrayed before her.

"I don't actually see it that way," Alice said. "This *is* your thing. You're the one doing the coming-out, aren't you? And say what you will about it, it's a rite of passage in your life, which is a big deal. So in my opinion, your debut is *the* place for you to wear a dress of your own design."

"Really?!" Amanda gaped. "Even if the rite of passage is all anti-feminist and antiquated and stuff?"

"Eh," Alice said with a dismissive wave. "That's kind of par for the course when it comes to rites of passage. If I could show you my bat mitzvah pictures, you'd scream. I look like this little *mouse* being squished between my parents and this barrel-chested rabbi with hair growing out of his nostrils. It was like—"

"—like a Woody Allen movie?" Scottie asked with a painful sigh of recognition.

"Exactly like a Woody Allen movie," Alice laughed. "But here's the thing. As hard as that ritual was, it was also something I was meant to do. Just like, maybe, being a debutante is something *you're* meant to do, Amanda."

Amanda looked at her dress-parts and bit her lip.

"Think about the other clothes you've made," Alice said, putting a hand on Amanda's shoulder and squeezing. "You didn't trash those Chanel suits. You took them and mixed 'em up. You made them your own—but with all due respect.

"There's no reason," Alice went on, "you can't approach being a debu-tante in the same way. Make the dress your own. Make the rite your own. Even make the Chalk Prince of Chicago your own. But with all due respect."

Amanda pressed her fingertips to her lips in a clear effort to keep from crying again. She nodded hard. But when she cast another glance at her dress, it was with fear.

"The thing is, I don't know if I *can* make this thing my own," she whispered. "I thought I had a handle on what I wanted to do with the dress, but now I've lost it and I don't know if I can get it back! I don't think I have it in me anymore."

"I know it's scary," Alice said with a nod. "But I think you can get it back if you want to bad enough. Look how far you've come with your knitting. You were plenty scared of that in the beginning what with counting stitches and following patterns. You've overcome an incredible amount."

"I guess," Amanda agreed quietly. "It wasn't enough to get me into Parsons, though."

"Yet!" Scottie, Tay, and Bella chimed together.

Alice gave Amanda's shoulder another squeeze, but this time, as she spoke, she looked over Amanda's head at Scottie.

"You still have time," she said. "When you're ready, when you want it—you can do this. I know you can."

Scottie froze.

Is she talking to Amanda or to me? she wondered with a dry-mouthed swallow.

Scottie suddenly began to feel light-headed. She looked at Amanda's dress—a beautiful thing that Amanda had wanted to make her own, but had destroyed instead—and felt a jolt of recognition.

She thought about the life she had now—the Chicks and Never Mind the Frogs, Beck and Nina, even the easy vibe going on at her loft with her parents and CC. She had a beautiful thing.

But the more time goes by, she couldn't help noting, *the closer I get to having it ripped away from me.*

A moment later, Scottie shook her head. She didn't want to think about all that.

Because, for one, college is still ages away, she insisted to herself. *And two, Amanda's the one having a crisis here. Not me.*

So Scottie sprang into action. She grabbed a handful of satin and started scooping Amanda's dress parts back into the garment bag.

"We'll help!" she blurted.

Her friends looked at her quizzically.

"With the dress," Scottie explained. "Tay, Bella, and I can help you with it, right guys?"

Amanda looked instantly grateful. But then, she shook her head.

"Thanks, but . . ." She shot Alice a wavery look and Alice smiled proudly. "I have to do this on my own," Amanda went on. "It's *my* rite of passage and my dress so . . . I think I have to find my own way back to them."

"You are so right!" Bella cried, bouncing over to Amanda and enfolding her in a hug. "It's perfect that you're going to do this on your own. It's like you'll really be a grown-up after your debut. It won't just be symbolic. It's kind of like when the Liguru girls of Tanzania get their first period and are sent off to spend a week alone in a hut. I learned about that in Non-Western civ the other day."

"That's kind of a cool way to think about it, I guess," Amanda said. "I mean, without the whole menstruating alone in a hut part."

And she was right. Scottie, of all people, knew that.

Like Bella keeps saying, It was me *who changed my life.*

She just hoped that, like Amanda, she could find the strength to do it all over again.

16 *(Duplicate Stitch)

"See, care packages can be very dicey," Scottie said.

It was late Sunday morning and she was slouched on her bed talking on her hands-free cell while she strung some purls into her latest memory quilt square. This one was intarsia'd with a fluffy, blue-gray cat modeled after CC's mother. Not that CC cared. She was curled into a tiny ball at Scottie's hip, snoring raspily as she napped.

"I *could* just stockpile a bunch of cramming classics for you," Scottie told Beck. She finished a row and turned her needle around to keep going. "You know, Twizzlers, chocolate malt balls, Twinkies, Slim Jims, Smartfood, of course . . ."

"Of *course*," Beck said. Scottie could picture him grinning.

"But as we both know," Scottie countered, "mid-study cravings can be very fickle. One minute, you've *got* to have a mocha Frappucino, the next, you could care less about coffee but you'll die if you can't get your hands on some Bugles."

Now Beck was full-out laughing.

"So I'm going to give you a rare opportunity, Beck Snyder," Scottie said, on a happy roll now. "I'm going to let you put in an *order* for your care package. Tell me what you want. A bag of all-black Jelly Bellies? A tub of popcorn from the Davis Theater? Penny's pad thai? Or how about cereal? Your Cap'ns, your Pebbles . . . you name it. Well, within

• • Chicks with Sticks

reason. If you want frozen hot chocolate from Serendipity or something, we might have a problem."

"What do I want?" Beck wondered out loud. "What I want is . . ."

Scottie heard the rustle of pages flipping, the *click-click-click* of a push-button ballpoint pen. They were the telltale sounds of a man drowning in school work. Scottie nodded sympathetically and made a decrease in her quilt square.

"I don't know," Beck sighed finally. "I've got a pretty big stack of ramen noodle packs here, so I'm good for food. What I *really* want is for my finals to be over already."

"Are you telling me," Scottie asked incredulously, "that you'd choose to subsist on ramen noodles when I can give you any snack you want? Did I *mention* the all-black Jelly Bellies?"

Beck laughed again, but wearily. "Okay, first of all," he said, "*you're* the one who likes all-black Jelly Bellies. And Good 'n Plenty. And even the little after-dinner anise seeds they give you at Moroccan restaurants. Which is all just gross, if you ask me."

"It's true," Scottie admitted with a laugh. "I do have an unhealthy licorice fixation."

"Second," Beck went on, "it's an incredible offer, but my philosophy exam's tomorrow at four and I'm *so* in the weeds. I'd love to see you—"

"And my snacks," Scottie interjected.

"And your snacks," Beck agreed, "but I can't afford to lose the study time."

"I'd just pop in," Scottie promised, maybe meaning it. "I'll leave the junk food in the doorway and back away slowly. You won't even know I'm there."

"Uh-huh," Beck said dubiously. "So not even a kiss hello?"

"Maybe a little kiss," Scottie allowed.

"And what about a kiss good-bye?"

"Well," Scottie said, "it'd be rude to leave without saying good-bye, wouldn't it?"

"And you're telling me that *nothing* would happen between this hello and good-bye," Beck said. "No chatting? No sharing of snacks? No kisses that aren't of a hello and good-bye nature?"

"Not unless you're looking for an excuse to blow off your studying," Scottie said innocently.

"Like you?" Beck said.

"A, my finals are, like, a week away," Scottie defended herself. "And b, homework is what Sunday *nights* are for."

"Man, I miss high school," Beck groaned. "The work was so *easy*."

"Hey, Spanish Four is *not* easy," Scottie protested.

"Compared to college-level Latin?" Beck asked.

"Well . . ." Scottie searched hard for a valid comeback. "That's why you need a care package! To sustain you while you do all this hard work."

"I wish I could say yes," Beck sighed. "I'd much rather eat Jelly Bellies, even black ones, with you than read another word of Sartre. But I can't. I'm already flirting with a B-minus in this class."

"You're right," Scottie said. "This is kinda tragic though. First I can't ever see you because of finals, and then as soon as you're done, you're in New York for your entire winter break."

"Well, considering I haven't seen my dad since August . . ." Beck sighed.

"Yeah, I guess he deserves to see you, too," Scottie said, her voice full of mock-sulkiness. "At least you like your dad. Tay's in Milwaukee this weekend, as miserable as ever, despite her fabulous new skateboard and wall dots."

"She's still not over the Porsche thing, huh?" Beck said.

"I think she's adjusted, now that convertible season is over," Scottie said. "Lately she's appalled by his interpersonal skills. She actually went out to dinner with him and a woman last night."

"Really?!" Beck said. "Yuck."

"Yeah," Scottie said. "She IM'd me about it this morning. Tay actually doesn't mind the fact that her dad's dating. He had his first date about five minutes after he moved out of the house, so Tay's used to that concept. It was seeing her dad *on* a date that creeped her out. Apparently, he was really aloof all night long, totally holding his date at arm's length, even though she was clearly crazy about him. Tay said it gave her flashbacks to when her parents were married."

"Which wasn't a good time, clearly," Beck said.

"It pretty much left Tay's mom a nub of a woman," Scottie sighed.

"Maybe I should be grateful, in a weird way," Beck said, "that my parents seemed to get along pretty well. Y'know, before my mom decided to chuck it all and leave the state without notice."

Scottie swallowed hard. Talk about feeling young and naive. When it came to divorce, she knew there was no way she could completely get it. "Well," she said hesitantly, "my guess is, when your parents split, it sucks any way you slice it."

"You're right," Beck said softly. "How do you always know what to say?"

"Lucky guess," Scottie said, meaning it.

"I don't think so," Beck said. "Your care package offer. That's perfect, too. I wish I could take you up on it."

"Next time," Scottie said, trying to recapture the breeziness of the first part of their chat.

"There'll be plenty of 'em," Beck groaned. "I can't believe I have to endure finals for three and a half more years! Not that you'll be around for 'em."

"What?" Scottie said. Her voice suddenly shot up an octave.

Is this some sort of pre-pre-break-up priming? she wondered, suddenly going cold and sweaty. She dropped her quilt square and found herself scooping CC off the duvet, hoping the cuddle would brace her for the blow.

"Well, you'll be off at school somewhere," Beck pointed out. "I predict you're gonna end up at Emory or Duke or some other place where you don't have to spend six months out of the year in Uggs and a million layers of wool."

"Oh," Scottie said, her heart pounding with post-trauma.

"Well . . ." she began. As always, the college topic left her groping for something to say. "Well, don't be so sure about that," she finally said, with forced jocularity. "I'm a knitter. I'm all about the wool. What would I *do* if I lived somewhere where they don't need sweaters?"

"Good point," Beck said. "Maybe you should investigate schools in Maine."

"Why stop there?" Scottie said, trying hard to keep up the riffage. "How about Minnesota? Alaska!"

When Beck emerged from his laughter, Scottie heard another rustle of pages flipping.

"You've gotta go," she stated.

"I've gotta go." Beck sighed. "It's just Sartre and shrimp-flavored ramen for me for the rest of the day. I wish it could be you instead."

"Next time," Scottie said again. She was glad Beck couldn't see her face. He'd know she was working way too hard on her smile.

As she clicked her cell closed, Scottie wilted. She poked idly at her quilt square but didn't pick it back up.

This is a sign, she told herself. *You've got a whole Sunday free. It's time to face the apps.*

She stared at her closed file drawer for a long, dreadful minute.

And then . . . she flipped her phone back open.

Tay was in Milwaukee so Scottie started with Amanda. But Amanda was in the middle of a debutante tea.

"I shouldn't even have my phone on," she whispered to Scottie, "much less be answering it."

"How *did* you answer it?" Scottie asked.

"I'm under the table," Amanda said. "I pretended to drop the sugar cube tongs. The table cloth is very billowy. They won't miss me for a while."

Scottie laughed dryly. "Sounds like we could both use a break," she sighed. "When are you done there? Want to hook up later?"

"I have a date," Amanda said.

"With Jamison?"

"With my deb dress," Amanda breathed. "I figured it out, Scottie! I'm going to knit a corset to go with the skirt! I got this amazing, white silk yarn and some really juicy alpaca. I might even incorporate the boning from the original bodice but I haven't figured out how to do that yet. Anyway, I'm almost done sketching and I want to do some swatches tonight."

"Amanda, that's great!" Scottie said. "I can't wait to see it."

She tried to imagine herself giving Amanda similar good news: *I got over myself and finally applied to . . .*

But see, that was where the fantasy ended. So she nodded wanly when Amanda said, "Give Bella a call. I'm pretty sure she's planless today."

And Bella *had* been planless—until her parents had invited her to a four-hour yoga workshop they were attending that afternoon.

"This is the perfect opportunity to tell 'em about my whole political thing," Bella whispered as she got ready to leave. "After all the stretching and breathing, they're gonna be way zen. *And* we're going to their favorite vegan restaurant afterward. I'm going to break it to them there."

"Wow," Scottie said. Again, she couldn't help but feel a little wistful. "You're so brave."

"Well, I couldn't keep avoiding it," Bella said with a shuddery sigh. "I mean, eventually they were going to find out. Better that I tell them first. You know, deal with it on my own terms."

"Yeah," Scottie said, shuddering herself. "You're right, Bella. You're *totally* right."

But a few minutes later, Scottie found herself grabbing her backpack and heading for the door, only stopping in the kitchen long enough to peek at CC's food and water dishes—both were full—and scrawl a note to her parents.

AT THE COFFEEHOUSE, STUDYING. XO, S

She slapped the stickie note onto the iMac screen, grabbed her keys, and left.

Scottie shivered as she settled into her seat on the L. It was only one o'clock but already she could feel the evening looming. The sky had a dark and broody look to it and it was starting to snow. It was the perfect day to be cozied up at home with her cat, some yarn, and a *Project Runway* marathon, or even her Spanish notes.

But Scottie was heading to the South Side. She'd had a sudden impulse. Once she'd expunged visions of care packages or chicky knit dates from her mind, she'd started to envision an outing with Nina.

No, *the* outing.

When she was alive, Scottie's Aunt Roz had taken her out every December for what she'd called a "Ladies' Day."

Scottie had been four when Aunt Roz had first proposed it. Scottie'd jumped up and down and squealed, "Are we going to the *Nutcracker*? Are we gonna see the sugarplum fairy?"

Aunt Roz had scoffed. "Oh, *everybody* goes to the *Nutcracker*," she said. "And besides, I know you, Scottie. Those giant mice will give you nightmares for the next six months and your mother'll never forgive me. No, *we* are going to the miniature rooms."

Of course, Scottie thought this meant that she and Aunt Roz were going to be shrunken down to the size of non-giant mice. How else, she figured, would they fit into the miniature rooms?

When Aunt Roz came to pick her up on a snowy Sunday, Scottie had been so excited she couldn't stop hopping. She slipped some doll clothes into her coat pocket so she'd have something to wear once she'd been

• Chicks with Sticks

miniaturized. She folded the five-dollar bill her mom had given her to buy a souvenir into the tiniest possible square so she'd be able to hold on to it. She even brought her umbrella to protect herself from giant snowflakes.

Of course, a secret neurosis niggled at the back of her mind throughout these preparations: how would she and Aunt Roz get un-shrunk after they were done touring the miniature rooms? The worry needled at her but she decided not to think too hard about it. Aunt Roz, Scottie knew, would handle the unshrinking. She handled everything.

Naturally, Scottie had been perplexed when the miniature rooms turned out to be tiny dioramas. You peered *at* them rather than doing shrink-and-explore missions *in* them. She was disappointed until she started gazing into the rooms. There were sixty-eight of them—each from a different period in history—tucked into the walls of a shadowy maze in the basement of the Art Institute of Chicago. The walls were lined with raised platforms so little kids could see each room without having to stand on their tippytoes or be hefted under the armpits by their adults. The rooms were the most amazing things Scottie had ever seen. She and Aunt Roz spent two hours there, discussing each tiny scene at length.

Then they went to eat at the Walnut Room in Marshall Fields. Scottie had the chicken pot pie and Aunt Roz had the strawberry chicken salad and for dessert, they bought a box of Frango mints, which they nibbled at while they shopped. They spritzed each other with perfume, tried on lipstick, funny hats, and clackety clip-on earrings, and finally got serious at the end to buy Scottie a blue corduroy jumper with pockets that looked like dolls' faces. She wore that jumper about every other day for the rest of the winter.

The following December, they'd done it all over again, right down to the pot pie and strawberry salad. It became a tradition, and it had gone on as long as Aunt Roz had.

For the past two Decembers, Scottie had felt a mournful twinge every time she thought of those Ladies Days, but now she missed them in a different way. She missed them on Nina's behalf. As Nina's Big Sib, Scottie was the one who was supposed to make this sort of memory for her.

Yes, Nina's twelve, not four, Scottie told herself as the train wound its way through the loop, *and yes, Marshall Field's has morphed into Macy's. But the miniature rooms plus pot pie? I don't care how old you are—that's magic.*

Scottie burrowed her hands into her coat pocket and smiled giddily. She couldn't *wait* to spring her surprise on Nina.

Nina opened the door with the baby propped on her hip. He was wearing fuzzy footie pajamas and doing that shuddery, hiccuping thing that babies do after they've been on a crying jag.

Nina blinked at Scottie, then immediately glanced down. She was wearing jammies, too—flappy flannel pants, an oversized, long-sleeved T-shirt, and white socks that had that dingy, I've-been-sliding-around-in-these-all-weekend look to them.

Oh, no.

Nina's embarrassment was palpable. And that's when Scottie realized she'd made a mistake.

I should have called first! she thought. *Given Nina a chance to get dressed. To get ready to see me.*

A moment later, she realized, *Maybe I would have called, if I'd really been thinking about Nina when I hatched this little idea.*

There was nothing Scottie could do to undo her gaffe now. So she just smiled as widely as she could, waved at Nina, and said, "Surprise!"

It came out hoarse and belty; as awkward as Scottie felt.

"Mmmmm-waaaahhh!" the little boy wailed, launching himself right back into his tears. He burrowed his face into Nina's neck and sobbed, pausing only to peer out at Scottie resentfully.

"Oh, God," Scottie said. She reached out with her mittened hand to pat the baby's back. "I'm sorry, Tommy! I didn't mean to scare you."

"That's Teddy!" peeped one of Nina's little sisters. She'd just slunk up behind Nina and was peeking around her to grin at Scottie. "Not Tommy."

"Right!" Scottie said, slapping her forehead with her mitten. "Teddy! I-I knew that!"

"Do you know *my* name?" The tiny girl clasped her hands and giggled as she challenged Scottie.

"Um, Alexandra?" Scottie said. Nina had told her about all her siblings and she was *certain* one of the "littles" was named Alexandra.

The girl's cackle made it clear that Scottie had the wrong little.

"Alexandra's *two*," she corrected Scottie. *"I'm* four!"

"Which means," Scottie said, trying to recover quickly, "you're Anya, right?"

"Right!" Anya's wispy white-blond hair ruffled in the cold air but she didn't seem to mind as she bounced excitedly behind Nina.

"You want to come in?" Nina said. She nudged Anya out of the way and stepped back to give Scottie room. Then she grabbed Teddy's thumb and popped it into his mouth. Instantly, he hooked his forefinger over the bridge of his nose and stopped crying, but he still refused to look at Scottie.

While Scottie shrugged out of her snowy coat and unraveled her long scarf from around her neck, she became acutely aware of chubby little Alexandra and nine-year-old Katie staring at her from the living room door. Everybody was wondering what the heck she was doing there.

"See, I planned this amazing afternoon for us," Scottie explained to Nina. "It's this thing my aunt used to do called a Ladies Day. I guess I got so excited about the idea that I just came right over!"

"A Ladies Day?" Nina said,

Scottie smiled sheepishly.

"It starts at the Art Institute," she explained. "Then we go to the Walnut—"

"Go?" Nina said, her eyes going flat. "Go out? You mean today?"

"Well, that was the idea. But I can see you're not really dressed."

Scottie glanced out the window at the gloomy sky and roiling snow and forced a laugh. "Of course you're not!" she added. "If I hadn't gotten this crazy impulse, I'd totally be at home right now, wearing my lavender stretch pants and digging into a giant bowl of Golden Grahams."

Nina tugged at her T-shirt collar with a hesitant smile and explained, "Katie had this idea that we'd have an all-day slumber party, since it's so yucky out today. *And* because we're stuck at home," she added, looking a bit horrified. "My mom's at the nail shop all afternoon. I'm baby-sitting."

"Oh," Scottie said. It took a few seconds for it all to sink in. No miniature rooms. No pot pie. No Ladies Day. *"Oh."*

"I'm sorry," Nina said. She shrugged helplessly.

"No, no," Scottie jumped in to say. *"I'm* sorry. I should have called you first. In fact, I probably should have called your mom to check this out with her anyway."

For the first time, Scottie remembered that she had a handout from Big Sibs/Little Sibs dictating that very thing.

What was I thinking? she wailed inside her head. *I didn't get permission for this. I didn't check to see if Nina was free. And I neglected to notice that there's a giant blizzard brewing outside. What do I do now?*

It only took one more glance at Nina—looking uncomfortable, looking tired, and most of all, looking like she needed a friend to get her through this long day with the littles—for the answer to come to Scottie.

She had to find her inner Chick; to summon up Tay's pragmatism, Bella's warmth, Amanda's creativity, her own generosity, and the confidence of their entire quartet.

"You know what?" Scottie said. "I'd much rather hang with you here than go out in this weather, anyway. Maybe I could borrow some of your mom's pajamas?"

Within a few minutes, Scottie had traded in the delicate gold sweater and black pants she'd chosen especially for the Walnut Room. Now she was wearing some pink-striped flannel PJs.

When she emerged from the bathroom where she'd changed her clothes, she found Nina waiting for her in the hallway. The littles were clustered around her like Russian dolls—small, medium, and large—and Teddy was still latched onto her like a little marsupial, sucking his thumb noisily.

"You look like a mommy!" Anya said, pointing at Scottie's outfit and giggling.

"Yeah, I don't *think* so," Scottie teased the little girl. "I'm only seventeen."

But then she looked at Nina—only twelve—yet surrounded by little kids and loaded down with responsibility.

Scottie took a deep breath, shoved her babysitting fears away, and reached down to scoop up little Alexandra. With the toddler bouncing happily on her hip, she led the group into the kitchen.

"*This*," Scottie announced, "is gonna be fun. What movie are we gonna watch?"

"Nemo, Nemo, Nemo!" Anya cried, jumping up and down.

"Emo, Emo!" her little sister echoed, scrunching Scottie's pajama top up in her fist. Teddy's head popped up from Nina's shoulder. He grinned wetly from behind his fist. Then, with a shy glance at Scottie, he wedged his face back into Nina's neck.

Nina looked sheepish until Scottie admitted, truthfully, "I always wanted to see that movie! I just didn't have a kid to take me to it."

Scottie took care of microwaving a bag of popcorn and pouring it into a big, plastic bowl. Nina told her how to assemble sippy cups of milk for the littles and then they all piled onto the living room couch. The three little girls tangled themselves together and balanced the popcorn bowl on their knees. Scottie pulled out her knitting, which intrigued Teddy enough to make him crawl out of Nina's lap and come over for a closer look. Scottie found a wad of scrap wool in her bag and gave it to him. He chortled with delight and started waving it around.

Hey, this is going pretty well, Scottie marveled. *Just as long as nobody throws up.*

She glanced at the little girls. Alexandra was staring at the TV, looking pale.

Oh, no! Scottie thought. *She* is *gonna throw up.*

Instead, Alexandra slapped her hands over her eyes. "Sca-wee!" she shrieked. "Sca-wee shock!"

Scottie glanced at the movie. A shark with an Australian accent was leering at the little clown fish.

"Oh," she said, finally getting what Alexandra had said. "'Scary shark!' Don't worry, sweetie. It's just a movie."

"Too sca-wee," Alexandra declared, sliding off the couch and landing on the floor with a plop. She grabbed Scottie's hand and tugged at it.

"Candy-wand!" she demanded.

Nina rolled her eyes. "She does this every time," she sighed. "About two minutes into the movie, she gets scared and wants to play Candyland instead."

"Oh," Scottie said with a little laugh. Then she looked at Alexandra. "Well, I can play Candyland with you."

Alexandra nodded in a businesslike way and toddled over to a bunch of board games stacked behind the couch. She pulled out the Candyland box, set up the board, and picked up the red gingerbread man.

"I'm wed," she declared. Then she made her little plastic man hop all around the board until it landed on the Candy Castle. "I win!"

Nina peeked over the couch.

"Watch out," she said with a grin. "She cheats."

• • *Chicks with Sticks*

• • •

By the time Scottie got home, late that afternoon, she was exhausted. Not just from her afternoon of endless Candyland games and sippy cup refills. But from the emotional ping-pong game going on in her head.

Okay, yes it all worked out, Scottie thought, as she shed her snow-sopped coat and soggy boots just inside the loft door. *The littles had fun, and I gave Nina some babysitting help. But that's the thing. I should have known that* that *was what Nina really needed, way more than a trip to the miniature rooms.*

Scottie sighed and slumped into the kitchen. She spotted a new stickie note on the iMac, a note from her parents telling her that now *they* were out, doing dinner with clients in the suburbs. Hauling open the door of the Sub-Zero to scan the shelves for a snack, Scottie continued to berate herself.

Clearly, I needed that Big Sib training more than I realized, she thought. *Could I have been more clueless?*

She shook her head and let the fridge fall shut. She wasn't really hungry.

She didn't know *what* to do with herself, actually. Something didn't feel right.

As her eyes fell on the bowl of cat food under the computer desk, Scottie suddenly realized what was wrong.

She poked her head out of the kitchen, and called, "CC?"

Her voice bounced off the loft's hard surfaces and came back at her, sounding small and lonely.

Scottie frowned. CC *always* came out to greet her when she got home, either giving Scottie's ankle a perfunctory chin-rub before she resumed napping, or mewling plaintively until Scottie picked her up. But just now, CC hadn't come out at all.

Scottie took a closer look at the cat's funky, neon-green food and water bowls. They looked exactly as they had that morning. CC hadn't touched them!

"CC?!" Scottie yelled. She ran out into the main room and scanned all of CC's favorite sleeping spots. They were catless. Scottie called out again, then cocked her head, listening for a meow.

Nothing.

"Where *is* she?" Scottie muttered, gnawing at a frayed cuticle on her thumb. She ran to the loft door and poked her head into the hallway to see if CC had slipped out without her knowing it.

"CC!" she called.

When she heard nothing still, she began to tear the loft apart. She pulled the quilts off all the beds to see if CC had burrowed under a duvet for warmth. She peeked beneath every piece of furniture and even looked in all the kitchen and bathroom cabinets. Then she really began to panic. She was just pressing her cheek to the laundry room wall, trying to get a view behind the washer and dryer, when she heard it.

Eow.

It was an almost indiscernible squeak.

"CC?" Scottie cried.

Eow.

There it was again, even weaker, but definitely close by. Scottie flipped open the wicker clothes hamper and pawed through it, but found nothing.

Eow.

There was a pile of her dad's shirts set aside for dry cleaning on the floor next to the hamper. Scottie grabbed the top shirt and found beneath it . . . CC. The cat was curled into a ball, looking as tiny and bedraggled as she had in her runty kitten days. Her eyes were half-closed and she barely lifted her head to mewl painfully.

"Oh my God!" Scottie cried. Scooping up her poor kitty and cradling her to her chest, Scottie ran into her room and grabbed her phone. Then, she stopped short.

Who could she call? It was 5 P.M. on a Sunday. The vet wouldn't be around and her parents were stuck in the suburbs.

Alice! Scottie thought. She'd owned Monkey for years. Surely she might know what to do.

But Alice didn't answer her phone.

Next Scottie tried Bella, but she was clearly still in yogaville because her cell was turned off.

Eow.

CC sounded like she was in pain, and she was shivering.

"Oh *God!*" Scottie shrieked. Instinctively, she speed-dialed the most levelheaded person she knew—even though she was in Milwaukee.

Tay answered after the third ring.

"I need help!" Scottie blurted before bursting into tears. Through terrified sobs, she managed to say, "CC's sick. *Really* sick. And there's no vet in the office and—"

"Scottie!" Tay interrupted, as no-nonsense as Scottie knew she'd be. "Where are you?"

"H-home," Scottie cried. "I just found her."

"Hang on," Tay said. "I'll be right there."

"What?" Scottie said. "How—"

But Tay had already hung up.

17 ✴ (Twist the stitch)

Twenty minutes later, Tay marched into Scottie's loft, her cell phone clamped to her ear with her shoulder.

"Oh my God," Scottie cried. "I'm so glad you're here. Why *are* you here? I thought your train from Milwaukee didn't come in 'til eight—"

Tay gazed at Scottie balefully and held up her hand.

"Uh-huh," Tay muttered into her phone. She motioned to Scottie for a pen. Scottie leaped to grab one from the cup on the computer desk and Tay scribbled a phone number onto the palm of her hand.

"Thanks," Tay said flatly before clicking her phone shut. Then she looked at Scottie and held up her palm.

"The number of a veterinary ER," she said bluntly. "Do you want to dial, or should I?"

"You're the best!" Scottie cried, whipping her cell out of her pocket and dialing quickly. As she waited for someone to answer, she led Tay back to her room, where she'd made CC a nest of super-soft, hand-knitted afghans on her bed. CC was curled up in the center of the blankets. Her little belly heaved with every breath, and she continued to meow weakly.

Tay sat gingerly on the edge of Scottie's bed and gave CC's head a little pat. Tay was vociferously *not* a cat person, so Scottie was touched by the gesture.

The phone at the ER was still ringing. Scottie gnawed on her cuticle while she waited for someone to answer. She was just breaking out in a cold sweat when finally, someone picked up.

"Acute Care Pet Clinic of Chicago," said an impatient woman's voice. That's when Scottie started crying again. Not in panic, this time, but with relief. This person on the other end of the phone would tell her what to do, which was essential because Scottie couldn't have felt more lost.

She sobbed. "My cat is sick."

Within a few minutes, Tay and Scottie were in the back seat of a cab, whizzing South on Damen toward the animal hospital in Bucktown. It was futile to ask the driver to veer from lane to lane a little more gently. Cab drivers *always* drove as if they were speeding someone to the ER.

Scottie braced her legs against the cab's front seat in a vain effort to keep the cat carrier on her lap from jostling.

"Thank you so much for helping me, Tay," she said. "I was so scared, my hands were shaking. I never could have tracked down this kitty ER on my own."

"I'm sure something would have come to you," Tay said. One of her mittened hands was fisted under her chin and she was gazing out the car window into the growing storm. "You've always been a good Googler. You found Stockpile, didn't you?"

Scottie smiled briefly, then peered through the mesh window of the cat carrier for about the dozenth time. CC was still curled up in a tight ball, her face covered by her fluffy tail. Without taking her eyes off the cat, Scottie asked Tay, "So who did you get the number from? John?"

"My mom," Tay said in a clipped voice.

Scottie looked up at Tay, her eyebrows raised.

"Oh," she whispered.

Oh . . . wow.

Tay was still in major avoidance mode when it came to her mom. She tried to tailor her schedule so she and Laura would see each other as little as possible. And when they did run into each other, Tay was stone silent, sidestepping any and every attempt her mom made to "bond" with her. Laura was about the *last* person Tay would want to go running to when she needed help.

But Tay *didn't need the help,* Scottie realized. I *did. Tay reached out to her mom for* me.

"Tay, I—"

"My mom's in a book club," Tay explained, cutting off Scottie's umpteenth thank-you. "Of course, it's teeming with cat ladies. I really don't get why women dig cats so much. You'd think they'd be more into dogs, who actually love you back. Cats are so aloof."

"CC's not. She's always been so sweet . . ." Scottie's voice trailed off. If she kept talking about CC, she might break down completely. So, she steered the conversation toward Tay.

"So you came home from Milwaukee early," she choked out. "Talk about fate."

"No fate to it," Tay said. "I never went."

"Wait a minute," Scottie said. She frowned in confusion. "Wasn't this your weekend to go?"

"Yeah," Tay said deliberately. She looked at Scottie with the same flattened, defiant eyes that she usually reserved for authority figures. "I just didn't."

"How—"

"It was easy," Tay barked. "I told my mom I *was* going, and I told my dad I *wasn't.* Finals to study for and all. Conveniently enough, my parents aren't on speaking terms, so there was no way for either one of them to find out."

"So your mom thought you were calling from the train?" Scottie asked, feeling bewildered.

"Luckily, there was a cell phone tower in range," Tay said sarcastically.

"But, Tay," Scottie said. For a moment, her focus was diverted from CC. She twisted awkwardly in the bucking, weaving cab seat to stare at her friend. "Where *were* you all weekend?"

Tay looked into her lap and didn't answer for a long moment. Then she shrugged and said, "With John."

"With . . . John?"

"His parents were out of town," Tay said. She looked out the window again, then back down at her hands—anywhere, it seemed, except at Scottie.

"So you stayed at John's," Scottie stated, trying to wrap her brain around this. "All weekend. With no parents."

"Yyyyup," Tay said deliberately. Clearly she wasn't going to volunteer any more information. And Scottie knew she shouldn't ask. But suddenly, images of Tay and John began flashing in her mind. She saw John wrapping his lanky arms around Tay in the hallway and holding her so close that there wasn't a centimeter of space between them; John drinking in the smell of Tay's hair like it was a cup of gourmet coffee; Tay's melty face whenever she allowed John a rare public kiss.

Scottie tried not to ask. It really wasn't her place to ask. But . . . there was no way in the world she could *not* ask.

"So you . . ." she stuttered. "I mean, did you . . ."

"Did we have sex?" Tay provided. She kept her gaze on her lap now. "No."

Only when Scottie exhaled did she realize she'd been holding her breath.

"We were going to, but . . . no," Tay said.

"Oh," Scottie breathed. "Um, why not?"

"Good question," Tay said, shaking her head and huffing in disgust.

"One I asked myself a hundred times after *it* didn't happen last night. And guess what the answer is. You'll never guess in a million years."

"Did something bad happen between you guys?" Scottie asked tremulously.

"What, like a fight?" Tay said. "No." Then she shook her head in disbelief and almost-yelled, "What happened was I backed out. Me! Which is crazy. I mean I was *ready*."

Scottie felt her cheeks go blushy. For all the hot and bothered make-out moments she'd had with Beck, she had no idea what *ready* felt like.

"And I don't just mean, y'know, physically," Tay explained. "That was actually the easiest part to get on board with."

"Really?!" Scottie gasped.

Tay nodded dismissively and went on. "It was the *relationship* stuff that got me freaked," she admitted. "I mean, having sex would have made us officially 'serious.'"

"Weren't you already there, though?" Scottie asked. "You've been going out for so long."

"Yeah, but it didn't feel serious," Tay said. "Not that it was *casual*, but . . . I guess I always felt like we were still separate entities. Sure, we were each other's Saturday nights and John was the one who carried my books to school. . . ."

Scottie gaped at Tay, who needed a guy to do her heavy lifting as much as an NBA player needed help changing a lightbulb.

"In a figurative sense, of course," Tay said with a tiny smile.

Relieved at the bit of levity, Scottie smiled back.

"But sex," Tay said, shaking her head. "I felt like it would turn us from John and Tay—two people who were going out—into JohnandTay. We'd become this cemented entity, you know? There'd be an unbreakable pact between us. It's all so . . . *heavy*.

"And things would get less fun, too," Tay went on. "Because we'd always be trying to find time alone so we could do it. And we'd probably start thinking about nothing *but* doing it, like those boring couples who are always mauling each other in the hall at school. . . ."

"Well, you've got me convinced," Scottie said, trying to keep the lightness going. "Sex? Bad. But what did John say?"

"He thought all that stuff was just me looking for excuses," Tay sighed, finally meeting Scottie's eyes. "And on my way over to your house, I realized he was right."

"Oh," Scottie said. "Then what's the real reason?"

"My *mother*," Tay blurted. She sounded flabbergasted—but also pretty certain. "It's *her* fault."

"Really?!" Scottie squeaked again. "You're about the last person I'd expect to be worried about being caught by your mom."

"I'm not worried about being caught by her," Tay scoffed. "I'm worried about becoming her."

"What?!" Scottie would have laughed if Tay hadn't looked so distraught. "That's ridiculous!"

"No, it's not," Tay said. "It turns out, my mom was quite the badass when she was my age."

Scottie snorted.

"I'm *serious*," Tay said. "My dad told me."

"Your *dad*?"

"Hey, when there's an entire weekend to kill in Milwaukee, even me and my dad can get a little chatty," Tay admitted. "He said I reminded him of my mother. When I almost threw up in his precious Porsche, he clarified: I reminded him of how my mother *used* to be, back when she was in high school, when my parents first met."

"What happened?" Scottie said.

"I think my dad happened," Tay said. "They got together when my mom was seventeen and by the time they were nineteen, they were engaged. In other words, they were 'serious' from the beginning. I think my mom just got lost. She was my dad's girlfriend, my dad's fiancée, my dad's wife, *my* mother. She never got a chance to figure out who *she* was. And now, as you can see, she's kind of just this big piece of Velcro, looking for someone to stick to. At the moment, that someone is me, but before that, it was definitely my dad. That's why they split up—one of the reasons anyway. He was totally stifled by her."

"Whoa," Scottie breathed. "But Tay, you'd never let that happen to you! Neither would John."

"I bet that's just what my mom thought," Tay said. "But I think that's the thing about sex. You can't exactly plan for how it might mess with your head. I don't want to lose myself in this relationship. *Any* relationship. Especially not when I'm sixteen."

"So, what did John say?" Scottie asked breathlessly.

"Well, I didn't tell him all *that* stuff," Tay said. "I just said no. He tried to be understanding about it. He's *John*. Of course he did. But I know he's totally confused."

"Why don't you tell him what you just told me?" Scottie said gently. "About your parents."

"Ungh," Tay groaned, dropping her face into her hands. "I don't want to get all psychobabbly with John. I mean, talk about unsexy."

"I don't think John could find anything about you unsexy," Scottie laughed.

"Except me pushing him away," Tay said broodily. "Here, we had this whole, y'know, romantic thing planned."

Scottie had to stifle a snort. She couldn't believe the word "romantic" had just come out of Tay's mouth.

"And then I went all aloof on him," Tay said. "Like a cat. Like *my dad*. Ugh!"

Scottie heaved a big sigh. "So, basically," she said, "you became your dad in order to avoid becoming your mom?"

"Ohhh," Tay moaned. "Mr. A'll just *love* this. He's gonna go all Sigmund on me."

"It does seem to have all the makings of a Greek tragedy," Scottie admitted.

Tay's laugh was dry and self-deprecating. But her face was as sad as Scottie had ever seen it.

"Tay . . ." Scottie began.

But she didn't know what to say! She didn't even know how to begin navigating all the issues swirling around this conversation.

"John loves you," was all Scottie could think of. "He'll get over this."

Lame, lame, lame, Scottie scolded herself.

Tay, Scottie could see in her eyes, agreed.

"The question is," Tay sighed, "will *I* get over this?"

"I . . . I don't know," Scottie stuttered.

Tay shook her head bitterly and turned to stare out the cab window again. "We're almost there," she muttered. "How's the cat?"

Scottie peeked back into the carrier, grateful for the deflection. CC was still curled up, still looking awful.

"Almost there, Ceece," Scottie whispered. "Everything's gonna be okay."

Then she peeked at Tay's pale, troubled face and wondered, *But how?*

Scottie, Tay, and poor CC waited for an hour in an exam room that smelled like antiseptic and dog kibble. Finally, the vet marched in. He looked just as you'd expect a vet working the Sunday night shift in the ER to look—hassled.

"I'm Dr. Bryson," he announced, barely glancing at the girls. As he scanned the form a nurse had filled out when Scottie first came in—the one that said CC hadn't eaten or drank for at least a day—Scottie brought CC over to the mustard-colored examination table.

"Hmm!" Dr. Bryson grunted. He began manhandling CC. In his large, calloused hands, the kitty looked even more vulnerable, tiny, and miserable.

"Any blood in the stool?" he asked curtly.

"Um, no, I don't think so—"

"You would know if there was," he blurted. "Has she been drinking more than usual?"

"Less, actually," Scottie said. "For a day or two? I sort of didn't realize it. You know, I just figured, 'Oh, her bowls are full. She doesn't need any food or water.'"

"A day or two?"

"Let's see," Scottie said, looking at the ceiling. "I usually feed her in the mornings before I go to school, so I know I put fresh food and water in on Friday. And yesterday? Um, I *might* have—"

"So basically, you don't know how long it's been since your cat has eaten *or* drank," Dr. Bryson said.

Tears sprang to Scottie's eyes as the vet scooped CC up and peered into her eyes, then pulled her lip down roughly to examine her gums.

"Your cat needs you to be there," Dr. Bryson scolded Scottie. "She doesn't know that you're caught up in the homecoming dance."

"I'm *not* caught up in the homecoming dance," Scottie murmured, looking at her feet. But she still felt wretched.

Briskly, Dr. Bryson finished his examination and pronounced, "Hepatic lipidosis. Looks like a classic case. Of course, we have to run some tests to confirm."

"Hepatic lipi . . ." Scottie couldn't even remember the term, much less understand it.

"Lipidosis," Dr. Bryson said, scribbling something on CC's form. "Fatty liver syndrome. Unless she starts eating asap, CC's liver may become saturated with fat that she can't metabolize without a whole lot of help. You're going to have to syringe feed her a high-protein solution and give her medication. Now, do you have someone who can help you *remember* that? Your parents, perhaps?"

"I'll remember," Scottie said. A single tear rolled down her cheek. She felt like a little kid who'd been stuck in the corner. "I promise.

"All right then," Dr. Bryson said briskly. "I'll take CC to the lab to get some blood drawn, and we'll call you tomorrow with confirmation and prescriptions. Meantime, you can go ahead and start giving CC her protein solution tonight. The nurse will show you how to use the syringe."

"Thanks," Scottie rasped, unable to look directly at the doctor.

"It's lucky that you came in when you did," Dr. Bryson said curtly. "Another day or two and it might have been impossible for CC to recover. She has a chance now, but it's going to take some work on your part."

Scottie could only nod. As Dr. Bryson carried her mewling cat out of the examination room, Scottie felt a stab of remorse. She collapsed into the molded plastic chair next to Tay's.

"I can't believe this happened," she cried. "She was fine yesterday! But I should have noticed that she wasn't eating!"

"That doctor was a jerk about it," Tay said.

"I deserved it," Scottie insisted, shaking her head hard.

"Scottie," Tay sighed. "You have a lot going on. We all do."

"Yeah." Scottie sighed. "I was out all day today."

"Oh yeah?" Tay said, perking up a bit. "Tell me about *your* crazy day. It might make me feel better about mine."

"Well," Scottie began, "I had this whole adventure planned for me and Nina. . . ."

Just as Scottie finished her story about her afternoon of apple juice instead of Frango mints, Candyland instead of miniature rooms, a nurse opened the exam room door with CC cradled in her arms.

"Ceece!" Scottie crooned, gingerly taking her cat from the woman.

"Stay here just a few more minutes," the nurse instructed, "and I'll be back with CC's supplement and some syringes."

"Okay," Scottie said, nodding eagerly. As she scratched CC's head and whispered sweet nothings into her ears, she glanced up at Tay—and froze.

Because Tay was giving her a squinty, skeptical stare.

"What?" Scottie said.

"Ladies Day?" Tay said.

"I know," Scottie said with a laugh. "It's a goofy term. But let's remember, my aunt made it up when I was four."

"I'm not talking about the name of the thing," Tay said. "I'm talking about the thing itself."

"What's wrong with it?" Scottie said, her grip on CC tightening a bit.

"What's wrong with it is you're not four," Tay said.

"Okay, let's not forget who ended up eating most of the Rice Krispie treats at your SSO," Scottie protested. "This wasn't me being immature! This was me doing something special for Nina."

Tay shrugged. "Okay, whatever you say," she said. "I mean, you're right. It *was* a nice impulse. Just like it was awesome of you to brave Stockpile to get me that skateboard. Or to paint Bella's French fry bus or go to Amanda's horrid debutante party. It's just—"

"What?" Scottie demanded. "What's wrong with trying to be a good friend?"

"Nothing!" Tay said. "But Scottie? You don't have to make such an *event* of it! If you eased up on the nostalgia trips, the memory quilt, the annual Chicks with Sticks whatevers? We'd still *be* the Chicks, y'know. Even if you, say, *went away to college,* we would—we *will*—still be the Chicks. You can't stop time, Scottie. What's more—you don't have to."

Scottie stared at Tay. "I know that!" she said quickly. "Of course, I know that."

But the next moment, Scottie ducked her head and busied herself with wrapping CC in her blanket and tucking her back into her carrier. She suddenly felt shy and weirded out—the way you feel when you see yourself in a candid photo and notice the bad posture or slight double chin that you never knew you had.

"Wow," Scottie said shakily. "Does Mr. A know that you've totally co-opted his therachat?"

Tay laughed sympathetically. "The therachat sucks, doesn't it?" she said. "Especially when it's dead on."

By the time the girls left the ER, the snow had piled in huge drifts. Their cabdriver inched home via residential streets, braking half a block before each stop sign to avoid skidding into the next intersection. Tay and Scottie each gazed out their own windows, too consumed by their thoughts to make conversation.

Even in silence, though, Scottie took comfort in Tay's presence.

Would it really be the same, she wondered, *if we had just said all those things on the phone, hundreds of miles apart?*

As if on cue, Tay's cell phone rang. Scottie could tell by her hushed, hopeful tone that it was John calling.

"Listen," Tay began, "I think I sort of . . ."

She gave Scottie a quick glance. ". . . figured some stuff out. Can I call you after I get home so we can talk?"

Her face softened as John answered. Scottie was happy for her, and was about to say so when her own phone chirped.

"Scottie!" It was her dad, sounding worried. "The weather's horrible. Why aren't you at home?

"Dad, CC was sick," Scottie said quickly. "Really sick. Tay helped me take her to the animal ER in Bucktown. I'm on my way home in a cab now."

"Oh, no," her dad said sympathetically. "Is she okay?"

"I think she's gonna be," Scottie said with a shuddery sigh. "So are you still in Lake Forest?"

"Yeah, I'm afraid we're stuck here," her dad said. "The clients have a guest room. Three of them, in fact, and they've graciously offered to let us stay over tonight so we don't have to brave the expressway in this snow. But sweetie, if you need us home to help you with CC, we'll figure out a way."

Scottie pictured her loft—the tall windows encrusted with frost, the cement floors radiating cold, the stormy darkness obscuring the ceiling rafters. It would be kind of nice to spend the evening with her parents, breathing in the aroma of her mom's latest juicy painting while her dad made his famous olive oil popcorn and put on a Netflix.

Or is that just me again, Scottie wondered, *trying to stop time?*

Tightening her jaw, she said to her dad, "No. You guys should stay there. Besides, it'll give you a chance to sell them more paintings."

"You read my mind," her dad chortled. "They've already committed to one, but now I'm working on getting them to take a triptych."

"I'm sure it'll be a deal by breakfast," Scottie said.

"Are you going to be all right without us? Want me to have Beck's mom check in on you?"

Again, Scottie had to resist the security blanket. "Nah," she said. "I'll be fine. I'll see you after school."

"All right. Oh, wait! I almost forgot to ask—before you left, did you see the package I left out for you?"

"The what?"

"On the coffee table," her dad said. "You didn't see it?"

"No," Scottie said. "What is it?"

Like she had to ask. She could tell by the excited swoop in his voice that it had to be something college-related.

"Oh, I'll let you see for yourself."

"Oh-kay," Scottie said apprehensively.

"Whoops, gotta go. The Mankoffs want to show us their wine cellar."

As Scottie flipped her phone closed, she realized the cab had almost reached her building. She turned to Tay. "Are you okay?"

"Yeah," Tay said slowly. "I think I am. What about you?"

Scottie still felt weird and didn't hide it.

"To be determined," she said with a shrug.

"Ain't that a universal truth," Tay said with a weary smile.

"Thanks for coming to CC's rescue," Scottie said.

• Chicks with Sticks

"Well, CC's just lucky that she's nicer than Monkey," Tay joked. Then she turned serious. "And I know you would have done the same for me," she said. "No matter what."

"How could I," Scottie wondered, her voice going plaintive, "if I wasn't even here?"

"You'd figure out a way," Tay said with a laugh. "Some crazy, convoluted way, yeah. But still."

Scottie laughed, too, then slipped the cab fare through the taxi's Plexiglas window and gave a Tay a quick hug good-bye.

When she got inside, she took her time setting CC up in her fluffy nest of afghans and administering her first dose of protein fluid. Then she changed into sweats and wool socks.

Finally, there was no more avoiding it. She padded across the vast loft floor to the TV area and looked at the coffee table. She saw a yellow, padded envelope, already ripped open. Resting on top of it, in an unmarked, plastic jewel box, was a DVD. Scottie picked it up and turned it over, certain there'd be some university logo on the back.

Instead, she found a lime green stickie note.

"Oh my God," Scottie breathed.

> *Well, here it is! Shearling has already been accepted into the NYU Undergrad Film Festival and my documentary prof says I should totally send it to Slamdance. You're gonna love it.*
> *Hugs,*
> *Jordan*

18 ✶ (Cast off all stitches)

Scottie stared at the DVD for several minutes before she found the courage to pick it up and slip it into the player. Then she wedged herself into the cushiest corner of the red couch, drew her knees up beneath her chin, and pressed PLAY.

The movie opened with a crudely drawn cartoon of a barnyard accompanied by a familiar song plinked out on a toy piano. Only when an animated sheep wearing funky rectangular glasses waddled into the frame did Scottie recognize the ditty: *Old McDonald had a Farm, E-I-E-I-O . . .*

After the bespectacled white sheep came one with red spikes sprouting out of its woolly head, then a pretty white lamb with long, fluttering eyelashes.

"Okay, I get it," Scottie whispered. She stiffened as she waited for the Scottie sheep to make its appearance.

The last sheep was runty and wobbly—much like CC—and black.

"Oh come *on!*" Scottie said. "The black sheep? She's got to be kidding."

Before she could get more indignant, the movie shifted into live action—home movies of Scottie and Jordan as little kids. There was Jordan dressed as a fairy princess for Halloween, and Scottie skulking in the background as a black cat. There was Jordan, age nine, doing a triumphant "stick" at a gymnastics meet, and Scottie with cake smeared all over her face at her seventh birthday party.

Over all this footage, a rumbly-voiced narrator read nursery rhymes: *Hansel and Gretel, Beauty and the Beast,* and *Rumpelstiltsken.*

Scottie could only assume that she was playing the part of the troll.

Scottie didn't think the film could get worse, but then the talking heads began. Jordan had intercut sound bites from their parents—telling the infamous Jabba the Hut anecdote, among others—with those of a woman Scottie didn't recognize.

"Birth order," the woman said, raising her eyebrows haughtily, "is far more significant than some would have you believe."

A black screen popped up with a title in blocky white letters: DR. FRAN ALTSCHULL-HASSAN, SOCIOLOGIST.

"Oh my God," Scottie bellowed. "Even her titles are pretentious."

"Sisters in particular," Dr. Altschull-Hassan droned on, "are prone to developmental effects. The firstborn is the extrovert, the star, because she *has* to be to distinguish herself from the interloper, her younger sister."

"Interloper?" Scottie screeched. "Who *is* this person?"

"The newer sibling, meanwhile," said Dr. Altschull-Hassan went on, her eyebrows traveling so high now, they almost met her hairline, "has to work very little to be the stand-out in the family, which can lead to an endemic laziness that, ironically, renders her the much less interesting of the offspring."

"What?!" Scottie screamed, partly because she was outraged and in part because she didn't know what the heck the sociologist was talking about. The only thing that was clear was that this whole movie was a blatant bashing of little sisters in general, and Scottie in particular.

The film cut back to more home movies of little Jordan generally being fabulous, while Scottie waddled in her wake. By now, the movie wasn't even getting to Scottie. She was just shaking her head in incredulous disgust—until she came to the scene with Aunt Roz.

It was a film snippet Scottie had seen so many times that she recognized it instantly. Jordan was riding a carousel horse with no hands while Scottie clung to Aunt Roz's legs outside the merry go round's fence, crying.

The sight of Aunt Roz, laughing and petting Scottie's crooked pigtails more than a decade ago, brought quick tears to Scottie's eyes. She felt a familiar tug of nostalgia. But instead of being a cozy kind of nostalgia, it was repulsive. In Jordan's hands, some of Scottie's most precious childhood memories now looked ugly.

Scottie started crying for real and hit STOP on the remote.

Jordan wants nothing more than to make me look pathetic, she wailed inside her head. *Why?*

But the question hadn't even finished ringing in her head before she knew the answer.

Because it's easy, Scottie thought. *Because all through our childhoods, Jordan was the star, and I was the wallpaper. And I pretty much stayed that way until the Chicks came along.*

Scottie dropped the remote onto the coffee table and drifted out of the TV area. When she reached her bedroom, she gave the sleeping CC a quick stroke, then sat on the shaggy white rug next to her bed. She didn't even have to peek beneath the bed skirt to find the Lucite box she'd stashed under the box spring. She knew exactly where it was. She slid the box out, popped off its lid, and beheld the contents—three stacks of knitted squares. So far, Scottie had made nineteen of them. She sifted through them now, skimming her fingertips over ridges and bumps, scratchy and soft, fuzzy embroidery and airy, full-of-holes lace; over all the memories Scottie had committed to yarn.

She picked out the square with the fuzzy, 3-D baseball, a throwback to the afternoon the Chicks had knitted at Wrigley Field. Then she found the one striped with red ribbing that simulated the Australian licorice Bella brought to almost every SSO. The amber square intarsia'd with a tiny athletic sock instantly carried her back to a gross frat party—

complete with boozy jocks doing sock slides across the floor— that the Chicks had gone to last year.

Each square was busy with activity—not just the click-swishes of Scottie's needles but all the forward motion of the Chicks with Sticks.

Except the images didn't look like that to Scottie anymore. Suddenly, they had become static. Fuzzy fossils. Been there, done thats.

Scottie had wanted to make a blanket of all these memories and burrow beneath it, wrapped up in the past. But now, her quilt squares didn't feel like a clever sort of photo album or an homage to the friends who'd changed her life.

They felt like a stopped clock, just as Tay had pointed out.

I put so much work into these things, Scottie thought. Crying hard now, she tossed the squares back into their plastic box without stacking them. *And why?! Because every time I finished part of my memory quilt, I could take another step backward.*

The Big Sibs/Little Sibs office was disheveled and chaotic. The cantaloupe-colored walls were pin-pricked by a rotating gallery of children's art and the olive vinyl arms of the chairs had been picked at, probably by the same restless fingers that had made the art. A young receptionist sat at a faux wood desk before a bank of office doors, answering calls on a retro-looking phone.

Scottie had loved the office's warm shabbiness when she'd come here for training several months ago. Today, she loved it even more—because she was sure it was the last time she'd see it.

She had a sudden impulse to turn around and leave—to spend her Monday afternoon doing her usual dodge-it dance of homework and knitting at Joe. But one quick recall of the day before—from her misbegotten "ladies day" to CC's pained meows to the wobbly black sheep in Jordan's film— made her stalk up to the receptionist, her face tense with determination.

"I'm Scottie Shearer," she said to the girl, who had a book open on the desk in front of her. "I made an appointment this morning?"

The receptionist swung her curtain of blond hair over her shoulder as she grabbed an appointment ledger and slid her finger down to the 4 o'clock slot.

"Yup," she said. "Just have a seat. I'll tell Carlie you're here."

"Carlie?" Scottie said. "The director?"

"The very one," the girl said, sounding bored. She flipped a page in her book.

"I'm not—?" Scottie said haltingly. "Um, I usually talk to Lily. The middle school coordinator?"

"Well . . ." The curtain of hair flipped again as the girl glanced up at Scottie. "Not today."

"Um, okay," Scottie said miserably. She slumped into one of the vinyl chairs and began to pick at some foam padding poking out of its arm.

Twenty interminable minutes later, the receptionist hung up her phone and said, "Scottie? You can go in now." She pointed with her ballpoint pen at the far left office door. It was plastered with crayon drawings, some stickers, and a whiteboard scrawled with messages that reminded Scottie of KnitWit. Still, as she dragged herself to the door and knocked tentatively, she felt like she was reporting to the doctor for a shot.

The nameplate next to the door even confirmed it: CARLIE DONATO, PH.D., EXECUTIVE DIRECTOR

"Come in," said a surprisingly young-sounding voice.

Scottie opened the door expecting to see a woman in a suit sitting behind a desk, shuffling important papers or something. Instead, Carlie was standing in front of a big wall calendar, scribbling a date into a box with one hand and swigging from a Diet Coke with the other. She wore skinny black pants and a couple of jersey tops layered on top of one another. Her flippy/funky red hair had random, bleachy streaks in it and her short round nails were painted chocolate brown.

"Ugh, can you say *busy?*" Carlie exclaimed, turning to grin at Scottie over the top of her Diet Coke can.

•• *Chicks with Sticks*

"Yeah, um, that's why I was surprised I was talking to you," Scottie said apologetically. "I usually talk to Lily?"

"Ah, but when you come in to quit, you talk to me," Carlie said, her grin holding steady.

Scottie almost gasped. How had Carlie known? When she'd called the office that morning, Scottie had simply asked them for the first opening in Lily's schedule. She hadn't told them what she was planning.

She squirmed even harder now, looking shiftily out the window to avoid Carlie's eyes.

"Scottie," Carlie said quietly. "Why don't you sit down and tell me what's going on."

Scottie glanced back at Carlie and realized her face was not unsympathetic. She was motioning at the two beat-up easy chairs shoved against the wall opposite her desk.

Scottie chose the chair next to the window. Carlie began to flop into the other one, but before her butt could hit the cushion, she popped up again.

"Forgot your file!" she chirped. She tapped her temple with a finger and rolled her eyes as she went to pluck a manila folder off her desk. "Crazy day here, today. *Crazy*. Not that that's unusual."

Scottie sighed. This was going to be even harder than she thought.

Carlie flipped through a stack of papers in the folder. "Nina Walczak, age twelve," she murmured, skimming through a report. "Says here she thinks you're great."

"Well, you probably haven't talked to her since yesterday," Scottie sighed.

Carlie's breezy demeanor quickly went serious. She leaned forward, an elbow on each knee, and stared at Scottie. "What happened yesterday?" she asked.

For once, Scottie didn't want to squirm around in her seat and beat around the bush. She already respected Carlie too much for that. So she quickly spilled everything about her clueless—and selfish—desire to take Nina out the day before. About not planning and not calling. About making Nina feel embarrassed and apologetic.

"I mean, I guess we had fun in the end," Scottie said, looking at her hands, "but I totally went about things the wrong way. Talk about forgetting all that training."

"I see," Carlie said.

"The point is," Scottie went on, "I don't think I'm really good for Nina. Seriously? I think *I* need a big sib more than she does. Which is pathetic because I'm totally privileged."

"Well, if you're the kind of person to blow off a commitment you've made," Carlie said, "then I'd agree that you're not good for Nina."

Not one to mince words, is she? Scottie thought with a cringe.

But the fact was, she agreed with Carlie.

"It's not that," she said. "I keep my commitments. Once I can stand to *make* a commitment, I definitely keep it. And I'll be honest with you. I only made this one because of my school's community service requirement."

"Oh," Carlie said flatly. Scottie could see her face go hard, her eyes flicker toward the wall calendar and her long to-do list for the afternoon.

"But once I met Nina," Scottie pressed on, "I actually forgot about the requirement. I forgot to tally up my hours with her each week and I forgot all that training about 'healthy interfacing.' Yesterday wasn't even my regular day to meet with her. I just went over there because I wanted to. So believe me, I'm committed."

Scottie felt her face go squashy as she added, "I just think Nina would be better off with someone else. I'm not proud of quitting, but I'm doing it for her sake, not mine. For once."

"Really," Carlie challenged her. "What if Nina feels otherwise?"

"That'd be because she doesn't realize what I'm really like," Scottie blurted. "We've spent all this time in my world—the places where I'm comfortable. We've knitted at cool coffeehouses and hung out at hip yarn shops and painted a French fry bus with my amazing friend, Bella."

"Okay, am I supposed to know what a French fry bus is?" Carlie asked.

"No," Scottie assured her. "Except that it was yet another safe place for me. I have these three friends and we do everything together. They sorta give me strength, you know? But see, whenever I have to leave the little world we have together, I pretty much freak."

"Nobody likes to leave their comfort zone," Carlie said, still looking a bit skeptical. "But Scottie, it sounds like you already have with Nina. You weren't really interested in being a Big Sib, but you tried it, and you connected with it."

"Yeah," Scottie admitted. "But lemme tell ya, that's the only thing I've gotten right this year. And yesterday, I think I messed even that up."

"Oh really," Carlie said. She crossed her arms and slouched into her chair like a kid. "So you're just a big screw-up, is that it?"

"Yes!" Scottie shrilled. "Carlie, you don't understand. I've spent this entire semester in major denial! I'm so scared of . . . I don't know. Every-thing. Life! I haven't sent in *any* college applications! I haven't even filled them out! I haven't been to one campus, unless you count visiting my boyfriend at Northwestern. I'm a mess!"

By now, Scottie's eyes were burning and she had to blink hard and clench her fists to keep from bursting into tears.

She'd often wondered what it might feel like to say all the things she'd just said—to hear the words out loud. She'd imagined that, after the awfulness of her admission wore off, maybe, just maybe, she'd feel relief.

But . . . nope, Scottie thought. *No relief here. Just pure, unadulterated awfulness.*

She felt even worse when she glanced at Carlie and saw her wearing a bemused smile.

Great, Scottie thought. *I tell her my tragic secrets and she thinks it's funny. I should get her a ticket to Jordan's movie.*

"You know," Carlie said, twisting a tendril of red-gold hair around her finger, "I went to UCLA because it was down the street from the house where I grew up, and more important, a few miles from my boyfriend who was a year younger than me and still in high school."

Okay, where is she going with this? Scottie was so curious, she forgot the awfulness and began to listen intently.

"I bounced from major to major," Carlie went on, gazing at the ceiling and shaking her head at the memory. "First I was psych, then I was philosophy. Philosophy led to anthro and anthro led to history. Finally, when I showed up at the counselor's office looking to declare a double major in French and poetry, they turned me away and told me to get myself together. That's when I realized that what I was *really* majoring in was sidestepping. If I focused on rearranging my class schedule every three weeks, I didn't have to think about the big stuff. Who was I? What did I want to do with my life? How would I survive next year when my b.f. graduated from high school and flew off to *Le Cordon Bleu* to become the next, great, bad-boy chef?"

She returned her gaze to Scottie. "Sound familiar?" she asked.

"Uh, that would be a yes," Scottie said miserably. "So . . . then what?"

"Well, by the time I woke up, I'd pretty much frittered away the semester," Carlie said. "I took out a loan to pay my parents back for the wasted tuition, took a leave from school, and found a gig working at a year-round camp for at-risk kids. Which made me feel like a fraud, because I felt like I was just as at-risk as they were. And p.s. can I tell you how much I hate the term 'at-risk?' I've banned it from all the Big Sibs/Little Sibs literature."

"Smart move," Scottie said.

"It's good to be the king," Carlie joked before going intense again. "Anyway, you can guess what happened next."

"I'm thinking . . . the brainstorm that led to Big Sibs/Little Sibs?" Scottie said.

"Yeah-huh," Carlie said. "I broke up with the boyfriend, transferred to Northwestern and eventually put myself on the Ph.D. track in child and adolescent psych. In short, I kicked myself out of my comfort zone."

Scottie felt inspired and terrified all at once.

"Of course, not everybody needs to go to such extreme lengths," Carlie said. "Some of us just need to take a couple steps."

"I know," Scottie said. "I guess coming here to quit was my first one."

"Well, I think the coming here was a good step," Carlie said. "The quitting, not so much."

Scottie bit her lip.

"Listen," Carlie blurted. "My job is really about protecting and caring for Nina, not you. But I gotta say, if you were to stick it out here? I think it would be good for both of you."

"I want to," Scottie said, feeling tears well up in her eyes. "I do. If only because Nina's so great. But what if I flake on her?"

"Well, forgive the blunt question," Carlie said, "but is that something you've done before? I'd say ninety-five percent of being a Big Sib is simply being a good friend. Can you do that?"

Scottie thought about the Chicks—about all they'd been through together, and all the things they'd done for each other. When she answered Carlie, it was with absolute certainty. "Yes," she said, "I can."

"Then I really think it *would* be good for Nina if you continued on as her Big Sib," Carlie declared with a bright smile. "Maybe dealing with your denial would help you do that."

"See, that's the thing," Scottie said. "I want to! I want to apply to some schools, for one. I think I'm finally ready. But—"

"But what?" Carlie said.

"But it's all so overwhelming," Scottie choked out. "It's almost Christmas break, which means the application deadlines are about a minute away. I haven't gotten letters of recommendation. I haven't written any essays. I don't have a clue where I even want to go. It's all too much. It's too late!"

"Hello!" Carlie said with mock impatience. "Did I *not* just tell you about my disastrous-slash-amazing first year of college? I guess I'm not the best Aesop, but Scottie? The moral of that story was—it's never too late."

"You really think?"

"I think I can give you one of those recommendations, even," Carlie said. "If, that is, you get your butt into gear."

"Thank you," Scottie said with a quick whoosh of breath.

This was the part where was supposed to hop out of her chair and rush out of Carlie's office, butt fully in gear.

But somehow, Scottie couldn't seem to loosen her grip on the chair arms. And that whole inhale/exhale thing? That was proving difficult, too.

"I know," Carlie said softly, patting Scottie's white knuckles. "It's hard. Even with a kick-ass letter of recommendation from the likes of *me.*"

Scottie shot Carlie a wobbly smile, but couldn't bring herself to laugh at the joke.

"Maybe it would help," Carlie suggested, "if you reached *into* your comfort zone—and asked some of the people in it for help."

An hour later, Scottie burst into her loft and called out, "Dad? Are you here?"

"Over here, honey." Her dad was watching TV, half-reclined in the corner of the red couch. CC was curled up next to him, looking quite comfortable.

"Dad," she said, taking a deep breath and heading toward him. "I have something I have to tell y—"

Suddenly, Scottie froze. A voice—a familiar voice—drifted at her from the television.

"The firstborn is the extrovert, the star . . ."

"Aw, man," she whispered through gritted teeth. "That damn sociologist!"

Her dad must have been thinking the same thing, because he shook his head and grabbed the remote. With the click of a button, Fran Altschull-Hassan was replaced by Oprah talking about her cocker spaniels.

"Did you watch this?" Scottie's dad asked her.

"Yeah," Scottie sighed, flopping onto the couch next to him. "I did."

She gave CC a scratch behind the ears and got a small dose of comfort from hearing her purr. The kitty definitely seemed to be feeling better.

"Sweetie," her dad began, "you know I often don't get your sister's movies, so maybe I'm missing something here, but on the surface, *Shearling* comes off as—"

"—not so nice?" Scottie said. "Uh, *yeah*, I got that part, too."

Her dad frowned. "When an artist is young and scrambling for material," he said, "she can tend to be a little melodrama—"

"Dad," Scottie stopped him. "You don't have to make excuses for Jordan. Yes, I pretty much hate this movie. And yes, I think she took some low blows. But at its heart—I think Jordan sort of got things right."

Her dad frowned at her in confusion. Behind the couch, Scottie's mom poked her head out from behind the long, canvas curtain that hid her painting space. Clearly, she'd heard the beginning of Scottie's confession. Looking intrigued, she ambled toward the couch, wiping her hands on a pomegranate-stained rag.

"The whole thing about me being this Jabba-like lump whose sister ran circles around her?" Scottie said, looking at both her parents now. "I'd say that's pretty accurate. After all, Jordan's kicking butt at NYU and I . . ."

Scottie's mouth went dry and she felt sweat start beneath her arms. But she took a deep breath and pushed the words out. "I haven't done a thing about getting into college," she admitted in a rush. "I haven't filled out any applications. I haven't even looked at all the pamphlets you gave me."

Her dad's mouth dropped open, while her mother's stiffened into a tight line. Her mom grabbed her dad's shoulder and squeezed.

"The appointment I told you I'd make with the guidance counselor?" Scottie blurted, talking super-fast so she wouldn't be tempted to stop. "I blew it off. Because I felt so scared of going off to college that I couldn't deal. With any of it!"

"But Scottie," her dad said quietly. "I could have helped you. I *offered* to help you at every turn. Every. Turn."

"I know," Scottie wailed. "I should have taken it. But, I don't know. I got totally overwhelmed. I thought it would pass, but it didn't! And then the days kept going by and it was getting to be too late—and too embarrassing—to ask for help. Soon, things just got so awful that I started to think I didn't want to go to college at all!"

Scottie wrung her hands and avoided her dad's stricken face as she admitted, "But now I realize I do. I *do* want to go—and maybe not even to a school in Chicago. But most apps are due on January first and school's almost out, which is gonna make it hard to get recommendations and I still don't even know where I want to apply and—"

Scottie paused to inhale and summon up the supreme humility it would require to beg her parents for help when her mother made a strange sound.

It sounded like a snort. A giggly sort of snort.

Scottie glanced up at her mother and was stupefied to see her biting her bottom lip, clearly trying to hold back laughter. She was looking at Scottie's dad, whose face had also softened from a mask of disappointment into a twitching attempt to suppress a smile!

"Okay, *what* is going on here?" Scottie demanded. "I tell you that I'm drowning, that I've screwed up bigger than I ever have before, and you think it's *funny*?"

"Well, when Jordan did it, we didn't think it was funny," her dad admitted. "Not at all. But you know, the second time around, you have a little perspective."

"Wait a minute," Scottie screeched. "Jordan?!? Jordan the ballerina sheep? She did this, too?"

"Except she didn't come clean until mid-January," Scottie's mom said, coming around from the back of the couch and plopping down next to Scottie. "She had to apply late to NYU and she was automatically wait-listed."

"Okay, where was I when all this was happening?" Scottie said. "How come I never knew?"

"Jordan begged us not to tell you," her dad said with a shrug. "She was so embarrassed."

"Oh. My. God," Scottie said. "So this runs in the family?"

"Scottie," her mom said, picking at a pomegranate-colored cuticle with her thumbnail, "why do you think I pull all-nighters before every gallery show? Artistic integrity?"

"And why do you think I was so hard on your case?" her dad added. "It's okay to be scared about next year. It's a big step. But, I couldn't make it for you. Ultimately, you had to commit on your own."

"I have. I'm ready," Scottie promised. "I'm terrified and clueless, but ready."

"Then let's get started," her dad said.

"Right now?" Scottie said.

"Why not?" he replied. "As you know, I've got a *lot* of thoughts stored up to share with you. And since your mother is quite good at pulling all-nighters . . ."

"I'm yours," her mom offered, giving Scottie's head a quick stroke. "We can start by researching online."

"And I have phone numbers of several alumni associations," her dad added. "Tomorrow, we can set up some phone interviews with people who've gone to the schools you're interested in, to give you a taste. That, combined with virtual tours on the college's websites can take the place of campus visits for now. And you've still got four more days of school, right? So that's plenty of time to ask some of your teachers for letters of recommendation."

Scottie nodded as she popped to her feet. "I'll go get my laptop," she said. "And all the brochures you gave me. Don't worry. I'm going to do everything I can to make this work."

"Oh, I'm not worried," her dad said. He stood up and put his arm around Scottie's mom's shoulders. "We know you can do this."

Scottie shot her parents a skeptical look. "You sound pretty certain," she said, "for people who nicknamed their daughter Jabba."

"Hel-lo," her dad said in his best attempt at girl-ese. "You were three and it was just baby fat."

Scottie laughed. Just a little.

Her dad got serious again, too.

"Honey," he said, "You know that you aren't that little girl anymore, don't you?"

"You really think that?" Scottie squeaked. "When I just Jabba'd my way through this whole college application thing?"

"Sweetie," her mom interjected. "You came to us before it was too late, which was a pretty brave thing to do. And that's just one of many brave things I've seen you do.

"Think about the world you've created for yourself these past few years," she went on. "You started knitting when nobody else got it—including us. And you didn't stop there. You created a whole world for yourself with your friends and Never Mind the Frogs, and now with Nina. If you ask me, *that's* what makes an artist."

"But you know I don't want to be a fiber artist," Scottie said, feeling herself start to go squashy. "I don't know *what* I want to do. That's the whole problem."

"I mean an artist of life, Scottie," her mom said, reaching out and putting a hand on Scottie's cheek. "You have time to figure out the particulars. Plenty of it."

As two tears squeezed out of Scottie's eyes, she threw her arms around both her parents. Her fierce hug was one of gratitude, but it was also a good-bye. Or at least, the beginning of one.

She was finally feeling ready to say it.

As Scottie headed to her bedroom, with CC tagging along behind her, she shook her head in disbelief.

I'm actually gonna do this, she thought.

And that elusive relief she'd hoped for? She was finally feeling that, too. It felt so good, in fact, that she suddenly wanted to come clean to *everybody.*

I could ask Tay to read my essays, she mused, *since she has such an excellent B.S. detector. Amanda could coach me in interview etiquette and Bella could help all four of us do calming prana while we wait for the results. . . .*

She grinned as she yanked open her file drawer and pulled out the stack of college brochures and applications. Slyly, she found the one from her dad's alma mater, University of Michigan, and put it on top of the pile. Then she scooped up her laptop and said, "Come on, CC."

As she and her cat ambled back down the hall, she already felt her fear dissipating into a memory—one of those memories that quickly becomes hazy and surreal.

It was replaced by the much more vivid images of Scottie's friends. She could just *see* their faces right now—all sympathetic and bemused— just as she could often hear their voices in her head, keeping her company, asking for advice, and steering *her* straight.

And when it was time, next fall, to say good-bye to them? They'd help her do that, too.

I don't know how I forgot, Scottie chided herself, *that even when I'm alone, I've got the Chicks right there with me.*

 *(KnitWise)*

"I'm sorry, Amanda," Tay said, thrusting out a bony hip and crossing her arms. "But you cannot curtsey in that thing. It's too cool for curtsys."

"Oh. My. God!"

Amanda—who was sitting crosslegged on her bed with hot rollers lumped all over her head—stared at Tay. *Tay* was staring at Amanda's debutante gown floating on a dress form, as ethereal as the wisp of foam on a cappuccino.

Amanda looked down at Scottie and Bella, who were sprawled on her bedroom's lush white carpet knitting twin head kerchiefs to celebrate spring.

"Did one of these curlers singe my brain," she asked them, "or did I just hear Tay Cooper compliment a *dress?*"

"Oh, get over yourself, little *debbie*," Tay said. She loped over to Amanda's pink, flowery easy chair, flopped into it, and picked up her knitting. "Just because I don't wear the things doesn't mean I can't appreciate them. Or, at least, this one."

Scottie looked over at the dress, which Amanda had finished just a few days ago. Tay was right. It was amazing. More than that, it was *Amanda*, from the sheer spiderweb of silky threads that composed the corset to the soft, swooping knitted embellishments that tumbled down the length of the silk-satin skirt. It was angelic with an edge; gorgeous, but not without irony. It would help Amanda float above the parts of tonight's coming out ball that she deplored—the "cow-at-auction" parade, the gazillion-course dinner—and embrace the parts that she liked, like having a dance with her dad and trading deb disses (and kisses) with Jamison.

"I can't believe the ball is just a few hours away," Scottie said, pausing her clacking needles to gaze in awe at the dress. "Your very last deb duty."

"I prefer to think of it," Amanda said with a sly grin, "as my very *first* project for Parsons."

"Oh, really?" Scottie said. "Already working on that professor's pet award, are we?"

"Hey, there's a reason the acceptance letter comes in a big, fat envelope," Amanda said. She grabbed a chocolate-covered pretzel rod from a tub on the floor and took a happy chomp out of it. "There was a *long* to-do list in there. I have to buy a sewing machine and tons of other supplies. I have to make a portfolio of designers I admire. *And* I need to show up at school with a garment that's ready for critique."

"Wow," Scottie said. "All I have to do is buy a shower caddy and some notebooks."

"Don't forget your big foam 'Number One!' finger and your maize-and-blue pom-poms," Tay teased. She pointed at Scottie with one of her double-pointed needles before resuming her knitting. "I can't believe you're actually going to a Big Ten school."

"Hey, Michigan is *not* just rah-rah," Scottie said with a laugh. "Unless you want it to be. I mean, there are crunchy corners of the campus and wonky ones. There's a lefty newspaper and a huge engineering school . . . it pretty much has it all."

"Including a campus full o' midwesterners," Amanda said, grinning as she dusted pretzel salt off her hands. "It'll be like you never left Chicago."

"Har, har," Scottie said with a purse of her lips. "Besides, you know that's not true. It'll be *nothing* like Chicago—because none of you guys will be there."

Scottie smiled. It was a sad smile, yes, but a smile nonetheless.

Who knew college was what I wanted all along, she mused with a little laugh. *It's crazy, how appealing it's become—the idea of starting from scratch.*

Maybe that was because—when she arrived at her freshman dorm and her class schedule full of 101's—she *wouldn't* be starting from scratch, not really. She'd be starting from the Chicks; from a place where she wasn't the overshadowed sister, or the girl in Gapwear just trying to blend, or even the angst artist bent on sabotaging herself.

She'd be the girl she was right now, whose best friends were this unlikely trio of blueblooded fashion grrrl, wild-haired peace-and-lovenik, and snarky skateboarder. The girl whose romance had changed completely when her boyfriend went away to college—yet stayed the same in all the ways that counted. The girl who'd finally realized that her comfort zone wasn't nearly as small and cramped as she'd thought.

No, it's more like knitted wool, Scottie thought. *Warm and strong, but surprisingly stretchy.*

"Hey look," Tay said, pulling Scottie out of her knitty reverie. She was pointing at her again. "Isn't this the part where Scottie *used* to get all squashy?"

"Yeah," Bella said, a wicked gleam in her eye. "But she's, like, the opposite of squashy."

"She looks like she *wants* to ditch us," Tay declared.

"No," Scottie laughed. "You guys—"

"Well, it's just too bad if she does," Amanda said, hopping off the bed with a clack of her curlers. She bounced over to her closet and flung the door open. Then she pulled four big, white cardboard boxes off a shelf. As she plunked the boxes onto the floor, she added, "Because when you go off to college, you're taking us with you."

"What?" Scottie squawked. She cocked her head at her friends as they shot each other conspiratorial grins. "What did you guys do?"

She reached for one of the boxes, but Tay barked, "Wait! We should open 'em all at the same time."

"Yeah!" Bella said, scooching across the carpet to sit next to Scottie. Amanda and Tay scrambled to the floor, too. The four girls formed a circle around the stack of boxes. Amanda grabbed the top box, then Bella and Tay, and finally Scottie. Scottie's box sagged slightly with the weight of its contents, but when she shook it, she heard nothing.

"No guessing," Bella scolded her. "You'll know soon enough."

"One . . ." Amanda said, gripping the top of her box.

"Two," Tay said, even though she let them know with her eye roll how corny she felt doing it.

"Three!" Bella sang out, so loud that Scottie would have covered her ears if she wasn't *dying* to open her box. All at once, the four cardboard covers fluttered into the air, landing on the floor beyond their circle with a series of thwacks.

Scottie stared at the burst of color in her box. It took her a few seconds to comprehend what she was seeing. But when she focused on a fluffy, blue-gray cat embroidered onto a square of gold wool, she got it.

These were her memory quilt squares.

Correction: it was her memory *quilt*! The squares had been sewn together with big loops of rainbow-colored yarn.

"What?!" Scottie gasped. She pulled the blanket from its box and shook it out. She saw a KnitWit square here, her Buttered Toast square there. But she also spotted several squares she didn't recognize. One had French knots that unmistakably formed one of Bella's groat muffins. On another square, a chocolate bon-bon had been intarsia'd with luscious angora. Still another square was embroidered with a skateboard, its deck emblazoned with the pseudonym for Tay's blog, T.C. BOIL.

When Scottie gave her friends a stunned look, she saw that they were unfolding three identical quilts!

"But how—" Scottie cried. "When did you—? You *guys!* What did you do?!"

"We stole your quilt squares!" Bella cackled as she draped her own quilt over her lotused legs. "Remember, during that SSO at your house last February? When we made you go the market on the corner for ice cream? While you were gone, we dug around your room and found the squares and *stole* them."

"And we spent the winter copying them," Tay said.

"We made a bunch of our own squares, too," Amanda noted proudly. She pointed at one where she'd intarsia'd a pair of long white gloves, just like the ones she'd be wearing at her ball that night. Of course, these gloves were embellished with two sprays of hot-pink fuzz at the wrists.

"We made four of each square," Bella said, "then stitched them together in the same order."

"This is amazing!" Scottie said, her voice choked with emotion.

The more she pored over the blanket, the more new goodies she found mixed in with her own squares. Tay had crocheted a tug-of-war rope, an image Scottie immediately knew was a symbol of her back-and-forth life with joint custody. Amanda had knitted up an electric guitar, a nod to Toby, her first love.

And of course, there was no question of who had made the square with the crimson "H."

"Bella," Scottie said, grinning as she touched the red letter. "I still can't believe that you, queen of crunch, are going to Harvard. The oldest university in the country. The place that basically *invented* The Man."

"Hey," Bella said with a sunny shrug. "The Kennedy School of Government is there! It's a no-brainer."

She added, with a grateful smile, "And my parents are totally on board with it. It only took them a few weeks to stop teasing me about my business suits and start going to aldermens meetings. My dad even ordered a subscription to *The New Republic* and he's making a list of political action committees who might want to give me financial aid."

"The perfect parents strike again," Tay said with a rueful smile. Then she turned to Scottie. "Hey, speaking of no-brainer, how is it that you never noticed we'd absconded with your precious squares?"

"Yeah," Amanda demanded. "We had this elaborate lie concocted for when you found out we'd taken 'em."

"It was a charity art contest," Bella chirped.

"To benefit the gorillas of Rwanda," Amanda added.

"Gee, I wonder how you came up with that," Scottie joked. Then, as she stroked her beautiful quilt, she shrugged. "I guess I kind of . . ." she laughed dryly, *"forgot* about my memory quilt. I got so busy, you know, scheduling college visits and interviews, and hanging with Beck and Nina. And then there were all those Frogs meetings and SSO's. . . ."

"I think what you're trying to say," Bella said sweetly, "is you were too busy making more memories to dwell on the old ones."

"That's exactly what I'm trying to say," Scottie said. Finally, her eyes started stinging and her throat choked up. To hide her face, Scottie gave her quilt a closer examination. On the bottom left-hand square, she spotted some embroidered initials: TC.

"Tay," Scottie asked, struggling to speak through all the emotions clogging up her voice. "Did you put this one together?"

"Yup," Tay said. "It's even got some handspun yarn in it."

Tay searched her own blanket.

"I got Bella's," she announced.

"Amanda made mine," Bella said, running her fingers over her quilt.

"And I've got Scottie's," Amanda said, shooting Scottie an emotional look.

Scottie nodded hard, too touched to talk—until, she saw two more sets of initials on her quilt, in the corner opposite Tay's.

"JO," she said. "That must be John."

"Yeah, he helped with the stitching," Tay said, unable to keep a love-sick smile from creeping onto her face. "We've been knitting together a lot lately."

"Clearly!" Scottie pointed at the soft, burnt orange tube Tay was working on double-pointed needles. "What is that that you're working on, anyway? It's not your usual black."

Tay shrugged and gazed into her lap.

Scottie looked at Bella and Amanda. They seemed as incredulous as she was.

"Tay!" Amanda said. "Are you being . . . coy? *You?!*"

"It's just a pair of fingerless gloves," Tay retorted. Then she added, oh so quietly, "For John."

"For *John?*" Scottie, Bella, and Amanda exclaimed together.

"But what about the Curse of the Boyfriend Sweater?" Scottie asked.

A couple of years ago, Tay had knitted a sweater for an undeserving crush and—just as the curse predicted—had her heart broken the moment she gave it to him. Ever since, she'd refused to knit so much as a sock for John, no matter how much he'd begged.

"I know, I know," Tay said sheepishly. "And I know it's a big step but now, it just feels right. I'm finally ready to . . . knit for my boyfriend."

"Ah!" Bella screeched, covering her face with her hands while Scottie and Amanda burst out laughing.

When she'd recovered, Scottie's eyes drifted back to her amazing quilt. "So who do these other initials belong to?" she wondered. "LC?"

Tay's smile was even more sheepish now.

"Uh, that would be Laura Cooper," she admitted.

"Your mom?!" Scottie gasped.

"I caved and taught her how to knit," Tay said. "Turns out, she's pretty good. Once she got knit and purl down, she was off and running. She discovered these wacky knitting blogs I'd never heard of before and she's already made a major dent in my 'Three Hundred Sixty-Five Stitches' desk calendar."

"That somehow doesn't sound like the actions of someone made of cling wrap," Scottie said.

"It somehow isn't," Tay agreed. "I have to admit that time spent with my mom over the needles? It hasn't totally sucked."

"Wow," Scottie said. She ran her hand over her quilt again and added, "I guess in just a few months, we'll all be knitting with new people, huh?"

"Especially you," Amanda said. "I'm sure you'll have a Never Mind the Frogs outpost set up in your dorm by the time you leave freshman orientation."

"Yeah, I will," Scottie admitted with a laugh. "Won't be the same, though."

"That's the point, I guess," Bella said. "You know, growth, change—"

"Yeah, yeah, yeah," Tay cut in. "C'mon, you guys, we're not gonna get all mushy and philosophical, are we?"

"Too late, dude," Scottie said, pointing at their quartet of quilts. "We already have."

It was only then that she spotted another new square in her quilt. It was right in the center of it, actually.

An initial hovered in each of the square's corners: A, B, T, and S. In the center were more initials. They were the same letters the girls had carved into Joe's fireside coffee table years ago—right after sealing their friendship with a bundle of burning sage and some heartfelt words.

$$C \text{ w/ } S$$

Scottie didn't even try to hold back. She let the tears come as she traced those soft letters over and over with her finger.

She gazed at her three best friends through her tears and realized that she'd been wrong the night that she'd shoved her quilt squares away under the bed. She'd thought then that snuggling up under her memories was a step backward—the opposite of growing up.

But now she realized that, if she was ever going to grow up, she had to take her memories along for the ride. That went double for her friends. Sure, come fall, they were going to scatter across the country. But in their hearts, where it counted, they weren't going anywhere.

Like this memory quilt, Scottie knew the Chicks with Sticks would be with her—wherever they were—always.

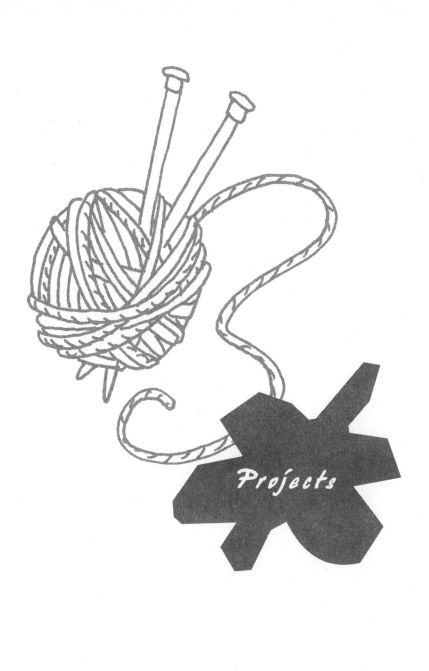

Projects

Converti-mitts

Knitting for your boyfriend is a big step, but if Tay can do it, so can you. Then again, there's no harm in protecting yourself from the Curse of the Boyfriend Sweater by not making your honey a sweater. Instead, try something small—yet sweet—like these open-ended mitts. Way better than a convertible car, they let your guy's fingers be free (the better for hand-holding or texting you) yet keep his hands fashionably toasty.

Note the smaller size for girly hands, because you deserve some knitty love for yourself, too.

MATERIALS AND TOOLS:
- 150 yds bulky yarn, to knit at 3.5 stitches per inch
- Set of 5 US #8 double-pointed needles, or size to achieve gauge

GAUGE:
15 stitches = 4" over seeded rib check pattern

SIZES:
These mitts are very stretchy and should fit a wide range of hand sizes. The smaller women's size will be best for boys with small hands. Men's should fit the average guy. And if you have

a basketball-playing b.f. like Tay, go XL by casting on 36 sts and working the seeded rib check pattern over 19 instead of 15 sts.

SEEDED RIB CHECK PATTERN:

Rounds 1, 3, 5: K3, *p1, k3; repeat from *.
Rounds 2, 4, 6: P1, *k1, p3; repeat from *, end k1, p1.
Rounds 7, 9, 11: P3, *k1, p3; repeat from *.
Rounds 8, 10, 12: K1, *p1, k3; repeat from *, end p1, k1.

DIRECTIONS:

Left mitt: CO 28 (32) sts and join to work in the round. Work in k2, p2 rib until cuff measures 2". On the next round, increase 1 on each side of first st to begin thumb gusset. Begin to work seeded rib check pattern across the next 15 sts, arranging needles as necessary so that two carry the pattern sts and two carry the palm-side sts. Continue to work palm side in k2, p2 rib. Thumb gusset will be in k1, p1 rib; take new sts into pattern accordingly. Increase 2 more sts for the thumb gusset every 3rd round; new sts will always be outside the old gusset sts so that the gusset takes on a triangular shape. After the 12th round of seeded rib check, there should be 9 gusset sts. For women's size, put these 9 sts on waste yarn; CO 1 new st to bridge the gap and continue the round. For men's size, continue as given until there are 11 gusset sts, then put on waste yarn and CO 1 st. Take new bridge st into k2, p2 rib pattern. Work until you have completed 2 repetitions of the seeded rib check pattern, then switch back to k2, p2 rib for the entire round. Continue in rib until the mitts reach the tops of the wearer's ring and index fingers, then bind off in pattern and break yarn, leaving a tail to weave in. Rejoin yarn to pick up the gusset sts, twist a new st up on either side of the held sts, and pick up 1 st above the hole: 12 (14) sts. Work the thumb in k1, p1 rib until it reaches the joint below the tip of the thumb. Bind off in pattern. Weave in all ends.

Right mitt: Work cuff in p2, k2 rib. Continue to work as for left mitt, but reverse the thumb shaping: after working the first row of seeded rib check sts, increase 1 each side of the first st on the palm side to begin the thumb gusset.

Wear the mitts with the finger-covering rib cuffed back for free fingers, or uncuffed for extra warmth.

Last Gasp of Summer Headbands

You've been there—the first day of school is looming but it's still sweltering. You need a way to look fabulous and keep your sweaty strands off your neck. Yarny headbands do it all. Scottie free-formed hers, but if you're not up for pattern-free knitting yet, use these easy guides to create your own customized looks.

Ribbonesque:

Want a knitty substitute for a slender ribbon? I-cord is perfect—and a very speedy knit. Use a fun color, novelty, or self-striping yarn.

YOU WILL NEED:
• Double-pointed needles

Cast on desired number of stitches (4–8, depending on thickness of yarn and desired bulk of cord).
K the row. Slide to other end of needle without turning work.
Rep until cord is desired length.
BO all stitches.
Tie it on!

Wide and Winsome:

This stretchy number is wide on top of your head and narrow behind your ears and neck. It's cute, comfy, *and* an easy knit. We're talking garter stitch with a few increases and decreases, people. That means you can make yourself a whole collection of them. If you want to mix it up, try substituting elastic string for traditional yarn.

YOU WILL NEED:
- Knitting needles of choice (between sizes 6 and 8)
- Embroidery needle

CO 6.

Work in garter stitch for two (2) inches.

Begin increases:

K1, kf&b (knit front and back of stitch), k all—7 sts.

Repeat next row—8 sts.

K four rows.

K1, kf&b, k all—9 sts.

Repeat next row—10 sts.

K four rows.

K1, kf&b, k all—11 sts.

Repeat next row—12 sts.

K 4 rows.

K1, kf&b, k all—13 sts.

Repeat next row—14 sts.

K all rows for four (4) inches.

Begin decreases:

K1, ssk (slip slip knit), k all—13 sts.

Rep next row—12 sts.

K 4 rows.

K1, ssk, k all—11 sts.

Rep next row—10 sts.

K 4 rows.

K1, ssk, k all—9 sts.

Rep next row—8 sts.

K 4 rows.

K1, ssk, k all—7 sts.

Rep next row—6 sts.

K all rows until tail is desired length for fit.

BO all sts.

Whipstitch together ends. (See Memory Quilt project for whip-stitch instructions.)

Slide on!

The Chicago Debutante's Corset

Amanda knitted her corset for her debby ball gown, but you *can dress this girly wonder up or down. Wear it as a strapless top with a full skirt, or cinched over a T-shirt and jeans. String a pretty ribbon through the back eyelets, or leave 'em empty for a lacy look.*

We're not gonna lie to you—this corset's gorgeous lily-of-the-valley motif is challenging. On the other hand, the cinched-in waist is a cinch because the diagonal ribbing in the side panels provides shaping with no increases or decreases.

MATERIALS AND TOOLS:
Debbie Bliss Cathay, 5 (5, 6, 6, 7, 7) skeins
US #5 circular needle, 20" or 24"
Stitch markers
Crochet hook (optional)
1"-wide elastic tape, long enough to circle your chest
Elastic thread (optional)

SIZES (measurement at the hip bones):

XS	S	M	L	XL	XXL
28"	32"	34"	36"	38"	40"

The pattern is very stretchy and designed to fit closely, so knit the smaller size if you're in between. Yarn allowances are based on a finished height of 14" (14", 15", 15", 16", 16") plus top edging and a swatch for gauge.

Gauge: 21 sts and 29 rows = 4" x 4" in stockinette

DIRECTIONS:
CO 156 (174; 186; 198; 210; 222) sts and join to work in the round. Work 8 rows in k3, p3 rib. Place a marker at the join. From now on, the corset is composed of four panels: two side panels of diagonal ribbing, the lily-of-the-valley panel at the front, and the eyelet panel at the back. Place markers between them according to the stitch counts below. The join falls at the beginning of the left side panel, so you'll work each row of the panels in the order given here. Repeat the instructions for each panel in turn until you reach the desired length. You can try on the corset at any time by slipping half the stitches to another circular needle or to a piece of waste yarn.

Left-side diagonal rib panel:
Work over 33, (36, 36, 36, 39, 39) sts.
Sizes XS, XL, XXL:
Rnds 1-4: K2, *p3, k3* repeat from *, end k1.
Rnds 5-8: K1, *p3, k3* repeat from *, end k2.
Rnds 9-12: *p3, k3* repeat from *, end k3.
Rnds 13-16: P2, *k3, p3* repeat from *, end p1.
Rnds 17-20: P1, *k3, p3* repeat from *, end p2.
Rnds 21-24: *k3, p3* repeat from *, end p3.
Rnds 21-24: *k3, p3*, end k3.

Sizes S, M, L:

Rnds 1-4: K2, *p3, k3*, end p1.

Rnds 5-8: K1, *p3, k3*, end p2.

Rnds 9-12: *p3, k3*, end p3.

Rnds 13-16: P2, *k3, p3*, end k1.

Rnds 17-20: P1, *k3, p3*, end k2.

Rnds 21-24: *k3, p3*, end k3.

Repeat.

Lily-of-the-Valley panel:

Work over 48 (54, 60, 66, 66, 72) sts.

Set-up row: K6 (9, 12, 15, 15, 18), p6, k24, p6, k6 (9,12,15,15,18). You should have a panel of 24 stitches flanked on either side by 6 purls and 6 (9, 12, 15, 15, 18) knits. Continue to knit or purl these flanking stitches as given. The lily pattern is worked on 23 stitches, not 24, so you will need to work a single decrease in Round 2. Instead of ending k6, k2tog as given below, try k4, k2tog, k1, k2tog.

MK = Make Knot: (k1, p1, k1, p1, k1) all into the same stitch, making 5 sts from one; then leapfrog the 4th, 3rd, 2nd, and 1st of the new stitches over the last new stitch and off the needle. Take care not to leapfrog the yo off when working the right side of the motif.

Rnd 2: Ssk, k6, (yo, k1) twice, sl 1-k2tog-psso, (k1, yo) twice, k6, k2tog.

Rnd 3 and all other odd rows: K23.

Rnd 4: Ssk, k5, yo, k1, yo, k2, sl 1-k2tog-psso, k2, yo, k1, yo, k5, k2tog.

Rnd 6: Ssk, k4, yo, k1, yo, MK, k2, sl 1-k2tog-psso, k2, MK, yo, k1, yo, k4, k2tog.

Rnd 8: Ssk, k3, yo, k1, yo, MK, k3, sl 1-k2tog-psso, k3, MK, yo, k1, yo, k3, k2tog.

Rnd 10: Ssk, k2, yo, k1, yo, MK, k4, sl 1-k2tog-psso, k4, MK, yo, k1, yo, k2, k2tog.

Rnd 12: Ssk, (k1, yo) twice, MK, k5, sl 1-k2tog-psso, k5, MK, (yo, k1) twice, k2tog.

Rnd 14: Ssk, yo, k1, yo, MK, k6, sl 1-k2tog-psso, k6, MK, yo, k1, yo, k2tog.

Repeat, working Round 1 as a regular odd row from now on.

Right-side diagonal rib panel:
Work over 33, 36, 36, 36, 39, 39 sts.
Sizes XS, XL, XXL:
Rnds 1-4: K1, *p3, k3* repeat from *, end p2.
Rnds 5-8: K2, *p3, k3* repeat from *, end p1.
Rnds 9-12: *K3, p3* repeat from *, end k3.
Rnds 13-16: P1, *k3, p3* repeat from *, end k2.
Rnds 17-20: P2, *k3, p3* repeat from *, end k1.
Rnds 21-24: *P3, k3* repeat from *, end p3.

Sizes S, M, L:
Rnds 1-4: P1, *k3, p3*, end k2.
Rnds 5-8: P2, *k3, p3*, end k1.
Rnds 9-12: *P3, k3*.
Rnds 13-16: K1, *p3, k3*, end p2.
Rnds 17-20: K2, *p3, k3*, end p1.
Rnds 21-24: *K3, p3*.

Repeat.

Back eyelet panel:

Work over 42 (48, 54, 60, 66, 72) sts.

Set-up rounds: K all sts for the first two rounds.

Rnd 3: K6 (9, 12, 15, 15, 18), yo, sl 1-k2tog-psso, yo, k24, (24, 24, 24, 30, 30), yo, sl 1-k2tog-psso, yo, k6 (9, 12, 15, 15, 18).

Rnd 4 and all even rounds: Knit.

Repeat Rounds 3 and 4.

When corset is long enough to cover bust, you may choose to make phony seams to give it a more structured look: drop the K stitch on either side of the diagonal rib panels (4 stitches in all, but do them one at a time) and ladder it all the way down to the top of the ribbed hem. Using your crochet hook, pick up the loose stitch. Draw through it the first "rung" of the ladder. Then draw through two rungs at once. Alternate drawing through one and two rungs until the stitch is all the way back to the top, and put it back on the needle. This will create a raised line that looks like a seam.

Work 8 final rounds of k3, p3 rib. Remember to make an extra stitch somewhere in the first round of ribbing to reestablish your original cast-on number. Cast off all stitches.

Sew in elastic tape around the top of the corset, making sure the tape will be slightly stretched when you wear the garment. If desired, hand-stitch lines of elastic thread through the ribbed panels on the inside to accentuate waist shaping.

Make tulip bud edging as follows:

CO 8 sts.

Row 1 (Right side): K5, yo, k1, yo, k2.

Row 2: P6, knit into front and back of next st (kfb), k3.

Row 3: K4, p1, k2, yo, k1, yo, k3.

Row 4: P8, kfb, k4.

Row 5: K4, p2, k3, yo, k1, yo, k4.

Row 6: P10, kfb, k5.

Row 7: K4, p3, k4, yo, k1, yo, k5.

Row 8: P12, kfb, k6.

Row 9: K4, p4, ssk, k7, k2tog, k1.

Row 10: P10, kfb, k7.

Row 11: K4, p5, ssk, k5, k2tog, k1.

Row 12: P8, kfb, k2, p1, k5.

Row 13: K4, p1, k1, p4, ssk, k3, k2tog, k1.

Row 14: P6, kfb, k3, p1, k5.

Row 15: K4, p1, k1, p5, ssk, k1, k2tog, k1.

Row 16: P4, kfb, k4, p1, k5

Row 17: K4, p1, k1, p6, sl 1-k2tog-psso, k1.

Row 18: P2tog, bind off next 5 sts using p2tog st to bind off first st; p3, k4.

Repeat Rows 1-18 until edging is long enough to attach along the top, across both side panels and the front of the corset. (Leave the back panel unedged to be sure the corset remains stretchy enough to pull over your head.) Cast off on a WS row, leaving a very long tail with which to sew on the edging. Pin edging in place while wearing corset, then sew down.

Weave in all ends and block lightly if desired.

Scottie's Memory Quilt

Some folks scrapbook, others journal. But how many people do you know who knit their memories? There are countless ways to construct a memory quilt. You can embroider or intarsia squares with images of precious events, like the Chicks did. Or you can weave scrap yarn from favorite projects into cool new patterns. (Break out your stitch dictionary!) Anything goes, as long as you keep your squares a uniform size so you can patchwork them neatly together. That means paying attention to gauge. (Yes, we know that's boring, but you'll thank us for the tip later.) Knit enough squares to make the shape you'd like—whether it be a bed-size rectangle or a doll-size square—then sew them together with a whipstitch. That's an overhand sewing stitch used to join two finished edges. Select a sturdy yarn in either a neutral color that will let your squares shine or an accent color that will add to the quilt's fun. We recommend joining individual squares into rows first, and then connecting the rows to form the larger piece.

MATERIALS AND TOOLS:

A quantity of knitted squares, arranged so they make a quilt of desired size and shape

A large embroidery needle

Whipstitch:

Start with the front sides of your pieces facing you and the edges to be seamed placed together. Insert the sewing needle from the right square through the first edge stitch (the bottom corner) and through the first stitch on the left piece from the back side.

Pull the yarn through, carry yarn over the top of the work, and insert sewing needle into next stitch on each piece.

Keep repeating this process, joining one stitch from each edge with every stitch.

Be sure to keep your stitches tight and even so your quilt will be firmly constructed.

Tie off at ends of stitching and weave in ends to finish.